The Forgotten Mission

The Forgotten Mission

Gus Leodas

ZEBRA BOOKS are published by KENSINGTON PUBLISHING CORP. 475 Park Avenue South New York, N.Y. 10016

Copyright © 1982 by Gus Leodas.

Revised Edition Copyright © 2006 by Gus Leodas.

Library of Congress Control Number:		00-192194
ISBN 10:	Hardcover	0-7388-3818-7
	Softcover	0-7388-3819-5
ISBN 13:	Hardcover	978-0-7388-3818-2
	Softcover	978-0-7388-3819-9

This is a work of fiction. Names, characters, places and incidents either are the product of the author's imagination or are used fictitiously, and any resemblance to any actual persons, living or dead, events, or locales is entirely coincidental.

This book was printed in the United States of America.

To order additional copies of this book, contact:
Xlibris Corporation
1-888-7-XLIBRIS
www.Xlibris.com
Orders@Xlibris.com
2119

TO THE BEAUTIFUL LADIES IN MY LIFE:
CAROLE, DEANNA, AND LAURA,
ABSOLUTE GEMS IN A SEA OF GLASS.

PROLOGUE

JULY, SEVERAL YEARS AGO

THE DISTANT BLEATING of sheep was provoked by the crowing of the cock at the hour that roosters awaken their immediate world. Cow bells clanged in the damp meadow and birds sang in the yawning sky; a morning symphony from the trespassing tenants of Shuller's Land, a neglected stretch of land bordered by stunted scrub oak and black pine.

Near the three-room house, the doorless weathered barn that leaned precariously from old age waited for a strong wind to complete the collapse before someone discovered its horrible secret.

Wisps of mist clung low at the forest's edge sheltered from the rising sun that had dissipated the gray pall in the flats. The house and barn had cleared of mist, but rivulets of dampness clung to their wooden frames.

The front door clicked open and a weary, middle-aged man—stocky, with salt-and-pepper curly hair and naked—shuffled onto the porch and stood next to the rocking chair. His bare feet left footprints in the moisture.

He rubbed his body to stimulate his blood hoping the wet chill would subside, and looked up squinting at the tall oak's dead branches that once guarded the house from the sun. To the man, the dead oak was the perfect monument, the perfect landmark for this forsaken property now covered with weeds. He watched as the light from the east began to expose its nakedness.

He breathed the Monday southwesterly breeze with contentment, listened to the distant symphony for a while, stretched his arms as a tenor accepting the crowd's adoration and with middle fingers jabbing the air shouted to the dawn, "Go to hell world. Go to hell!"

He grinned from ear to ear with satisfaction, returned to the house, closed the door and went back to sleep.

PART I

ONE

SHULLER'S LAND WAS a potato farm and had been a large producer. The last crop was planted in 1942 the year the land died from the horror of that one long night.

Mitchell Pappas came to the land renting for six months from May to October, the time he felt capable of writing a novel in isolation. His last novel, *Murder by Murder,* appeared on the bestseller list for almost a year.

He had seen the small advertisement in *Suffolk Life* the previous year when he stayed in East Hampton with his wife, Helene, and though now informally separated amicably, she was his literary agent.

Mitchell never met the owner of Shuller's Land. The real estate agent handled the transaction. Carter Borden, the agent, had a smile and face Mitchell wanted to punch. He paid Borden in advance. The property was the perfect place for him and wanted to minimize the risk of anything going wrong with the transaction. After signing the lease, he learned that no one else had lived on Shuller's Land since

World War II. Borden reminded Mitchell of his first wife, Virginia, who never told him the entire story about anything.

She would tell him bits and pieces, but never the whole. He referred to her as a used rug merchant who showed the first roll of the rug never unfolding the entire rug.

And she persisted until she got her way, pecking away like a woodpecker until the tree finally fell, always complaining about something or other—almost all he deemed trivial. He wondered after a time what had turned the wonderful girl he married into a blight to live with, and contributed it to lacking children. She couldn't bear and didn't want to adopt. Add his late hours at the office and the mixture became explosive.

In those days, he was an account executive at J. Walter Thompson, the advertising agency. He accepted the job when a personnel director recruited him on the Columbia University campus.

His wife wasn't an asset in the business world that dominated his life and evolved to a travesty in his private life, so he virtually ran from her. They divorced after eight years.

Ten years ago his world caved in. He lost his job due to a major account loss and a management change. For three months he tried without success to find a position. Depression set in and he began to feel unwanted in the advertising field. Then he caught his wife with another man in his bed, stormed from his Westchester house and disappeared.

Two years later, he had a best-selling novel and with it, acclaims.

Mitchell had run from society to Key West. He withdrew twenty thousand dollars from his savings account and left everything else to that 'bitch'. He wasn't sure why. Maybe he felt sorry for her—or for himself. Or did he still love her?

It was a good time to leave the rat race. He also attributed his flight from his surroundings to male menopause. The hell with it, he thought. Gauguin left his family and went to the South Pacific to paint, to get away from the world. And look what happened to him. Mitchell wasn't setting any precedent by his action.

Mitchell rented a room in Key West, walked the beach and thought. His lazy, aimless thoughts began to form passages and he started putting words together; creating.

He hadn't written book-length before and found solace in creating fiction. He brushed up on his grammar in the library, read a few books on how to write and develop characters and began to write.

The first story was weak. After thirty pages and a week's work he threw it away—dull, boring and terrible. His writing wasn't that sacred. His style was like many others. He determined to write in a story-telling sense: an entertaining and compulsive read.

He used to skim bestseller novels when the story meandered. He felt an author should put his readers on a train to the ending in a straight and interesting line—without excessive embellishment of characters and places, the local stops on the trip. Many authors meandered, and he wasn't able to sustain interest.

Mitchell wasn't about to write like them or follow a pat style formula for writing a novel—creativity has no boundaries. And if editors or publishers didn't like his style the hell with them.

Mitchell was lucky. He found an agent in New York who loved his style and his story—a fast-paced murder mystery based on a real murder in Key West with some unique twists. The agent found the publisher, and writing became his lifestyle.

"The owner pays us a fee every year to maintain the house," said real estate agent Borden. "That's why the house is in good condition. Everything else," he shrugged, "well, it needs people. And love. The animals on the property belong to an adjoining farm about one mile away to the east. They eventually go home. The neighbors maintain the farther fields for their use. But you should have total privacy. We've alerted them to stay away from the house to suppress their curiosity. People around here drop in unannounced.

"I don't know why the owner holds on to the place. With today's real estate prices the land is worth a fortune—a fortune. The owner decided to rent the place to offset the expenses and taxes and you're the first tenant. Call if you need anything."

Shuller's Land was perfect for Mitchell's personality. He was considered by some to be a bit eccentric, not that he was a writer, a bestseller author of mysteries and suspense, but because he always felt more creative living in an abnormal manner away from the routine methods of living and working.

His outburst at the world every Monday morning, rain or shine, hot or cold was defiance—no longer needing to commute to a nine-to-five job in the Monday morning rush hour. Time was his now and exaggerating that fact was inspiring and satisfying, leaving his mind clear to think out the riddles and mazes in his stories.

His wife, Helene, was wonderful. That's why he kept her as his agent. He still loved her but couldn't live with her for long durations. The fault was his.

*   *   *

Mitchell awoke at ten o'clock and shaved. He tried to convince himself to grow a beard and eliminate the nuisance of shaving but couldn't tolerate facial hair. He shaved religiously, the one neatness about him.

He thrived among the unkempt. His bed remained unmade, pants lay on the floor where removed, the shirt was tossed over a chair and the socks were crumpled in balls next to shoes widely separated. The kitchen was worse; a four-day backlog was in the sink and on the counter. The laundry piled in a corner. Why not—who was going to see it?

The house needed attention though the plumbing and electricity worked. The furnishings were vintage 1930s. There were numerous cracks in the plaster and the windows opened with difficulty. He wondered how living there in the winter would be and if the wood burning stove in the living room was adequate to heat the entire house. It looked old.

Mitchell made coffee then, still nude, went to his jeep and brought in the two bags of groceries; supplies for three weeks. He prepared breakfast; two eggs and bacon then sat pondering his novel and the adventures of his characters, leaving the real world behind.

At three o'clock the story became baffling. Something was missing, needing more intrigue, another angle or device. The manuscript was fiction based on an actual murder that turned out to have been committed by the butler. That's what intrigued him. The world had already stopped believing that butlers did it. The real story wasn't powerful enough to make a major novel—to be selected by a major book club giving it bestseller status.

Besides, he had his reputation and pride. He had to turn out a masterpiece in keeping with his standards and fame. The world expected nothing less. He had to add the proper ingredients, now elusive.

At 3:20 he gave up and decided to walk in the woods hoping to find a solution in the fresh air. A sunny July day with the temperature in the low eighties dictated wearing shorts and sandals. On previous walks, he headed north automatically as a magnet toward the North Pole then circled south and back across the weed and dirt road, over two miles. He enjoyed the tranquility in the latter part of the afternoon when the world was tired from the sun.

From the house the road went past the dead oak that once provided the Shuller house the only shade in the expanse. The weeds had encroached on the road that still had definition. Twenty yards from the tree its course curved and headed west to the forest. He began to head north then decided to follow the road toward the south woods, and realized it was his first trip in that direction.

Mitchell walked leisurely, hands in pockets pressed against the thighs with thumbs out. Reaching the trees, he stopped and looked back across the open field. The oak hovered as an eerie gravestone reigning over the loneliness.

What a desolate place he thought, his story problems forgotten. Who lived here? Why didn't someone live here? Why abandoned by its owner? Ah! Who gives a damn, he concluded.

He walked among the pine needles where the weeds were sparse in tree shade. It was the oxygen in the woods, the extra advantage that stimulated his thoughts, why he loved the woods. He attributed the mental surge to the oxygen plants and trees generated.

Within five minutes, his thoughts left the pleasant surroundings and returned to his book. The road led to an opening in the woods by a fifteen-foot gully that ran approximately sixty feet until it inclined to the woods again.

He nearly walked by the dark object in the gully as he gazed at the road in intrigue and fantasy. The object lingered as a black mass in his peripheral vision. The sun shone bright on that side hindering his vision. Then he turned and saw the object.

Time had dulled the exterior and rust covered the roof. The sun couldn't find anywhere to reflect. The chrome rotted years ago. He stared at the abandoned blue Ford pickup truck. The out-of-the-way gully *would* be a likely place to dump a truck in this area. But something was peculiar about the way it had settled there, nearly parallel to the road.

Somebody drove it down, he thought— dangerous but possible. If pushed, wouldn't it have gone straight down and hit the opposite bank head on? He was creating intrigue again. He decided to explore the derelict—because it was there. He had no destination or timetable and curiosity hummed.

Mitchell entered the gully from the far end where the decline was shallow. He walked around the truck treating it as a deadly enemy playing possum. In the open back were remnants of what were two fifty-pound seed sacks, a rusted chain and a toolbox.

The toolbox stimulated him. What was in it? He reached in, grabbed the box and placed it on the hood. Rust clung to his fingers. He rubbed them together.

An attitude formed; a pirate about to open Captain Kidd's treasure chest.

"Avast, lads!" he said aloud. "Stand back you scum before I run you through. We have found it at last!"

He rolled his eyes with mock greed.

The lock was stubborn. He hit the lock hard with a rock. The box opened readily. He unclasped the two latches and lifted the top to expose an adequate tool collection: hammer, hoses, fuses, screwdrivers, pliers, assorted screws and nails, and miscellaneous gadgets; rusted and corroded. If someone abandoned this heap, why would they leave the tools? He put the toolbox back.

The truck's front end was dented. With difficulty, he raised the creaking hood. One end had separated from the body. All parts were in place. He lowered the hood to its original position and headed for the cab. Both windows were open subjecting the interior to the elements. The passenger door was wedged closed. His force couldn't open it. He gave up. With effort, he was able to open the driver's door. Spiders owned the interior. He cleared the webbing with a stick as spiders darted to safety from the onslaught.

The foul odor was repelling. He climbed behind the wheel then shifted to open the glove compartment. The compartment had no lock, and was stuck. He pulled with agony in his fingers and succeeded. Inside was an unopened pack of Lucky Strike cigarettes, a yellowed road map of Long Island and an envelope. He carefully opened the brittle and discolored flap and withdrew folded papers; an insurance policy with a company in Missouri and a registration certificate preserved better than the envelope. Why leave the registration?

The truck was registered to Henry Shuller, age forty-two. Mitchell's mind spun a web of intrigue. The truck belonged to the farm owner. The registration year was 1942. No one has lived on the farm since, almost abandoned. If the truck were dumped, wouldn't Henry Shuller take the registration and his toolbox?—A valuable commodity out here in the boonies? In 1942 the country needed metal. Shuller could have sold it easily. Why dump it?

Mitchell decided to hold on to the registration and wrapped it in the envelope placing it in his back pocket. He closed the glove compartment. Then he noticed the key was still in the ignition; a single key attached to a chain with a rusted American flag charm. *Damn!* That was baffling, also. But if Shuller abandoned the car, what good was the key to him?— And the registration. He put the registration back in the glove compartment.

Then he saw the tip of the handle sticking up wedged between the seat and the passenger door. At first, he thought it part of the door. He grasped the end and pulled.

His eyes widened.

The Luger was still in good condition. Spiders had made a home in the barrel. He examined the Luger and checked the cartridge after suppressing an urge to press the trigger to see if it still worked. The cartridge was full.

He looked for identification marks, but couldn't find any. Should he take the Luger or leave it? He had no desire to carry it on his stroll. Someday he'll come back. What was a loaded Luger doing here?— Probably a war souvenir. He had other matters to solve. He forgot Shuller and his former possessions.

Curiosity lingered. He walked around the truck one more time checking the ground for something that naturally didn't belong there. He found only sand, rocks and weeds.

Mitchell climbed the incline to the road and continued his southward stroll in the forest, his mind on his fictitious butler. In an hour he walked over two miles, oblivious of the real world as a fictitious mist clouded his mind. He was heading north having explored the property's lower portions, still far removed from human life. He knew a neighbor was to the east. Though he hadn't met him yet, he could hear his farm equipment. But the woods were thick and provided privacy. In frustration he gave up on his book. He would look at it fresh tonight.

The scent of the forest felt divine and he focused on his environment—the birds, tree toads and two rabbits living merrily in their habitat. Brown leaves covered the forest floor in a thick layer. The earth was never exposed as the incessant foliage inundated it every year to supply acid and nutrients to the soil. The leaves crunched in freshness beneath his sandals and the crisp crackling sound was euphoric in his mood. Pine and oak branches were low in this area. He skirted them, bending and weaving to protect his eyes, becoming work requiring conscious thought. He returned to the road where the weeds continued to tickle his exposed feet.

The road curved away from the forest and followed the edge of the tree line for a quarter mile before curving easterly toward the house after meeting the road from the north.

He looked to the sky showing his sharp features to the sun. He closed his eyes and let the warm rays flow through him. The sun felt good, but wild gyrations of dots and flashes on his closed eyelids forced him to level his head and open the eyes. Traces of purples and reds faded, and there were no obstructions when he looked toward the barn.

Mitchell noticed that the leaning barn was more lopsided from the front. The barn was a derelict building, useless to him, and never paid attention before. To pass the time he decided to explore to see what 'treasures' it held.

The pine siding had turned gray-brown—a valuable commodity in his friend's modern homes. He marveled at how it stood upright with its severe preference to leaning toward the house as if having a need to touch it.

Attached to the barn was an extension with a sloping roof with three wide openings that faced east. The agent told him it was a potato storage shed. Someone carted the doors away.

He checked the potato storage area first. The long rectangular room was empty—no implements. The ground was level and smooth. He walked around finding no interest in the emptiness, visualizing the room filled with potatoes after the harvest. He went outside again and to the barn.

Mitchell stood in the open doorway surveying the interior.

The doors had fallen; one lay flat, the other leaned against the side. The sun provided spotted light through the holes in the roof. The darker reaches had good visibility. He flicked on the three light switches and, to his surprise, three bare bulbs turned on.

To the right were eight stables with harnessing hanging randomly. He swung open the stable doors, went inside and probed. The earth in all was level except for the last one, which pitched toward the rear. On the other side was more open area. Farm tools lined the front wall by the tractor and its various implements. The tires had leveled. A pitchfork and an ax were on the ground. He picked them up and placed them next to the other tools, near the shovel.

Remnants of hay bales lay by the tractor and behind. He found nothing of interest on that level. His attention turned upward. He climbed the ladder to the loft with cautious footing and careful, went from one end to the other checking his footing with every step. The loft felt hard, secure.

He examined some holes in the roof and concluded they were irreparable by him. He walked around carefully; probing—nothing interesting, except some bird nests that hadn't been occupied for some time. He descended the ladder and pushed against two support poles to test their strength. They felt firm. The rear door was locked with a crossbeam. He probed along the back wall then the west wall toward the tractor.

Mitchell would have missed it if the sun hadn't gleamed off the tiny exposed steel area. He parted the dirt and straw and picked up the dagger. The swastika shocked him. There were imprints on the guard and on both sides of the handle.

Lugers and Nazi daggers!

His curiosity increased. Was there something else lying in the dirt? He took the pitchfork from the front wall to use as a broom where he found the dagger, made wide sweeps along the west wall then around the poles. He uncovered several pieces of short-length rope. He held the strands, examining, wondering who put them there. Were they cut? They looked it. With age it was hard to tell. He let them fall. Then he swept along the south wall.

On the fourth stroke the pitchfork unearthed a black wallet near the last stable. He picked it up, dropped the fork and hurried outside to daylight for a better examination. He blinked to adjust to sunlight and opened the wallet with expectation.

The wallet lacked pictures and identification, but the billfold pocket possessed ten, ten-dollar bills. Alexander Hamilton seemed pleased to see daylight again.

"A wallet with one hundred dollars and a dagger," he marveled. He took the hundred and put it in his pocket. "Well, we finally found some treasure, mates!"

Mitchell was about to discard the corroding wallet then decided to search for secret compartments. His novel-oriented mind flowed again. A loose flap was where pictures should have been. He reached in, pulled, but nothing was there.

Mitchell squeezed the leather and felt resistance. He tore at possible openings. Something was in there. A closer examination revealed an inner layer to the billfold pocket. He yanked it and found a German Army identification card, surprisingly well preserved and a photo of a soldier from the chest up. He turned to let the sun light it better and adjusted the distance from his eyes to focus.

Corporal Carl Dieterman, age eighteen, number 021433724.

Who was Corporal Carl Dieterman and what the hell was his wallet doing here?

TWO

THURSDAY, JUNE 18, 1942.

THE EARLY MORNING HOURS.

THE TUMULTUOUS ATLANTIC was passive that day with waves cresting at two and three feet though the sky was overcast. Below, U-boat 337 headed for the United States and the South Fork of eastern Long Island for an historic spy mission, a prelude to an invasion by Germany.

Lieutenant Commander Guenther Krupp—he made it a point to tell all that he wasn't a member of the industrialist Krupps who built U-boats at the Germania Shipyard at Kiel—was unhappy with his mission and wished some excuse or reason would justify its cancellation.

The war in the Atlantic was at its peak as Hitler's sea wolves continued to devastate shipping and war ships. The U-337 was one of the fiercest sending a total of nearly 75,000 tons of shipping to the bottom not counting two British warships. Krupp needed to be in the action; pursuing, preying, setting tonnage records, not ferrying passengers.

Commodore Karl Dönitz gave him the U-337 in 1941. And here Dönitz was ordering him to ferry soldiers to set them ashore at East Hampton. Krupp couldn't understand that. He cursed the mission's inconvenience, wasting the vital performance of the U-337.

He loved his U-boat, acclimating to the tight world of action, boredom, discomfort and terror. The crew lived worse than he, occupying quarters packed with bunks and hammocks amidst instruments and torpedoes. The four passengers made the situation stifling, adding more body odor to the stench of bilges, cooking, clothing, diesel fuel and cologne that the men used to wash the seawater from their faces. And constant noise, a drone that sometimes forced his ears to ring and hum as an engine.

Nerves were frayed easily in such an environment and cheers from a sinking were psychiatrist's couches, an excellent release.

Krupp was considered a top-ten U-boat commander of the sea wolves. He ranked with illustrious daredevils like Guenther Prien, who commanded the war's first daring raid in October 1939 in Scapa Flow sinking the battleship Royal Oak and killing eight hundred thirty-three officers and crew. And with Wolfgang Luth, who sank more than 200,000 tons; and Karl-Friedrich Marten and Erich Topp with close to 200,000 tons.

Krupp was a warrior with the scent of war buried deep. Thirty years old, he felt as an ancient warrior and looked older. Lack of sun paled his skin.

Darkening rings surrounded his eyes and his sharp features and narrow lips betrayed any form of kindness.

But ferrying passengers? Was Dönitz angry with him? Wasn't his tonnage level good enough to keep him in the top ten?

This ancient gladiator couldn't understand why Dönitz was sending four young German soldiers to America. The group leader, Kretschmer, seemed to be about thirty. The three others looked like children who couldn't be more than twenty-two or three. What harm could they do in America that would outdo the damage U-boat 337 would have done had it used this ferrying time to sink a battleship or a destroyer? What war was this to be against America? Sending children! Thank God this mission would be over in a few hours.

Carl Dieterman, the youngest, wondered why the U-boat commander never smiled at him or his comrades since they came aboard. It seemed that Krupp looked at him scornfully—probably because Dieterman was nauseous and sick the first three days aboard. Dieterman couldn't help it. The cause was the stale air, and he wondered continuously how anyone could live for any time in this underwater Devil's Island.

*   *   *

Commander Krupp gathered his passengers in the compact wardroom to review final preparations.

"Sergeant Kretschmer, we will be reaching the Long Island coast in less than two hours. I suggest you prepare yourself after this meeting. I understand you are to land with uniforms. Are we agreed?"

The soldiers wore white sweatshirts. Krupp wasn't a stickler for uniform regulations with the overcrowded conditions inflicted on his command.

Sergeant Heinrich Kretschmer was annoyed.

"Yes, but civilian clothes will give us an advantage if we're seen."

"I agree. The decision isn't mine. You are landing as soldiers of the German Reich, not as spies. Should you be caught in uniform, and the chances are great at landing, then you will be treated as prisoners of war. In civilian clothes you are spies subject to hanging. Somebody in the High Command is being considerate toward you. The moon is hidden. That is in your favor. I remind you it is dangerous to my crew to stay on the surface longer than necessary. Move quickly when outside. Two men will take you to shore on a rubber raft and return. When you reach shore do not delay my men for a second.

"You should know that another team in naval uniform landed safe last week—on Saturday, I believe—at Amagansett following the procedure you will be following. The naval team's plan was to take the train at Amagansett for New York City. Their mission, like yours, is to sabotage vital industry and transportation. By the way, another team was landed last week in Florida. Believe it or not, General Rommel bet Commodore Dönitz that your team would do better than the naval team." The soldiers smiled with pride finding the bet, if true, amusing.

"The train station in Amagansett is near the beach; your initial mission is a bit more risky. From East Hampton, you will make your way northwest to Riverhead and board the train from there for New York City. Command didn't want you taking the same line. So initially, the naval team has an advantage.

Sergeant Kretschmer, all your maps, train schedules and prime objectives are in this package. The package also contains forty thousand American dollars in tens and twenties. This money should keep you housed, clothed and fed for several years. And here, for each of you, is one hundred dollars to tide you over until the money can be safely divided—when you find permanent lodging."

Kretschmer took the cardboard package and distributed one hundred dollars to each, in ten-dollar bills.

"We," continued Krupp "may never meet again. And yet, we may. Being this close to foreign soil again is dangerous. Once a month on the twenty-second, you are to transmit at midnight to a U-boat in the Fire Island vicinity. You know the assigned frequency. Make sure the money, the ten thousand each, fills your needs for at least two years. Before then we should be in America to join you. Then I'll be happy to see you again." Krupp was pleased with that. "Your official classification for identification when transmitting is Landwolf Three-three-seven. Sergeant Kretschmer, who is your radio man?"

"Corporal Carl Dieterman."

Dieterman raised his arm. Krupp underlined the name on his clipboard notes. It figures, he thought. And a corporal yet!

"Have you any questions?"

He lacked confidence in the four. He wasn't hopeful for their success. They looked like losers. It was his instinct, like knowing if he bet on a specific favorite horse he would lose. But then, he didn't select the foursome—maybe the preceding team would be successful. Their looks and inexperience may be deceiving. Krupp wouldn't have picked these men for this assignment—or any assignment. Maybe the Army knew what it was doing.

There were no questions.

"Good luck, Landwolf Three-three-seven, good luck." Krupp turned to leave—*and good riddance.*

"Sir."

"Yes, Sergeant Kretschmer?"

"May I use your wardroom for a few minutes to review added instructions with my men?"

Krupp nodded approval and left, closing the black curtain.

Heinrich Kretschmer was a tough militarist and a sadistic bastard according to his men. He stood before them, hands brushing his crew cut. He was tall and broad shouldered, and had a pointed nose with wide nostrils that flared when angry, which was often. He was thirty-two, a career soldier and unmarried and had no known relatives.

"I don't like delaying wearing civilian clothes until after we land. But orders are orders. After we land, we head for the sand dunes, change clothes, bury the uniforms, sleep there then set out after nine o'clock when people are out and blend in as summer tourists. We won't have much food. We'll have to find that and shelter, if possible, until we reach New York City. I hope to hell it doesn't rain. It's bad enough we'll have to carry those suitcases. Avoid spending money. We may have to stay longer than Krupp thinks. We'll head into East Hampton then go north-northwest through the back woods and roads to Riverhead.

"Memorize the map and route I've laid out. We'll stay off the roads at darkness. We all speak English well, a touch more British than American but we'll get by. We could be taken as New Englanders.

Remember to pronounce the double-U. You look troubled, Lassen."

Corporal Erich Lassen, twenty-one, and Corporal Peter Lehmann, twenty-three were the munitions experts. Lassen was in the army two years and was the only son of Max and Gertrude Lassen of Berlin. Lehmann, also in the army two years, had a wife in Brandenburg.

"It may be dangerous staying in those dunes at night," said Lassen. He had a sad face, with sad eyes and a frowning forehead. "If there are patrols, we might get caught. And if the naval team got caught, the whole coast will be on alert. Then we could get caught. I'm for moving inland right after we change. The mist will help us and we should be able to move unseen. Peter and I have munitions, explosives to carry, and Carl has the radio. We'll be obvious walking around like that in the daytime. I say we stay to the woods at all times. Let's forget about acting like tourists. Let's do our job unseen and unnoticed. It's a long trip to Riverhead and may take longer than we expect."

Kretschmer pondered the suggestion.

"You impress me, Lassen, an excellent suggestion. You are right. We could get caught with our pants down." He laughed. "Lehmann, what's on your mind?"

Lehmann also had a crew cut but had a more stoic Aryan face with a small space between his two front teeth.

"Erich's thinking is good. I agree."

"I didn't ask you if you agreed. Do you have any other suggestions?"

"No."

Kretschmer looked at Dieterman, amused.

"Dieterman, you look scared."

"I'm not, Sergeant. I may look timid, but I'm not."

"What? Did you and Lehmann go to the same school? Don't you people listen? I didn't say you were timid. I said scared."

"I'm not. Are you?"

Kretschmer stared at him surprised at his comeback. "You're right, Dieterman. You're not timid. What do you think? About the dunes?"

"You're in charge. I'll go with what you say. But Erich is right."

"That's very diplomatic, Dieterman." Then he leaned toward them, glaring. "We've never worked together before. I'm sure you've been told about my reputation. Let me warn you. I don't make mistakes. This is a war mission. Remember you're soldiers and everyone is the enemy. Everyone. We will complete our missions successfully for General Rommel, for the Fatherland. If any of you does anything to prevent that, I will kill you."

They knew he meant it by the flare in his nostrils.

The urgency to fill army quotas deprived Carl Dieterman from completing his high school education. He was drafted six months ago and trained in radio operation without seeing action. This was his first assignment and he accepted it because corporal stripes came with it.

He was five feet-ten inches, had a boyish face Kretschmer didn't think was supported with strength and conviction, close-cut blond hair, and blue eyes— and well-formed teeth and full lips. He could have used a bit more weight to fill in the area beneath his high cheekbones.

His parents, Dr. Wilhelm and Gerda Dieterman, died in 1939 in an automobile accident and he was forced to live with an aunt and uncle who he hated. The Army offered freedom. He had lived in Leipzig, a city in southern Germany.

Dieterman sat alone among the chaos of his comrades in the crowded bunk area. His thoughts were elsewhere, envisioning the mission ahead; the landing, the inland travel, the train trip; New York City and the first sabotage. But failure loomed. Kretschmer was right. He was scared. What if he got caught? How would he react? Spies were hung or electrocuted. Would he be brave knowing he was about to die? Would he beg for mercy? Would he do things he normally wouldn't do to save himself? Say things against his country, his family? Would he crawl on his knees and beg without pride and humility to live? He was trained to be brave, strong when captured. He had hours upon hours of lectures. Theory, he concluded, theory.

"Let's go, Dieterman. Stop daydreaming," Kretschmer barked. "Go stand by the ladder."

Dieterman reacted, grabbed his belongings and moved out following Kretschmer. They joined Lehmann and Lassen.

Krupp's attention focused on the periscope. He lowered the periscope and ordered the crew to surface. It was four in the morning.

"It's hard to see anything at this hour with the mist. The shore lights are barely visible. The odds are on your side."

The engines stopped. The hatch opened and fresh, moist air fought the stench to enter the U-boat. The landing party climbed up. The ocean was favorable and the sky moonless and dark. The mist diminished the sparse lights on Long Island. With drilled efficiency, the U-337's crew launched the raft keeping the guidelines taut.

Reaching the deck was a cleansing to Dieterman. He exhaled hard to rid his memory that horrible experience breathing the U-boat's atmosphere. From the conning tower Krupp watched the soldiers waiting. His U-boat was far offshore to be seen by coast watchers or Coast Guard shore patrols. When his two sailors returned after dropping the passengers on shore, he would wait a few minutes before starting the engines again to give Landwolf 337 time to get inland should an American hear the engines and panic, and sound an alarm.

Dieterman, Lassen, Lehmann and the luggage were in the raft. Kretschmer, waiting his turn, turned to Krupp, clicked his heels and saluted stiff-armed, silent.

Krupp returned the salute thanking God this nuisance mission was almost over, and not at all optimistic about those four soldiers.

THREE

THE INGREDIENT MISSING from the eerie scene were fog whistles thought Dieterman in his nervousness; like the movies where fog whistles of ships passing in the misty night glide across the water. His stomach was beginning to inform it wasn't happy about bobbing on those waves. His heart was pounding loud like the distant surf as the rubber raft neared the shore. Behind him, the U-boat had vanished absorbed by the mist. They reached where waves began to break. Their clothes dampened by mist and spray added to the morning chill.

The two sailors oared with trained vigor, oars barely audible as Landwolf 337 strained tense eyes for life on land. The dunes and beach between East Hampton and Amagansett were lifeless. Kretschmer and Lehmann had Lugers ready as the roar of churning foam and expiring waves increased.

Erich Lassen and Carl Dieterman held the luggage with both hands: the radio, the package with the maps and money, two large black leather suitcases full of explosives, fuses, timers and other explosive paraphernalia, and two medium-sized suitcases with clothing—more clothing and personals can be purchased in New York City. As they neared shore, the surf grew vigorous and angry. A sailor jumped into knee-high water and pulled the raft to shore for better control and to minimize his passengers wetting their shoes. They leaped from the raft to wet, but waterless sand by timing the tide's thrusts and pulls. They scanned the beach east and west then the dunes, and ran crouched to the low dunes splintered with beach grass.

They were at the edge of town. Tension eased to quiet alertness as they edged upward to look over the dune line. The dark was still. As expected, East Hampton slept. The landing succeeded.

The sailors vanished in the mist without a word on a dead-reckoning course to find the U-boat without a safety line to guide them back.

The soldiers mounted the top running low until finding a sand alcove thirty yards from the beach. Dieterman carried the radio and the money package. Kretschmer carried the two suitcases with clothes. The others carried the explosives. The soft sand made the weight seem heavier as their feet sank to the ankles, trampling beach grass.

Feeling secure, they changed clothes, buried the uniforms and stalked north to Montauk Highway. In the distance they heard the whine of engines. The U-boat was leaving. They crossed one by one, keeping low, moving fast in the sparsely residential area. The few houses were dark. The mist near the ocean was thick and the woods dense and dark to enter. The low-growing branches would be a hindrance.

Kretschmer decided against the woods and backyards. He chose to walk the first street heading north and for them to walk in pairs fifty-yards apart. Kretschmer and Lassen were first. Alert they proceeded unnoticed until a forest loomed. With trees came security. The woods were penetrable. Once in the woods, they bunched due to limited visibility.

They traveled for a half-hour and finally reached a clearing. At times, low branches and high brush made the journey difficult. Kretschmer decided they should rest until dawn's light. They settled and waited in silence, their attention eastward toward the sun. Dim daylight assured they were deep in the forest. Kretschmer left, making a circle of one hundred yards to reconnoiter.

Erich Lassen leaned against a tree tired from carrying the heavy suitcase, and watched as Sergeant Kretschmer surveyed. He should have been made the group leader, he thought. He was the one with the brains, with leadership qualities. Dieterman was young, inexperienced. Peter Lehmann had nothing but thoughts of seeing his wife again—all he talked about was how they made love all the time. No, Lehmann was not a dedicated soldier. Maybe Lehmann could find a woman to keep him in shape sexually. Then he could forget the soft nights in bed and concentrate on the mission.

Leaders were born, not made he believed, and he was a born leader whose talents were suppressed by being at the wrong place at the wrong time. The Army hadn't given him the opportunity to develop. It needed men and he a body filling a function. He felt that if the mission succeeded, he would be responsible. His brains were already correcting

Kretschmer's thinking. Staying in the dunes!—God, what a stupid idea. They would have been caught by now if a shore patrol were within hearing distance of that damn U-boat.

Why didn't Krupp allow more time before starting the engines? Idiot. Someone on land could have been convinced it wasn't a fishing vessel. Besides, what if that other team were seen or caught? The area would be heavily guarded.

He would have to learn how to handle Kretschmer; learn when to stand and fight and when to yield when Kretschmer was making stupid decisions. He didn't respect Kretschmer, but feared him. That big dumb sergeant threatened to kill if anyone screwed up. Lassen was convinced he meant it. No, he would question Kretschmer on critical decisions. The sand dunes decision was critical.

Kretschmer had returned, content.

"We should be safe here."

"Let's keep moving," said Lassen. "There may be patrols out and we're still near the shore."

"Don't get carried away with giving orders, Lassen. We're safe here. Besides, it's still early and dark. We'll wait another half-hour. Maybe we'll come across an empty house or a vacant cabin during the week. We could sleep there." He stared at Lassen. "Is that understood?"

Lassen nodded. It wasn't a major point to question. Kretschmer was partly right—it was dark and foggy. But the decision left him uneasy and rest was uncomfortable.

FOUR

IN THE LATE thirties and early forties, the farming community of East Hampton was evolving to prominence as an artist colony as such renowned painters as Ernst, Motherwell, Leger, and Wilcox settled here. Ernst married Peggy Guggenheim, a supporter of American artists, and soon East Hampton's artistic affluence spread.

Gavin Garland, a broad man with red hair and beard, with sparkling happy eyes that expressed his warmness and compassion for people, came to East Hampton in May 1942 with his wife and two daughters, renting two rooms in a boarding house on Main Street. Garland was considered destined for greatness as a leading American painter of rural and suburban life. He was a strong addition to the artist colony.

He woke at four-thirty on the morning of Thursday, June 18, 1942 and silently slid out of bed not to awaken Lorraine, his wife, and two daughters sleeping on cots along the interior wall.

On occasion, he rose early for the dawn light that inspired his paintings. He had prepared his utensils—easel, palette, brushes, folding seat, food, and paint—and packed them to strap over his shoulder. The pack was always ready, except for the food, to move at sudden inspiration.

Gavin dressed and entered the kitchen. Lorraine came in behind him, eyes squinting from the light. Bobby pins fastened her hair. She gave a sleepy-faced yawn.

"Where to this morning, lover? What else inspires you besides me today?"

Gavin kissed her. "I told you last night."

"Tell me again. I guess it didn't register or have I forgotten already?" She returned the kiss.

"I heard about an open area, a gully, out at a place called Shuller's Land that might be worthy. I called the owner and he approved my being there. He gave me directions."

"A gully? How attractive can a gully be?"

She rubbed her eyes open and massaged her oval face to stimulate the drowsiness.

"Shadows and light, love. That's the only gully I've heard of here. It's worth exploring for an unexpected aura."

"After fifteen years being married to you, I should know you by now and know everything, no matter how ugly is beautiful to you."

"Except for you. You're beautiful-beautiful."

He kissed her again, rubbing her rear.

"It may rain," she said.

"It's just overcast. It'll clear by noon. I'll be back by three, four. Now, why don't you go back to sleep? I must go to work to send our girls to college."

"That's ten years away. Let's go back to bed."

She winked and moved her eyebrows, beckoning. He grinned.

"Later."

"Your loss. Let me make some coffee before you go."

"Thanks, but I'm late already."

"How far away is this gully?"

"It's a good hike from town."

"Have a nice day, Gavin. Miss me."

"I will. Always do. You're my inspiration."

"No, I'm not. But it sounds good."

They kissed. He took the pack and left.

Outside, he harnessed the pack on his back, made a right on Main Street, a right on Route 27—Montauk Highway heading east—and then north into the woods.

Familiar with the surrounding wooded area, Gavin moved through the open areas skirting brush and low branches. He had an excellent sense of direction and moved confidently. The rising light assured he was headed correct. The mist had thinned considerably and visibility was nearly two hundred yards. He thought he saw people up ahead. Garland knew young people camped in the woods during the summer months, a common sight.

*   *   *

The half-hour had passed slowly for Landwolf 337 as they watched the day brighten and listened to the birds welcoming the day.

Dieterman bolted and whispered in panic.

"Someone's coming!"

Kretschmer turned toward the sound of boots

crunching leaves and twigs and saw a tall man with a red beard and backpack heading towards them.

As Gavin Garland approached the four men, he didn't see any camping gear—just luggage, a carton, and a radio. They were well dressed and clean-cut looking. He didn't feel threatened. Besides, he could handle himself well in any situation. His street upbringing in New York's Hell's Kitchen had toughened him for any situation or confrontation.

"Hello, there," Gavin called out waving.

"I'll handle this," Kretschmer whispered to his men and stood to greet the bearded man. The others smiled and waved back as Kretschmer walked toward the intruder.

"Good morning to you," Kretschmer said.

"Good morning," Gavin said again. He shook Kretschmer's hand and turned to greet the others.

"You guys are sure up early. I thought I was an early bird." He pointed to the luggage. "Couldn't you get a room in town? How . . ."

The words strangled in Gavin's throat severed by the dagger, thrust up to the hilt. He fell, gargling, hands at his throat and reddened by blood. His movements ceased abruptly. Dieterman, Lassen, and Lehmann were stunned, horrified. Kretschmer turned to them to stifle comments.

"Remember, we are German soldiers. This is war. We can't afford to have anyone identify us. And he saw us. This is what soldiers must do to survive."

Though shocked, Lassen was impressed with Kretschmer's efficiency. The dumb sergeant *was* a killer, but rightly so. Lassen reacted first.

"He's right, Peter, Carl. It had to be done. To let him go might have been risky." He turned to

Kretschmer, who had asserted command. "Shall we bury him?"

"It doesn't matter. Let's leave. I imagine it will be a while before others come this way. Take his valuables. Make it look like a robbery."

Kretschmer pulled the dagger from the throat oblivious to the grotesque expression on Gavin Garland's face, cleansed the blood by sticking the dagger into the ground several times then sheathed it beneath his sport shirt.

Lassen helped Lehmann pilfer the body. Kretschmer looked at Dieterman staring at the dead man whose eyes were wide open from the sudden shock.

"What's the matter, Dieterman? Never saw a dead man?"

Dieterman shook his head and mumbled a faint "No."

"Well, have a good look because that's your enemy. You kill before they kill you. Now snap out of it and get ready."

Dieterman stood solemn, holding the transmitter pack and the carton, unbelieving Kretschmer's ugly war philosophy. *This is war. You are a soldier. He is the enemy. Kill first.*

He tried hard to accept the killing, to find justification. He turned his back to the corpse to help him accept Kretschmer's command.

As they were leaving, Dieterman looked over his shoulder at the intruder and wondered if he had a family.

FIVE

GRACE CONNERLY TOOK a two-day vacation from her job as assistant story editor at the *Saturday Evening Post* to open her summerhouse in East Hampton and her ten-year-old son, Douglas, missed school because the opening was an exciting ritual. They left their apartment at 74th and York Avenue in New York City at six-thirty that morning and headed north in their 1940 Buick on the East River Drive to the Triboro Bridge and onto the Grand Central Parkway to Long Island.

Doug's bicycle was tied to the roof. The back seat and trunk were laden with clothes, food and utensils—the initial needs to ready for the summer. When readied, the future weekend trips would then be by railroad to save war-rationed gasoline. She'd leave the car by the East Hampton station.

"I hope it will be as exciting as last year, Mom."

"It should be, sweetheart."

"With Dad not here and all. You know."

"Unfortunately, Doug, the Navy needs him in the Pacific. But I don't mind as long as I'm with you."

She ruffled his hair and touched the face that had her features. Douglas smiled from his mother's attention that played to his ego.

Grace Connerly was a striking, beautiful woman, educated and poised—a Barnard graduate. Her first job was in an advertising agency as a junior copywriter doing industrial ads. She ran from there when offered a job at the *Post*. Advertising wasn't creatively challenging for her; at least, industrial ads.

She would have preferred to summer at Southampton, but her husband, Lawrence, didn't want to summer or vacation with, in his opinion, a bunch of snobs. He believed that snobs had no fun since they were always looking snobbish to impress upon other snobs that they were better snobs. His exaggerated theory usually made Grace laugh. But she agreed with him; a summer place was to get away from everybody.

They had bought the four acres three years ago and built the house a year later. The property was accessible by a paved dead-end road. The house was positioned well into the woods in the event the road was extended and traffic reduced their privacy. A dirt path weaved through the woods to the house. The area suited them. The house was far enough away from Main Street and close enough to the beach. Their place in the sun was tailor-made.

Then came the excitement seeing the home being built. They would stay at a boarding house in town and spend the days at the beach and watching the construction. The Connerlys would bring coffee and donuts for the crews. When the house was theirs, and before furniture arrived, they sat on the floor and had lunch sniffing the smell of new paint, wood and plaster.

The area was a playground of freedom for Douglas. Something Grace knew he needed. It took some time to adjust her city mentality that he could run and play out here without fear of traffic or cement bruises. When he needed male companionship, Grace would drive him to a friend's house or he would have friends over.

All was beautiful in her life except the war.

"You did a good job with that bike, Doug."

They were passing LaGuardia Airport.

"Jackson helped me." Jackson was the apartment building's doorman. Douglas was stretching to see the planes.

"You both did a good job. I couldn't have gotten ready without you." Grace was encouraging Douglas to feel needed. "Now you're the man in my life. You know you have work to do out there. All the things Daddy used to do. Can you handle it?"

"Sure," he replied looking at the planes. "I know what has to be done."

"Be sure to let me know if you need help."

"I will."

Grace smiled at her son. The bud of male responsibility was beginning to bloom.

*   *   *

Landwolf 337 moved northward through the woods often brushing inchworms and ticks from their clothes. Carl Dieterman felt Lassen and Lehmann accepted the killing as war because they were joking and laughing with Kretschmer. Why not, reasoned Dieterman? They were used to killing, taken dozens of lives with their explosives, and would take more. Was he the only one having a foul taste in his mouth and a weight in his stomach? The Army had toughened Lassen and Lehmann. Why hadn't it toughened him?

Another half-hour brought them to a clearing and a paved road. Kretschmer checked his compass and map.

"It's small to be on the map. It leads north. Let's get back in the woods and follow it."

Within a half-mile, the road ended and they saw the one-story house in the distance. The house was nearly square with cedar planking in board-and-batten style stained light gray.

"Get down!" Kretschmer hissed in a semi-whisper. Assured no one was outside, he waved Lehmann on. "Check it out."

Lehmann moved with stealth from tree to tree and pressed against the house, listening. All windows were closed on that side. He moved carefully and leaned out and checked the rear windows. Closed. He peeked in the kitchen window.

He circled the building then reported to Kretschmer.

"It's empty and looks like nobody lives there."

"Probably haven't opened for the summer yet. Let's go in. It's the perfect place to rest for a few hours. It will be dark walking in these woods when night falls. Is there a way in?"

"The back door looks possible."

"Okay, you check that. Dieterman, test the windows on the far side. Lassen, you take this side. I'll try the front. Move."

All entrances were secure. Lehmann attempted to pick the back door lock.

"Lassen, stand guard out there," Kretschmer ordered pointing toward the road. "Dieterman, break that window. We have no choice." He indicated a side window.

Dieterman took his handkerchief and placed it near the latch. With his Luger he hit the handkerchief and shattered a small area. The opening was large enough for his hand. He turned the latch and pushed the window open. He climbed in and opened a door.

The room was a large living/dining room with one door leading to the kitchen, the other to the hall. Two bedrooms were on the other side. The living room was decorated with rattan furniture, pictures and a large mirror. The furnishings were covered with white sheets. They spread out and checked the house then congregated in the living room. "Not a goddamn thing to eat." Kretschmer was annoyed. "Let's eat the crap we have. I'm starved."

About to settle at the dining room table to open their canned and dry food, Lassen pounded on the back door in panic. Kretschmer rushed to open it.

"There's a car coming!"

"Quick, get back in the woods."

Lassen took off, crouching. Kretschmer hurried to the living room window and saw the car through the trees.

"Dieterman, get out and hide in the woods on the other side. Hurry!"

Dieterman ran. Kretschmer and Lehmann shoved the luggage in a closet. Lehmann cleared the table and moved to the front to cover the right window near the mirror and couch. From there, he had a good view of the front door entrance and path.

Kretschmer pressed against the wall next to the living room door. Their Lugers were drawn. Kretschmer cursed to himself—nothing seemed to be going right.

SIX

GRACE CONNERLY WAS tired from the long journey and felt exhilaration at reaching their destination. She inhaled deep while taking in the scenery that belonged to her. She turned the motor off where the paved road ended.

"We're finally here. Okay, man of the house, what do we do first?"

She looked forward to this weekend with Douglas—an opportunity to get to know him better, to get closer, as a friend and companion by helping to fill the void from his father's absence. She would diminish maternal authority this weekend, time to do that at his age to some degree. For now, she would suppress mothering attitudes—except when necessary.

"Okay, let's see," pondered Douglas in his new role. "Why don't you go and open the windows and air out the place." He remembered his father saying that last year. "I'll start undoing the bicycle. Then you come back and help me take it down and then we'll take the rest inside. Good?"

"Perfect."

"Let's go lady. Get moving," he grinned.

"Yes sir." She saluted.

When Grace got out she absorbed another thankful survey and stretched her tired body. She loved being here, the flipside of her city lifestyle. Douglas began loosening the knots. Grace headed for the house. As she walked the path to the front door Lehmann watched her from shadows. When she neared, he pressed against the wall and couldn't see her where she stopped at the door. They heard the lock click twice and the door open.

Grace turned her nose at the stale air, hurried to the first bedroom and opened both windows. This was Doug's room. Some dust lay toward the corners, but a vacuuming will fix that. She would prepare his room first, help him unpack then let him start in the living room. She had left the closet door and the drawers open for circulation and they smelled fine. She wiped her hand quickly on the bureau and left dust tracks. Brushing her hands, she left.

She came back to the hall, entered the second bedroom and opened the larger window. She wiped the picture of her and Lawrence on her bureau and kissed his face. She took a cursory review around the room and left heading for the door leading to the living room.

Kretschmer and Lehmann could hear her footsteps. Lehmann hid behind the couch. Outside, Lassen and Dieterman watched Douglas.

Grace opened the door. The house was a bit chilly, but this room felt colder and breezy. She entered and headed for the window. She saw the broken window and froze. Her first thought was a burglary. But what could they take? Did somebody come in and stay here? Then an alarming thought occurred—Was someone here? She began to turn with apprehension.

"Don't move!" Kretschmer commanded. The voice was riveting.

There was upheaval in her body. Grace stayed still. "Now turn around slowly and come toward me," the voice ordered.

The voice was authoritative, demanding obedience in the face of harm. To her right, she saw a man rising from behind the couch and a strange gun pointing at her. Lehmann moved back to his position by the front window. She turned toward Kretchmer whose stern face studied her.

"What . . . what do you want? Why are you here?" Grace asked nervous, with heart pounding.

"Shut up. Come here to me and turn around. Do as I say and we won't harm you." She found some reassurance in his tone as she moved closer to him. She stopped three feet away. "Now turn around."

She turned slowly—obedient, looking over her shoulder to ensure Kretschmer wouldn't strike her with the gun.

"Don't look at me," he said. "Face front."

She did, hunching her shoulders expecting a blow. Kretschmer put the Luger behind his belt and pressed close to Grace. He reached around with his right hand and covered her mouth then wrapped his left arm around her body and pressed closer. The feminine scent made him forget the danger for an instant. He savored it.

"Don't fight or make a sound. Is it just you and the boy?"

She nodded.

"No one in the back seat? Sleeping maybe?"

Her head shook. The tremor in her body told him she was telling the truth.

"Lehmann, what's he doing?"

"He's untying a bicycle from the roof of the car."

Kretschmer loosened the pressure on Grace's mouth as she had difficulty breathing.

"Relax, lady. Everything's going to be all right once he comes in here. You do anything stupid and he'll get hurt. No harm will come to him. Or to you."

Her eyes still exhibited fright.

Dieterman lay prone behind thick brush and watched Douglas working. He was a bit deep in the woods to see Douglas clearly. He had a better view of the car's front. Lassen's view was unobstructed from his southern position.

Douglas began to wonder what was taking his mother long and kept glancing at the path. He had one more knot to go. It had taken him longer than expected. Jackson had made the knots tight and didn't want to cut the rope to use it again. His impatience forced him to call out.

"Mom! Hurry up!"

He concentrated on the knot and it loosened and untied. His fingers stung. He gathered all the rope and tossed it on the front seat. Then he leaned against the fender to wait for his mother. After ten impatient seconds, he decided to have the trunk ready for unloading. He pulled the keys from the ignition and opened the trunk. Then he emptied the back seat piling the boxes and bags by the roadside. Then he emptied the trunk. He leaned against the fender again and waited for his mother.

The next minute was nerve wracking. Impatient, he took a small suitcase, a bag with laundry products and headed for the house.

"Mom!" He called again when twenty feet from the house. "Mom! What's taking you so long?"

Then he became suspicious.

His bedroom window was open; the living room windows were closed. He went off the path parallel to the house to check the bedroom windows along the side. Open. On a straight line, skirting the possible danger, he went to the other side to check the kitchen, living and dining room windows. Closed. Was one broken? Why would it take her long to open the windows? Maybe she had to go to the bathroom.

Unsure, he went back to the path where he had stopped. He felt something was wrong. A chill ran through his body like the ones he would have when a horror movie overwhelmed him. He called his mother again, loud and waited for a reply. He walked with hesitancy toward the house with cropped steps as if walking a tightrope.

"Mom!"

He stopped ten feet from the front door. By now, the house had become a frightful monster. He was about to shirk it off as his imagination, but he saw movement in the window as he strained to look through the glass reflection. He thought he saw a man's shadow in the living room mirror. He looked harder, feet cemented in place, body leaning forward.

Lehmann shifted his position farther back to the wall, but his movement showed in the mirror. Douglas saw the movement of a human figure.

"Mom! Is that you?"

This time, his voice was weaker, questioning, a cautious yell tinged with fear. The fear grew and quiet panic set in. If his mother, why didn't she answer? He had to get away from there—to get help!

He set the suitcase and the bag on the ground.

"Hey, Mom! I'm going to leave the stuff here for you. I'm going for the rest. Okay?"

He moved backward, his eyes probing the windows and measuring each backward step. Then he turned and ran as fast as he could toward the road.

Lehmann saw him bolt, smashed the window and yelled, "Lassen! Dieterman! Get him! Get him!"

Grace Connerly nearly collapsed.

The man's voice propelled Douglas and he began to cry, fearing for his mother. He had to get help. Douglas flew out of the woods and with arms and legs flailing with all-out energy he raced down the paved road thankful he wore his sneakers.

Lassen and Dieterman chased him. Lassen was closer because of his position in the woods. By the time Lassen reached the road, Douglas was nearly fifty yards ahead. Dieterman was twenty yards behind Lassen. Douglas was swift and his lead increased.

Lassen was convinced the boy wasn't catchable. In frustration, he pulled the Luger at a full run, stopped, took random aim and fired.

Douglas went down with a scream tumbling and landing on his back, his hands trying to stop the blood rushing out his right thigh. He writhed in agony— the pain, searing.

Aghast that Lassen fired, Dieterman ran past Lassen to the fallen boy thrashing in pain. Lassen followed, stopped ten feet from Douglas and looked around to make sure no one heard the shot and was investigating. Breathless, Dieterman knelt by Douglas and tried to calm him as Douglas struggled to move away on his elbows. His eyes were filled with terror afraid the man was coming in for the kill.

Dieterman placed his hands on Douglas as a reassuring gesture.

"Stay still. I'll stop the bleeding."

Douglas didn't believe him.

"Stay still!"

Dieterman pulled his belt to make a tourniquet. Douglas continued to struggle backward, blood flowing, survival instincts controlling his mind. His panting was loud and erratic.

"Stay still! Stay still!"

Dieterman grabbed him.

"I won't hurt you. I swear!"

Douglas stopped moving. If the man planned to kill him, he would have done so by now instead of trying to tie the belt around his leg. Dieterman had raised his leg and was about to tie the belt when Lassen interrupted him.

"Not here, in the woods! Take him in the woods and tie it there. It's too open here!"

Dieterman conceded.

"Right. You're right."

He lifted Douglas upright, and with Lassen's help they half lifted and dragged Douglas about forty yards into the woods to the first wide clearing. They lay him down. Dieterman slid the belt beneath the bleeding leg. Lassen moved away from the kneeling Dieterman and checked the road from there. Dieterman wrapped the belt above the wound and tightened. Douglas was breathing hard, terrified. Dieterman gave comfort to settle him by holding his shoulders.

"The bleeding will stop soon. You'll be all right."

He watched the boy's glare dilute as he began to relax. Douglas felt the danger to him had passed.

"Where's my mother? What have you done with my mother?"

"She's fine, fine. Nothing's going to happen to either of you. What's your name?"

"Douglas."

"Douglas, mine's Carl. You shouldn't have run away. This wouldn't have happened."

Dieterman checked the belt. The bleeding was subsiding, but he knew the bullet had hit bone and the boy would need professional help soon. For now, stopping the bleeding was all he could do.

"I want my mother. I want to see my mother, please."

"I'll take you to her in a minute as soon as the bleeding stops."

Dieterman's voice tempered Douglas's fears and he began to believe this man wanted to help him; he wanted to believe. But then his eyes shifted from Dieterman to Lassen and the trauma returned. His senses screamed.

Dieterman looked at the boy's horror-filled eyes as they looked over his shoulder. What was frightening him? He turned quick.

Lassen was pointing the Luger at Douglas.

"Stand back, Carl." The demand was monotone and businesslike.

"Erich, he's only a boy! He can't harm us!"

"Move back."

"No, I can't let you. Have you lost your mind?"

He leaned forward to protect the boy's body. Douglas was now in panic crawling away on his back. Lassen remained unyielding.

"Carl, you're making this difficult."

"For God's sake! We can't do this!"

The explosion in Dieterman's ears was deafening.
The roar muted the impact of the bullet crushing
Douglas's face.

"Nooo!" Dieterman screamed. "Nooooooo!"

The body beneath him stopped moving.

He looked at the bloody mess of what was once a
child's face and his body shook and heaved.

Carl Dieterman vomited on the boy's shirt.

SEVEN

THE FIRST SHOT nearly stopped Grace's heart. The second shot and the time between were a nightmare of panic and fearing for her child. With the shots came the sense that all things human and right ceased to exist. It was war.

Kretschmer knew the danger had passed when he heard Dieterman's yell. That fool had objected to Lassen doing his job. He released his hold on Grace.

Rejecting the danger around her and with only one thought in mind, she tried to run to her son. Kretschmer restrained her. Lassen came into the room holding his Luger and nodded to Kretschmer. Grace knew by the way Lassen looked at her that he had killed her son. Her muffled anguish became louder and she cried. Kretschmer's hand squeezed her mouth deadening her scream.

"Quiet!" he ordered.

Grace disobeyed, her grief out of control.

"Lassen, where's Dieterman?" Kretschmer asked.

"He's outside throwing up."

"That figures," Kretschmer sneered.

Grace was beginning to smother from his hold.

Kretschmer became aware of his left hand across her right breast and he began to massage.

Grace struggled to breathe.

Kretschmer inhaled to absorb her cologne and clean, scented hair. The more she struggled, the tighter he held. Then he pulled the blouse open ripping the buttons off. Kretschmer spun her toward Lehmann.

"Stop fighting or that man will shoot you."

Lassen raised his gun. Grace looked at the Luger and retreated from struggling as Kretschmer eased his grip and her breathing came easier.

Lehmann and Lassen watched with contained desire as Kretschmer lifted the brassiere and exposed her breasts. He massaged each one slowly, whispering in her ear, "Hmmm, doesn't that feel good?"

The half-naked woman stirred Lehmann reminding him of his wife—same firm breasts with pink, blushed nipples. He watched, envious, impatient now for a turn to feel the softness.

"If you move, he'll shoot you," Kretschmer said.

He removed his hand from her mouth and breast. She clenched her teeth and closed her eyes, vibrating from hatred. Fear had died within her with the death of her child.

Kretschmer removed the blouse remnants and tossed them to the floor. His passion began to stir and he hardly heard Grace's clenched whisper, "God! Give me strength!"

Kretschmer undid the brassiere and it fell next to the blouse. He unbuttoned the skirt and it fell around her feet.

"Lift your feet."

She stepped away from the skirt.

Kretschmer pulled out his dagger and began to cut the panties from her, and then she stood naked, in shoes and socks. He sheathed the dagger.

He unbuttoned his pants and pressed against her, his hands around her, surrounding and massaging both breasts. His breathing grew heavier. Lassen and Lehmann became excited watching him.

War had turned the atmosphere to eroticism.

"Come here, Lassen," Kretschmer called as he kissed her neck. "I think she wants us both. Don't you, darling?"

Grace still had her eyes closed hiding from this nightmare, oblivious to his touches and kisses.

He pressed down on her shoulders. She resisted.

"Get on your knees."

He pressed harder. She opened her eyes. Lassen was coming toward her, undoing his belt. Kretschmer pressed again.

"On your knees. Now! Lehmann, you're next. But first, Lassen."

Lehmann's eyes flared with anticipation. Kretschmer pressed harder. Grace bent her knees slowly as Kretschmer pressed and she watched her son's murderer coming closer. She went to one knee.

Kretschmer eased the pressure. Lassen came closer.

Revenge began to erupt and a rage built as she watched that vile, snickering animal that killed her boy coming to attack her.

With wild abandon and blind rage, she sprang at Lassen her fingers gouging his face drawing blood as she screamed loud to summon the strength to gouge his eyes out.

"Bastard! *Bastard!*"

Lassen screamed from pain. Grace kept screaming piercing, incoherent sounds and clawing. Lassen tried to restrain her arms. Kretschmer tried to pull her away by the hair.

Lehmann shot her in the head.

She stood petrified for a moment. Kretschmer moved away and she fell backward with a shuddering thud. She was dead before hitting the floor.

Dieterman had stopped convulsing just before he heard the shot.

"Oh, God. No."

Weak-legged he rose and stood over Douglas mournfully then wiped his mouth as he hurried to the house, spitting to rid the foul taste.

Lassen, Kretschmer and Lehmann hadn't moved since Grace fell stunned by the turn of events and deprived their sexual toy. Lassen's face was bleeding, streaking his jaw then falling. He attempted to stop the flow.

Carl Dieterman fell limp against the doorway disgusted with the scene and his comrades. The woman was sprawled on her back, legs and arms spread. The pool of blood increased. Lassen and Kretschmer's exposed organs had shrunk.

"This isn't war and you're not soldiers," Dieterman scolded. "You are murderers of women and children—sadistic raping swine! Do you hear me? Despicable swine! *Do you hear me?*"

EIGHT

LASSEN AND LEHMANN put Douglas's body in the car trunk slamming the lid shut after removing Dieterman's belt. They took their food to the kitchen and ate after hiding their gear in the woods.

Eleven o'clock. Dieterman took his belt and went to Grace's bedroom exhausted from vomiting and disgust. He fell asleep.

Sitting around the dining room table, the 'swine' ate in silence. Grace's body lay ten feet away where she fell.

"We were caught off guard. Very foolish of us," said Kretschmer.

"Yes," said Lassen. "But I would have loved to have her. She was beautiful. I haven't had a woman in months."

The left side of his face was scarred and reddened from two deep scratches, one close to the eye. The bleeding had stopped, leaving dark lines.

"If you're so damn horny, why don't you do it now? She's still warm and she can't fight back,"

Lehmann said nodding toward Grace. "Put a towel over her face so you won't have to look at her."

"Don't be a wise guy," Lassen retorted.

"Let's get back to business," Kretschmer interrupted. "I'm debating whether we should go to Riverhead in the car. I'm tired walking in these damn woods."

"It's best we don't," answered Lassen. "Some permanent resident may recognize the car. We've come this far. And we shouldn't stay here much longer. Let's find a car away from East Hampton and the shore."

Lassen wondered how Kretschmer would react to his suggestion this time. Kretschmer didn't object to the initiative.

"Right. But we've got to sleep to be alert. Lehmann, you sleep for two hours. Tell Dieterman to do the same if he isn't already asleep. Lassen and I will stand guard. Then we'll sleep for two hours. I want to leave here before four-thirty. We'll find another place farther on where there aren't neighbors for miles. The country north of here should be more remote, farming country. We'll get a good night's sleep tonight. If the farm is isolated or abandoned, maybe we'll stay there an extra night and listen to the radio news if they have a radio. I wonder if that naval group got caught. I don't expect anyone else will be coming to this house today."

They awakened Dieterman and Lehmann in two hours. Lehmann took the watch by the road— Dieterman, the back woods.

Carl Dieterman leaned against a tree and tried to sleep uncaring anymore if he got caught to end the killing nightmare. If caught, he wasn't sure they would be hung as spies, but if anyone found out they killed three persons including a child . . .

He knew he would be considered as guilty as the others, an accomplice. To hell with guard duty—he needed more sleep to clear his head and rest his body from its shock. He slept for an hour and a half then woke as a soldier in combat, alert and startled.

He looked at his watch and seemed pleased to have wakened before the two hours. Kretschmer wouldn't have tolerated sleeping on guard duty. He would have gone berserk.

At 4:10, Landwolf 337 moved out in the direction of Shuller's Land.

NINE

HENRY SHULLER HAD much to be thankful for today; the planting started in early May was finished yesterday. The cool weather potato would be ready for harvesting in late summer and fall.

In late August he would kill the vines to keep the potatoes from sprouting. After years living with its numerous diseases and pests, he still loved to walk among the coarse, dark-green potato plants covering his land like a green carpet speckled with white flowers.

Now the land near the house looked neat, trim and rich brown with its scalloped rows planting mounds. He began the May planting in the northern fields hiring two local men, as he did each year, to help with the planting. At harvest time he would hire migrant workers to collect the potatoes. Then store the crop in the pitched-roof storage barn, keeping the doors closed during the day to keep the sunlight out and opening the doors in the evening to let the cool air circulate. When the potato storage barn became full, he would use the back half of the regular barn up to the last four and unused stables for extra storage. But this year the crop wouldn't be stored for more than a few days. The United States Army bought the entire crop.

He became concerned about a new problem, the golden nematode—a potato-ravaging worm discovered in America in 1941 in neighboring Nassau County to the west. The nematode infestation destroyed the Nassau crop that year. Authorities assured Henry and Suffolk County farmers that strict controls were being implemented to prevent the spread eastward.

The military became concerned on this attack on a vital food source. They informed Henry to expect a visit from Washington officials sometime in late July or August to inspect the crop. He wasn't concerned at all about this. His crop and dirt were clean.

Henry Shuller was a rugged, strong man at forty-two: a man of the land, of fresh air, of sun and daylight. He left the fields when darkness, cold, hunger or sleep prevailed. He thrived on fresh air. He felt as a caged animal on rainy days and in winter, impatient to begin a new day outdoors.

So were all the Shuller men since his family came here from Virginia to escape the ravages of the Civil War. An unconfirmed rumor came down the family chain that his great-grandfather had waylaid two Union payroll couriers and made off with five thousand Yankee dollars. He never admitted to committing the robbery or could explain to family members how he got the money to buy the land. "The good Lord always provides," he would say.

Henry's mother said the robbery was restitution for the land and home the Union Army destroyed.

And with that claim the Shuller pride was massaged. To them, this land wasn't just a farm, not just another piece of property. This was Shuller's Land!—A prideful proclamation to God, the world and the Yankees. Signs were posted accordingly.

Henry Shuller was the last in the male line, the last of the original Shullers. His wife, Martha, had a hysterectomy after the birth of their only child, Melissa, seventeen years ago. His family name would end with Melissa. He regretted never having the sons he wanted to help him around the farm and to carry on the family tradition and pride. Martha died from pneumonia in 1937.

Thoughts on marrying again were fleeting. Then came those lonely nights when he yearned to sleep next to a woman. The thoughts were prevalent during winter when he was caged and rested from working the fields. Maybe someday, someone would come along he would say to himself. Now he was busy enough raising potatoes and Melissa. He considered her prettier than his wife, and blessed by nature. She had his wife's finest features: the mouth and nose. Melissa often reminded him of Martha, and that was a blessing.

He named Melissa after his mother who died twenty years ago. Shuller tradition named the children after family members. He was named after his grandfather.

Melissa would be late coming home from school today, the last day. Then she would spend the afternoon with her best friend, Patricia Griffin, their nearest neighbor a mile to the east. He and Sean Griffin, Patricia's father, grew up together and were friends.

Shuller's house was small but adequate for two people. It had a kitchen, bedroom and a good-sized living room with good durable furniture, including a sofa that opened into a bed. He slept there. Melissa used the bedroom. In a corner of the living room was a standing RCA Victor radio with bands for standard broadcast, special services and short wave— a beautiful furniture piece with light and dark walnut veneers. He bought it for Martha eight years ago as a Christmas present.

He enjoyed listening to the radio programs with Melissa, a device to share an excuse for companionship. Their relationship had gone beyond father and daughter. Henry treated her as an adult. He never told her what to do, avoiding paternal authority. Now, he asked for her opinion and asked politely. He was pleased with his communication with his daughter.

But next year she would go to college, to New York University in Washington Square in New York City. Then he would be alone except for the weekends and holidays when she visited. He would plan to visit her. He hadn't been off the farm in years and a good opportunity to be among crowds again. This summer would be a special one for both, especially for him.

Four o'clock was early for him to start cooking. He prepared dinner when Melissa was late. He enjoyed cooking and taught Melissa how to cook. He left the house for the barn to feed Warrior, the sole stable occupant. He had two other horses. Having no real use for them he sold them the previous fall.

Warrior belonged to Melissa. She rode him regularly through the woods and when visiting the Griffins and others. On school mornings, he would drive her to the main road about three miles south to catch the school bus then pick her up at four.

Today she planned to walk the mile from the Griffins through the fields and woods.

TEN

LANDWOLF 337 REACHED the edge of Shuller's Land at 4:40 and at 5:15, reached the gully. They skirted around the gully and found the dirt road. With searching eyes they sought signs of human life, ears strained listening for farm machinery. They crossed the road towards the field and crouched near the edge of the woods. The fields were lifeless. The stillness added loneliness to the house and barn shaded by the large oak. A pickup truck parked near the tree.

They studied Shuller's Land.

"This looks like a perfect place—nothing around but privacy. It's small enough. There shouldn't be many people." Kretschmer's eyes followed the road from the house to the woods. "It looks like that road is the one behind us. Lassen, when you get to where the road turns toward the house, you and Dieterman stay behind with the equipment. Lehmann and I will go to the house like lost tourists and ask for directions giving us a chance to survey the situation. Let's go."

They moved into the woods then returned to the road and reached the turn. Dieterman and Lassen hid behind brush. Kretschmer and Lehmann headed for the house. They reached the field strolling casual.

"I don't like this, Sergeant."

"Why not?"

"It's open and far from the trees."

"It's isolated. Let's see what's there first and what we can find out. If it's wrong, we leave."

"What I'm saying is that we should move on and find an abandoned house. This one has people, and people mean trouble."

"What are you, another Lassen with you thinking? Don't think. I'll do that for you."

Lehmann retreated.

"We can handle it . . . if we have to," Lehmann agreed.

To Lehmann, that meant more killing, no survivors to identify them. Maybe the farmer had a pretty wife or someone to remind him of his wife.

Henry Shuller had fed Warrior and was in the kitchen preparing broiled chicken. Salad ingredients were on the counter. Coffee perked. The dishes and place settings were on the table. Melissa was expected in less than a half-hour. He opened the refrigerator for more lettuce. He was washing the lettuce leaves when he saw the two men through the window as they exited the woods.

Henry tried to recognize them. They didn't look familiar, but from that distance he didn't trust his poor vision. Obviously, they were coming to visit. As they came closer he became positive they were strangers.

It was early for those government men to come and inspect the fields. Must be tax assessors again, he thought. They were here last year and assessed him another seventy dollars. But now we were at war and farming was an essential industry, a vital commodity. If they were taxmen he didn't want them in the house. He dried his hands with the dishtowel, checked the oven then went outside to meet them.

The sky was gray and blue and the air, cool. He sat in the rocking chair on the porch, rocked gently and lit a Lucky Strike cigarette watching the visitors all the time deciding if they were tax people.

Kretschmer and Lehmann saw the farmer exit the house. They turned on their friendly personalities. The two men were getting closer conversing and laughing. Henry's impression was— jovial and friendly. Maybe they weren't taxmen. Kretschmer waved at fifty yards. Henry waved back, rocking. He decided to meet them by the road. They may be unfriendly. Damn tax idiots! He rose and headed for the road. No sense in being unfriendly if they weren't the enemy.

They approached, smiling.

"Good afternoon, gentlemen,"

"Hello, sir. Sorry to intrude on you like this but we're hopelessly lost," said Kretschmer putting on his best smile.

Henry smiled, relieved.

"For a while I thought you were someone else who's not welcome here. By being way out here I'd say you were lost. I'm Henry Shuller. Where do you want to go?"

They shook hands.

"I'm Nicholas Baxter," said Kretschmer, "and this is John Montgomery. We're visiting friends in East Hampton near Georgica Pond. We started out for a walk in the woods and here we are. Yours is the first house we've seen for miles."

"Yep. It's sparse out here. Here you've got to love the land or you'll die of boredom. I can tell by your accent that you're not from around here. New England?"

"Boston. We tired vacationing on Cape Cod. We heard Long Island's beaches were better, so here we are. A final vacation before we're inducted into the service in two weeks."

"I can't say I envy you. God bless you for doing your duty."

"Can you tell us how to get back?"

As Kretschmer talked, Lehmann stole glances through the windows for other signs of life. Warrior whinnied in the barn. He looked there expecting someone to come out.

"You go back to the road you came and turn left. It's about three miles to the main road. You'll know you're going right when you pass a gully on your right. You may be able to hitchhike from that road. It's not far from that point to the town."

"Wow. Three miles. Can we trouble you for some water before we go?"

Henry liked them. They seemed friendly and neighborly.

"Sure. Come along."

He turned for the house.

"What are you planting, Mr. Shuller?" asked Lehmann.

"Potatoes. The best damn potatoes in the world. Katahdins and Superiors, the all-purpose type. The Army will take the entire crop this year. I don't mind. They pay well. Chances are you fellas will be peeling them in a few weeks."

Henry laughed heartily. Kretschmer and Lehmann grinned.

"At least we'll know they're good," said Lehmann.

Henry opened the door.

"Come on in."

They entered the living room to the scent of food cooking. Kretschmer was pleased to see the radio.

"Wait here. Sit and relax, and I'll get the water."

Henry came back with two full glasses. They drank and returned the glasses.

"We appreciate this. Thanks," said Kretschmer.

"On second thought," said Henry. "I'm not expecting my daughter for a while yet. Maybe I can drive you to the main road. I'll leave a note for her should she get here before I get back."

Kretschmer and Lehmann acted delighted.

"Listen, why don't you wait in the truck and I'll be out in a minute," urged Henry.

"That's terrific of you to do that. Are you sure you won't mind?" Kretschmer said.

"Not at all. Go ahead. I'll be right out."

"Mr. Shuller," said Lehmann. "I thought I heard someone in the barn before. Maybe your daughter is in there or your wife?"

"No, no. That's just the horse. My wife passed on a few years ago. Go ahead. It's all right."

They went out content with what Henry said. Lehmann seemed unhappy the farmer was a widower. They conversed when they neared the truck.

"Lehmann, this is a good opportunity to have him drive us around the area. We'll deal with him later if we don't run into anyone else on the road. When we reach the bend in the road I'll make him stop the truck. You get out and help carry the gear to the house. And intercept the girl. It looks like it's just the two of them. Hop in the back and I'll sit next to him."

Lehmann climbed into the open back and sat on the edge. Henry had gone into the kitchen, lowered the oven to warm, placed the salad ingredients in the refrigerator, wrote the note to Melissa and left. Just like Bostonians, he thought. Never know where they're going. Harvard, bah! Out here, people help each other and he wouldn't have felt right if they had to walk to that road.

He closed the front door and looked east toward the woods and the Griffin place looking for Melissa. He called out to Lehmann.

"You're going to be uncomfortable up there young fella. It's a bumpy ride."

"That's all right, Mr. Shuller. This way you'll have more room. I don't mind."

Henry shrugged. "It's your rear end." He climbed behind the wheel, started the motor, shifted and headed for the west woods.

"Mr. Shuller?"

"Yes, Nicholas." He turned and saw the Luger. "What the hell is this?"

"Just drive. When you get to the turn in the road stop the truck and keep both hands on the wheel."

"If it's a holdup we keep little money here. I have maybe—twelve dollars and change."

"It's not a holdup. I need you to drive me around your property. That's all."

"Why the gun? I'd have done that if you asked."

"Now it's on my terms."

Henry wasn't one to frighten easily. But he was frightened for Melissa if these men were still here when she returned.

"If it's not money you want then what? Leave and we'll forget we ever met."

"Just shut up."

They entered the woods. Henry stopped the truck and the other two men rose from behind the brush. Now they were four. This disturbed Henry. They approached the truck.

"Lehmann, come here," Kretschmer called. Henry kept his eyes on the two walking toward him. The one on the left had scratches on his face. Lehmann hopped out the back and appeared at the window.

"You and Lassen wait in the barn and intercept the girl," Kretchmer directed. "Let Dieterman wait in the house." He turned to Henry, now white from fear. "Don't look concerned, Mr. Shuller. You'll be back in time to greet your daughter. No harm will come to either of you. We only want to stay at your place overnight."

Lehmann ran to the truck and took a suitcase from Dieterman.

"I didn't think you were from Boston. You're name isn't Nicholas, is it?"

"Doesn't matter. Make a right here and go north. Where does the road go?"

"It circles the property and comes around the other side."

"Good. Go." He waved the Luger.

Henry shifted and turned north.

"You're Germans, aren't you?"

"Germans?"

"You're Germans. German names. German looks. German gun. There's German blood in my ancestry."

"That's nice."

"What are you doing here? Why do you want my place?"

"Are there any other houses near here?"

"As you will see no houses. Why do you need to know the land?"

"I told you. My men and I plan to stay here overnight, maybe for a day or two more. If you cooperate no harm will come to you. We will take your Germanic ancestry into consideration. We don't harm Germans. And your daughter will be safe. We are soldiers of the German Army, not hoodlums. That's why we won't steal from you. We don't want your money, just some food and a place to rest. We are on a military operation. If you give us trouble I will shoot your daughter before your eyes. Remind yourself that your country started a war with mine. Not the other way around."

The cold stare penetrated Henry. He stopped conversing as silent panic came with awareness of the danger to Melissa. He didn't trust these Germans. They were soldiers, and soldiers in wartime weren't men anymore. They were killers and seducers. And that scared him, terrified for Melissa.

Now his thoughts were survival and escape—how to get Melissa away from the house or find her before she got to the house or how to get the intruders out. The last option seemed impossible. They were here to stay, taken over the house and wasn't sure they would leave them behind—alive.

His mind and thoughts jostled with the bumps.

Kretschmer's eyes kept roaming; absorbing—conscious that Henry's hands were still holding the wheel. He turned at every slight movement.

They had almost gone 180 degrees and were approaching the east road to the house. Henry tried to see, to pierce through the woods for Melissa. God, he hoped she hadn't arrived when he was gone. The woods were thick to see any distance. He regretted not cutting down those damn trees to expand the field. He didn't see her.

"Go back to the house," ordered Kretschmer. "I want to make a check."

Henry turned and didn't see anyone by the house. Maybe they were still in the barn waiting for Melissa. As they approached the barn Lehmann and Lassen came out.

"Anything?" asked Kretschmer.

"Nothing."

Henry was relieved.

"The northern sector looks good. We'll make a swing around to the south. We'll be back soon. Okay, Mr. Shuller, proceed."

Lassen and Lehmann returned to the barn.

Henry Shuller was thinking for his life, and Melissa's.

He made a left at the intersection and headed south. Now his mind schemed. He must somehow overpower his passenger, drive across the fields, intercept Melissa and go for the police—But how?— How? Kretschmer would shoot if he made a move. He was convinced. Maybe he should pick up speed and ram a tree and then run across the fields. Would that work? Negative. He sought answers—then he got the idea—The gully, maybe at the gully.

He drove faster with that thinking. The enemy would never expect him to ditch there. He held the wheel to brace. His passenger might get killed. The thoughts gripped the wheel until his knuckles turned white.

He noticed Kretschmer's attention wasn't as intent on him as on the road ahead and the woods to the right.

They were approaching the gully. He had to act, take the offensive. There was nothing else but this opportunity. He had to chance surviving the crash or catching him off balance and wresting the gun away.

The trees ended and the gully appeared.

Henry veered suddenly and Kretschmer panicked.

"What are you, crazy? Watch out!"

The truck headed straight down with Henry holding tight to the wheel and increasing pressure on the accelerator.

"Look out!" screamed Kretschmer bracing his arms against the dashboard.

The truck bounced against the opposite side. Kretschmer's head bounced against the windshield thrusting him backward, stunned. Henry grabbed the Luger, Kretschmer resisted and they fought.

The Luger flew from Kretschmer's hand and landed behind him, between the seat and the door. Kretschmer was dazed and weak. Henry punched him hard across the face and Kretschmer slumped. Henry looked for the gun but couldn't see it. He tried to start the motor again and again at the same time struggling to open the passenger door to push Kretschmer out. The door was jammed and the motor wouldn't turn. He opened his door, jumped out, and ran toward the incline with blind desperation.

He must reach Melissa!

ELEVEN

KRETSCHMER REGAINED HIS senses. Blood ran from a cut in his forehead. He looked up and saw Henry at the top of the incline. He hastily searched for the Luger. Frustrated, he gave up hoping the farmer didn't have it. If he did, wouldn't he have shot him? Convinced, he bolted out the open door and ran after Henry.

Henry tore through the woods until he reached the lower field, hidden from the house, and cut across it in a northeastern direction toward the Griffin farm. He looked over his shoulder repeatedly without seeing Kretschmer. He turned again about one hundred yards into the field and glimpsed Kretschmer coming out the woods.

Henry had difficulty running with heavy boots in the soft and planted earth. He left a path of crumbled mounds behind. The boots and the soft earth began to take a heavy toll on his breathing. Kretschmer was gaining; following Henry's path.

With arms and legs flailing, Henry reached the middle of the field. The boots like anchors.

Breathing became painful. Kretschmer was closer.

Now Henry wasn't running to save Melissa. He was running for his life.

He was strong and kept going. Suddenly, he stopped and turned to face Kretschmer. He felt sure he could overpower him. His strength would be sapped if he kept running—and he saw Kretschmer didn't have the gun.

Henry's maneuver startled Kretschmer. Now he was unsure if he could take the farmer. The daring offense was cause for caution. They were twenty yards apart, studying one another. Henry decided the best defense was an offense. He moved toward his enemy, hands ready, body prepared to pounce.

Kretschmer looked puzzled and stepped backward. Then he turned sideways with his hand under his shirt. With lightning speed, he spun and threw the dagger. Henry reacted quickly and leaned away from the badly aimed weapon. The dagger nearly buried itself in the soft earth. Now they circled each other as wrestlers.

Henry leaped and they tangled, colliding and falling. They squeezed, strangled, groaned, moaned, scratched and rolled in a cloud of dust. Henry's right arm became free and he punched and punched, making contact with Kretschmer's face and forehead. His arm pounded as a hammer, and Kretschmer's holds weakened until he stopped struggling.

Breathless, Henry staggered over him and with what strength remained, hit him again wanting to make sure he stayed out. He was breathing hard and was confused. He had to kill him! *Kill* him! The urge to kill the enemy was overwhelming, but overpowered by the need to intercept Melissa before she reached the house. Assured Kretschmer was out, he ran toward the woods and Melissa. He ran at full speed stretching the pain threshold in his lungs. When he reached the woods he slowed to have a look at Kretschmer. He was motionless on his back where Henry had left him.

Henry sensed freedom.

He slowed to a jog to conserve some energy. He had a distance to travel and his boots were lead. In another one hundred yards, he would reach the clearing then the road that led to the Griffins. Maybe from there he could spot Melissa. He had to move faster. Frightening thoughts of Melissa being at the house were propelling him.

Henry increased speed again and ran without changing course through the low oak and pine branches with his hands protecting his eyes. The forward rush and the continuing danger increased the pounding in his throbbing head blocking out the sound of his boots crushing leaves, twigs and brush.

Then he heard a noise behind him and his heart jumped. He turned.

Kretschmer was already in the air, landing on Henry before he could defend himself. Kretschmer pounded Henry with a thick branch. Henry struggled and took the first blow, groping to stop Kretschmer's arm from swinging again. He was off-balance and the blows kept coming. Everything became dim. Then black.

Breathless, dirty and bleeding, Kretschmer stood triumphant over the farmer, threw the branch away, straddled the unconscious enemy and choked him with both hands until Henry Shuller's last breath came.

TWELVE

MELISSA SHULLER AND Patricia Griffin were as sisters; best friends sharing private secrets about love and life; constant companions since childhood aided by the closeness of their parents.

In their rural environment the Shullers and Griffins were one family. The family relationship was gratifying to Henry Shuller and Sean Griffin having grown together as friends and neighbors. They were a bit concerned when they married if their wives would get along. If anything were to separate them, it would be the incompatibility of spouses. But Siobhan Griffin and Martha Shuller related beautifully and added to the cohesion. The families' closeness was the foundation for their social world. That camaraderie was continuing in their offspring.

Melissa and Patricia differed in one area. Patricia loved Bing Crosby and Melissa, Frank Sinatra; caught up in a popularity contest as to who was the better singer. They ran around in school the past month collecting votes and calling the results to a radio station in New York City. Bing Crosby won the school by twelve votes.

They also spent hours cutting pictures of movie stars from magazines and pasting them in scrapbooks. *Photoplay* was their favorite magazine Glenn Miller, their favorite orchestra leader and they could jitterbug all day to Benny Goodman.

The last day of school was usually in session for a few hours, but with the war the school board had scheduled a special auditorium program. Though the seniors had graduation ceremonies two days before, they were requested to attend this special event in their honor. They sang patriotic songs, and prayers were offered to those soon entering the armed services. Slogans—duty, honor and country dominated the day.

To Melissa and Patricia war was a glorious game adults played and talked about and a good excuse for parades. A word without connection to reality, death, pain and anguish, war didn't come to the Long Island suburbs. War always happened over there, somewhere to others.

But to be sure the local residents kept their shotguns and rifles clean.

Volunteer bomber spotters began to sprout throughout Long Island, eyes searching the sky. Ever since Pearl Harbor, rumors German planes were coming plagued the Island. So real was this belief that barrage balloons were floated over Lakeville Road in Nassau Country to entangle the Luftwaffe bombers. Radar bases were established to scan the sky. Powerful searchlights were at ready. The newspaper headlines told of impending invasions. The fear had started with misleading stories by *Newsday* such as, "Incendiaries Seen Likely Here.

Here's What to Do." The December 9, 1941 issue was erroneously headlined, "Axis Planes Nearing Coast." This, plus nationalistic fervor kept up the threat that an invasion was imminent.

Nationalism expected many seniors would join or be drafted by the services. Females were urged to join the women's corps. The atmosphere in the region, as in the entire country, was patriotic.

The school ceremonies took an hour longer when the last-minute guest speaker, the commandant of the Coast Guard station in Montauk, espoused glory serving the country. He showed a film about the Coast Guard. When the speeches and march music ended, Melissa spent fifteen more minutes in the school bus area saying farewell to friends and signing yearbooks. Patricia spent the time talking to one boy. By then, the bus was ready to depart.

Patricia Griffin had long reddish-brunet hair, freckles and a button nose everyone considered cute. She had an outgoing personality, like her mother, a ready smile that complemented her wide eyes, perfect teeth and plump cheeks punctuated with dimples. Her figure was just beginning to take shape.

Melissa had short blonde hair, blue eyes and an attractive face. Sadness was in her alert eyes, like the eyes and features of a Greek statue. She was more the quiet type—more serious as if losing her mother permanently dimmed the brightness in her life. Maybe because she had grown quickly with added responsibility being the only female in the house that she became independent and lonely sooner than Patricia. But below her mature facade, she was still the child waiting to become the woman. She had a dignity and poise about her, an attractiveness that made her better than average looking. She was third runner-up as the prettiest girl in school.

The bus was half-full, the normal load. Melissa and Patricia sat together toward the rear door, Melissa next to the window.

"Congratulations, Pat. Put it there. We're done at last."

They shook hands.

"Yup, we finally made it. It would have been better today without all that patriotic nonsense."

"The patriotism was all right," Melissa said.

"You know, maybe there's something to all that flag-waving. Why don't we run off and join the WACS or something."

"Are you kidding? Which Sousa march convinced you?"

"Yes, kidding." Patricia laughed.

"I can't wait to go to college, to be on my own. To spread my wings and leave the nest and find out what I'm all about as an independent person."

"I wish I could go with you," Patricia said.

"I spoke to your mother the other day. She approves you going."

"I know. So does my father. But with six kids coming up behind me, the burden will be heavy for my parents."

"I think you should change your mind. Your parents don't want you to be a martyr for them. They're concerned about getting you out into the world."

"I do want to be a teacher more than anything else in the world," Patricia said.

"But?"

"But it'll be a financial drain on the family."

"You keep saying that. You'll make it, Pat. I know you'll find a way. You're the resourceful one."

"A rich man will come along, sweep me away and educate me."

"If you can land a rich man with the knowledge you have now, why ruin it?"

They laughed again and Patricia entered a daydream.

"Wouldn't it be wonderful if we went to college together?"

"I would give anything for that, to be roommates. Please change your sacrificial mentality. Listen to your parents."

Saddened by the thought, Patricia said "Not likely."

Sean Griffin was waiting for them with his pickup truck at the bus stop. He looked annoyed sitting in the dust-covered green truck with its numerous scratches and dents.

"What took you people so long?"

"Sorry, Dad. Long program." Patricia sat next to him.

"Forget it. Come here."

He leaned over and kissed Patricia on the cheek. Sean Griffin was the same age as Henry Shuller and built about the same. He possessed a broad smile he attributed to his Irish ancestors. He had a wind-carved toughness in his face and hands like leather. He had thick eyebrows, a thin mouth, and a full crop of hair. He needed a shave, and the white in his stubble was visible.

"Congratulations, honey. You, too, Melissa."

"Thank you, Mr. Griffin."

"Well, you girls have reached another plateau in your lives. How does it feel?"

He shifted and headed for home.

"What's to feel?" asked Patricia.

"Terrific," said Melissa.

"Melissa, are you staying with us or shall I drive you home?"

"I'm going to your house. Mrs. Griffin said the other day that she wanted to see me today."

"I won't be able to drive you later, you know."

"I know. You still have planting. I was planning to walk. It's nice out. And I'm used to it by now."

"Did your father finish?"

"Yesterday."

"Good for him. Tell him if he has nothing to do to come over tomorrow and help."

"I will."

"Do me a favor will you, Melissa?"

"Anything."

"Will you please try to convince my stubborn daughter to go to college?"

Melissa became excited, and encouraged.

"Come on, Pat. Everybody agrees you should go. There's time to apply. New York University has room."

"Dad, we can't afford it this year. Maybe next."

"You see, Melissa. That's all I get. I've got a stubborn daughter and a considerate one. But one way or another, we'll get her there. We'll have to visit you in New York. That might convince her."

The Griffin house was a two-story, four-bedroom structure run with an iron hand by Siobhan Griffin, who looked older than her thirty-nine years. Patricia inherited her red hair and freckles. The seven children: Patricia and Mary Beth, fourteen; Robbie, thirteen; Maureen, ten; Jack, nine; Sean, Jr., six; and Kelly, four, made the place seem like a miniature Pennsylvania Station with its noise level, also.

Siobhan always looked forward to Melissa's visits. She regarded her as another daughter after Martha Griffin died in her arms at the hospital. Martha's last words for Siobhan were to look after Melissa for her. And in tears, Siobhan promised for as long as she lived Melissa would be her daughter.

She had grown to love Melissa as her own, raising her as her child and being the substitute mother. She filled Melissa's void. She educated Melissa about men, women, and other matters and secrets mothers share with daughters.

Time was approaching when Melissa would be leaving them, and the thought saddened her. She would lose both soon if she persuaded Patricia to go to college. She loved Patricia, of course, but felt a different and special kinship to Melissa attributable to her promise to her beloved friend, Martha. To Siobhan, the lifetime commitment was engraved in stone.

Out in this desolate area, Melissa and Patricia had become her friends and female companions helping her in every way with the children and the house. Her world was to be disrupted by their reaching the point in their lives when they had to make the move into adulthood and leave her home. When she pondered the future, it saddened her. She had younger daughters but she was a mother to them and them children to be raised.

Four large oaks stood as sentries near each corner of the house providing alternating daylong shade. An area on the eastern side was designated as the playground with appropriate bought and hand-devised facilities. Two tires swung from the two nearest oaks. The Griffin barns were to the right about eighty yards from the house.

Jack Griffin was leading Kelly, Maureen, and Sean, Jr. in a game of follow-the-leader when the pickup truck pulled up. Jack ran to the truck to the complaints of his abandoned followers and waited for Melissa to get out, jumping up and down. He had freckles and slightly rounded ears. When Melissa stepped down he jumped on her.

"Melissa, Melissa. I love you. I love you."

"Jack, take it easy." She held him.

"Give me a kiss, Melissa. I love you."

"How's my boyfriend?"

She kissed him on the forehead. Jack beamed and ran back to his game, to more complaints.

Melissa loved to stay here. She felt the pulsation and drone of a large family and decided to have a large family someday. Over the years, the Griffins had supplemented her life and made her less lonely. At times, she would spend days here. When her mother was alive she once spent a week with the Griffins. Her father encouraged her to visit the Griffins often. She did, for a while then less and less when she realized two years ago that in this desolation, her father needed companionship. Now, almost all nights were spent at home and most afternoons, when her father was in the fields, at the Griffins.

The extended school program took from the after-school time with the Griffins, leaving about a half-hour for today.

Siobhan Griffin was in the kitchen by the stove when Melissa and Patricia came in to the pungent odor of lamb stew. The kitchen was painted yellow with fluffy curtains on the window over the sink and yellow shades on the other two. Yellow was Siobhan's favorite color the color that best expressed her personality, warm and bright. The minute one walked into the room there was an atmosphere of welcome, love, and family. Melissa always felt at home here, as did strangers who spent more than a few minutes in Siobhan's kitchen.

The long kitchen table had a pale yellow tablecloth and yesterday's flowers in a vase, still looking fresh.

"Hi, Mom."

"Hi, Mrs. Griffin."

"How was it?" Siobhan asked stirring the stew.

"Boring, boring, boring," Patricia complained.

The girls sat at the table. Melissa jumped up remembering something.

"Can I use the phone, Mrs. Griffin? I want to call home to tell my father that I'll be late."

"Of course. How many times have I told you not to ask, just use it?"

"Thank you."

Asking was a courtesy Melissa always extended. The simple gesture was a reminder that she belonged here but not entirely. She didn't want to take advantage though she knew they loved her.

Melissa went to the living room where the long-necked phone stood on the lamp table. She dialed. It rang. She let it ring eight more times then hung up.

When she returned to the kitchen, Patricia asked, "Can you stay longer?"

"There wasn't an answer. He's probably in the barn feeding Warrior or something."

"Men are never indoors on a nice day," said Siobhan. "It's against their religion I think. Sit. We have a surprise for you. Patricia, go and get the kids."

"What's going on?" asked Melissa delighted. Surprises stirred her juvenile senses.

Siobhan entered the pantry. Patricia called the children from the window. "Come on. It's time!" Then she went inside and from the stair hollered up to the bedrooms.

Siobhan came out of the pantry with a homemade chocolate cake with a candle in the middle. Patricia came back. Melissa's eyes widened with happiness.

"What's that for?"

"It's for your graduation from all of us. Pat, get a match."

The others streamed into the kitchen with greetings for Melissa. Jack maneuvered and sat on her lap, his arm around her waist. Patricia struck a match and lit the candle.

"Ready kids? Let's start," Siobhan said.

And the kids sang "Happy graduation to you," to *Happy Birthday.*

Melissa blew out the candle and they cheered and clapped. Melissa beamed touched by the moment.

"All right, kids," said Siobhan. "Out. No cake until after dinner."

There were boos, hisses and complaints as they all left but Jack. He stayed on Melissa's lap.

"You, too, lover. Out," Siobhan ordered.

"I don't want to."

Jack hugged Melissa tighter hoping for support against his mother's outrageous demand. Melissa patted his head to console him.

Siobhan's hands went to her hips.

"Move, I said."

Jack gave up.

"I have to leave you, Melissa. Kiss me."

She did and the adults laughed calling him impossible. Jack left happier and he blew Melissa another kiss before he went out the door.

"That kid is insane about you," Patricia said.

"He has good taste," Melissa replied.

Siobhan cut a piece of cake, put it in a plate and passed it to Melissa.

"How about a cup of coffee with that?" Siobhan asked.

"Love it."

"Me, too, Mom."

Patricia cut a piece of cake for herself. Siobhan poured three cups.

"My father will kill me if I don't finish dinner later. But this cake is yummy."

"Melissa, honey, Pat and I were talking the other night about how much we're going to miss you when you leave for college."

"I'll be coming back and forth. I won't disappear. It's New York City."

"I know but it won't be the same."

Siobhan looked admiringly at Melissa in a wonderful, motherly way. Melissa thought Mrs. Griffin's eyes were a bit watery.

Melissa stood and went to Siobhan, who was about to sit, kissed her on the cheek and said, "I love you." Melissa kissed her again. "I love you very much and always will."

THIRTEEN

"WAIT, MELISSA. I'LL walk you halfway," called Patricia. Melissa had said good-bye and was on the road leading to her house.

"Great."

"I want to talk to you about something."

"Now what can you possibly tell me that's new?"

"I may go steady this summer with Buddy."

"Pat, that's great. When did all this happen?"

"Today."

"What did he say?"

"He came up to me after the ceremonies and asked me to wear his class ring."

"So that's why you two were off by yourselves. Did you take it?"

"I told him I'd think about it. So?"

"What do you mean, 'So'?"

"What do you think?"

"You like him, go ahead."

"I don't know. Going steady could get serious. I've never gone steady with anyone before. You know that."

"There's always the first time. It'll assure a good summer social life, anyway. Besides, he has a car." Melissa laughed. "Freedom."

"I know. That's why I'm thinking about it."

"You've been dating him on and off the past year. This will give you a chance to know him better. And who knows?"

"So you think I should?"

"Yes."

"I don't know about going steady. If I agree, he'll think I'd be willing to let him."

"Has he tried anything yet?"

"No, just what I told you already. He tried to feel my breasts. I know I let him, but I don't know about going further. And that was over my blouse. They are all so pushy, you know? All boys have on their mind is sex. They don't know what to do with their hands if they're not feeling some part of you."

"You'll have to control him."

"I probably can do that. If he gets out of hand, I'll give him his ring back. That is, if I don't like what he does." She nearly giggled. "I may just do it. I'm dying to try it."

"You and I both, Pat. But I'm going to save it for the man I marry."

"That's what I want to do. But I don't want to marry Buddy."

"Don't do it then. Or do it and don't marry him."

"He wants to know if he and I, and you and Scott could double-date sometime."

"Sure, Scott's nice," said Melissa.

"I think he's in love with you."

"He never said anything when we dated about two months ago."

"Maybe he's shy hoping for an initiative from you."

"I'll date with him. But he doesn't excite me, you know what I mean?"

"Ok. It's agreed. I'm going to go steady with Buddy."

"And I'll bet you five dollars you're no longer a virgin by September."

"Hmmm. I'm not going to bet. I may lose for the fun of it."

"Well, if you do, make sure he uses protection."

"Of course."

Patricia reacted to a sudden idea. She put her arm around Melissa.

"Why don't we lose the old cherry at the same time? Let's double-date, have a few beers and swing a little." She laughed, holding her tighter.

"You're crazy. I have a hunch I'm going to find my Prince Valiant in college. He's going to sweep me off my feet and take me away to a land that's far, far away—but not East Hampton!"

They shared the laughter. When the teenage conversation about boys ended they were nearing the woods. The woods marked the end of the Griffin property then came a wide Shuller field, the deep Shuller woods then the open area where the house stood.

"How far do you want to walk, Pat?"

"I'll go as far as your woods."

"That's a haul."

"I know but it'll give me a chance to think about Buddy. I never have privacy in my house and I need private time. The walk back will do me good."

"I can appreciate it. Sometimes though I have too much privacy. But if you're going that far come over and say hello to my father."

"I don't know. We'll see."

They passed the Griffin woods, entered the Shuller field, and headed for the Shuller woods.

FOURTEEN

SERGEANT HEINRICH KRETSCHMER covered with dirt and blood drying on his face, sat on the ground disheveled and exhausted heaving deep breaths to settle his racing heart.

He couldn't remember being that exhausted, not since he beat his girlfriend to death in 1939 for helping a Jewish family escape from the Gestapo. The Gestapo didn't know she was involved. Kretschmer found out after they both got drunk and she bragged about the incident; condemning the Nazi murderers who, she believed, were destroying Germany with their fanaticism and hate.

Kretschmer was the dutiful German soldier, Hitler's soldier to whom nothing was more sacred than the Fatherland and advancing the race. She became something vile, an enemy. How dare she talk about his uniform like that? How dare she help the trash of Germany?

He drove her outside of town, parked the car, made love to her in a wooded area then beat her to death with his belt. Then, he had swung and pounded until his strength was drained though she had died minutes before. He was never accused once he explained to the Gestapo why he killed her.

Visions of that ugly night returned, and regret lingered for depriving himself that beautiful woman who loved him more than anything. Now he looked at his fallen enemy, this obstacle, with scorn for reminding him those days. He spit contemptuous at Henry Shuller for putting him through a physical ordeal.

When his breathing became normal he rose aching and stood over his prey feeling elation—the elation of the gladiator who had defeated the Christian scum with the roar of spectators in his ears, like the roar of thousands who gathered to hear Hitler's speeches in the stadiums.

He had won the battle and the wreath of Germany. He won to continue fighting for Germany. The roar receded and he stood victorious.

He brushed the dirt off his clothing and headed back to the potato field to search for the dagger concluding it was stupid to have thrown it leaving him defenseless. His superiors wouldn't have been pleased with that maneuver. The enemy might have retrieved the weapon and used it against him. He was grateful to be alive after making such a blunder in his haste and panic. Had Shuller escaped the mission would be aborted and his golden opportunity to win the Iron Cross would be lost.

He positioned in the middle of the battleground in the field. At first he had difficulty plotting the direction of the errant throw. Then he selected an area and searched. He began to probe in expanding circles, and found it after five minutes. The dagger had pierced a planting mound and its handle was barely exposed. The weapon was indispensable to him. If lost he would have taken Dieterman's dagger. He had scorn for Dieterman, the weak link in Landwolf 337's chain. He would have gotten rid of that vomiting weakling at that summerhouse, but he needed Dieterman. And as long as he needed him, he had to tolerate his shortcomings.

He would feel better if Dieterman did something dramatic or heroic like killing an enemy to advance the mission of Landwolf 337. Maybe he would force Dieterman to kill the girl.

Sheathing the dagger, he headed for the woods and the road leading north back to the house. He wondered if his men had encountered that girl and thought about going back to the gully to look for his gun. He dismissed it as far to go and decided to go back for the Luger later, before they left the area. His priority was reaching the house, wanting to wash and change clothes and tend to his wounds.

He was satisfied with privacy at the Shuller property. Then he became irritable thinking of Dieterman.

The German gladiator hastened through the woods looking for the girl who should be approaching from his right. He approached with caution upon reaching the intersection with the east-west road that led to the house. He saw the house to his left. The woods to his right were clear and quiet. He pondered waiting there for the girl, getting rid of her now and leaving her body in the woods.

FIFTEEN

DIETERMAN, LASSEN AND Lehmann went directly to the house after the truck pulled away and placed their luggage in the living room. Lassen checked the bedroom.

"From the pictures in there and the size of the house, it must be a small family."

"The farmer didn't say anything about others. Only that his wife was dead and was expecting his daughter soon."

"Only two people living here," said Dieterman tearing the note Henry left for Melissa.

"How can you be sure?" asked Lehmann.

"There's two plates at the kitchen table."

"You're astute," said Erich Lassen. "Speaking of the girl, Carl, you wait here. Peter and I must wait in the barn should she come."

Lassen and Lehmann left.

Carl Dieterman continued to rip the note then placed it in an ashtray. Carl studied the room. He admired the radio and was tempted to turn it on.

The room was neat with minimum fine dust considering its location near the front door. In addition to the normal living-room furnishings, there was a picture of President Franklin Delano Roosevelt and a painting of a harbor scene. Appropriate, Carl thought, to offset the surrounding area of earth and trees. He checked the wood-burning stove, now cleaned and ready for winter use.

Carl wondered what the girl looked like and how old she was. Those thoughts led him to the bedroom. Melissa's room had a double bed with a walnut headboard, and a blue-based multi-flowered bedspread neatly tucked in at the corners. The walls were painted white, and the curtains matched the spread. On all the walls were pictures of male movie stars: Tyrone Power, Errol Flynn, Clark Gable and Robert Taylor—a family picture of the Shullers on her walnut bureau and a single portrait of Mrs. Shuller. He figured the girl was about eleven or twelve. Then Carl noticed Melissa's graduation picture on the night table. He picked it up.

Carl realized then that the family picture was taken years ago. When did her mother die? Himself an orphan, he felt he had something in common with the pretty girl smiling in the picture proud as a peacock.

He wondered how her mother died. Was it as tragic an accident as his parents? At least she had her father. He had no one. Only an aunt and uncle he couldn't tolerate, mainly because they didn't want him. They felt obligated to take him.

The uncle was an arrogant man who finally had a younger male to yell at and abuse and order around as if he were a dog. His aunt tolerated him being her sister's son, and because the state had given them almost all the inheritance, a substantial amount, to raise Carl.

Living with them was a nightmare. If he seemed scared or weak or gentle depending on who was calling him names, it was due to treading carefully around his uncle not to disturb him. Living over a medical office as a youngster also honed that direction. Toward the end knowing he was going into the army, Carl fought off one of his uncle's impulses to kick the 'dog' and he swung and broke his uncle's nose. And when he went down, Carl picked up a vase and smashed it across his face.

Shocked at this retaliation, the dog biting the master, his uncle bandaged his wounds, filled two glasses of white wine, toasted Carl and apologized saying that from here on in he would treat him as an adult. Carl relaxed took the glass then his uncle kicked him viciously in the groin. Carl doubled over in pain. He grabbed Carl's hair and thrust him upward and screamed at him face-to-face.

"When you leave this house for the army don't ever come back. If you do I'll kill you. Better yet, die in battle." He kicked him again in the groin and let him fall.

Carl erased his home life and went to the kitchen. The chicken scent was appetizing. He checked the oven. The chicken looked cooked. He turned off the oven, opened the refrigerator and checked its inventory.

In the hallway he checked the closet. The closet was full of clothes, winter clothing mainly and in the corner to the right, a shotgun. He took the shotgun out, fondling its stock. Good hunting gun, he thought. The cartridges were on the shelf among the hats and snowshoes.

Carl opened the barrel and looked through the empty, dark tunnels. He put the shotgun back and closed the door.

In the living room, he pulled the curtains aside to look outside. He didn't see anyone. He thought about his comrades and his position with them. So far three persons were dead. They were ruthless men and cold-blooded killers who tarnished honorable soldiers. Kretschmer killed the man with the red beard—Lassen, the boy. What human being would kill a child in cold blood? The vision of the boy made him feel nauseous again. Lehmann had killed the boy's mother.

Carl had no intentions killing anyone like that or raping anyone. He felt capable of killing, but only in the line of duty, or to save his own life.

Death loomed again, disturbing—and what of the farmer and his daughter? Would they kill them? He felt sure they would. He needed to find a way to save their lives without endangering the mission. Maybe he could convince Kretschmer to let them live—to tie them up or something. He was determined there would be no more unnecessary killings. To Kretschmer, everything was necessary.

He kept his eyes on the road leading to the west woods, in perfect view from his window, should the girl come from the west. The others in the barn covered the road from the east where they expected her to come from.

The more he thought about the owners, the more determined he became that nothing would happen to them regardless what his comrades thought or did to him. There would be no more killing.

Carl had decided to run to the barn as soon as the girl was apprehended to make sure nothing happened to her. The girl brought insecurity. He grew impatient and doubtful, and headed for the barn with determination.

Lassen and Lehmann were just inside the doors. When Lehmann saw him he called out, "Hurry up!" He checked the east road for the girl. "What are you doing here? You took a hell of a chance."

Carl hurried into the barn. Before they could say anything more, he pointed his finger at them defiantly, indicting them.

"This time try to remember that you are *soldiers*." His eyes widened to emphasize his order.

Lehmann and Lassen, surprised at the outburst, looked at each other blankly. Lehmann tried to soothe him.

"Carl, go back to the house. There will be no more killings."

"I have your word?"

"Yes."

Carl looked to Lassen for his answer. Lassen nodded.

"Peter's right, Carl. And I agree with him. No more killings. And you're right we mustn't forget our mission and we *are* soldiers. Go back to the house and relax. Put the radio on and take it easy. If it will make you feel better, we'll call you when we capture the girl and you can see that she won't be harmed. Agreed?"

Carl weighed Lassen's words then nodded agreement, turned away, checked the road and ran to the house.

Carl Dieterman sprawled out on the sofa, feeling better that his soldierly attitude had an effect on Lassen and Lehmann.

He relaxed and lowered his guard.

SIXTEEN

KRETSCHMER WAITED, IMPATIENT. Bent low behind thick brush, he cursed the girl for being late. He then realized she might have passed already. He stood, searched the road then jogged to the house.

As he approached the barn, Lassen and Lehmann came out and waited for him. Kretschmer was convinced the girl wasn't there by the way they looked over his shoulder.

"Get inside, fools!" Kretschmer hissed breathing uneasy.

They moved back inside. He followed them.

"What happened to you," asked Lehmann. "Where's the truck?"

"He tried to get away. The truck crashed in the gully. It's useless. I left the body in the woods. No one will find him there now."

Lassen seemed pleased with the outcome.

"One less nuisance."

"Anything happen here?"

"Nothing, Sergeant."

"Damn," he whispered under his breath. "I should have waited. She may have seen me. Just as well."

"What's that?" quizzed Lehmann not hearing what he mumbled.

"Is Dieterman in the house?"

"He's still there."

Kretschmer peeked out, eastward.

"You wait for her as planned. Stay alert. I'm going to wash up."

He dashed to the house. Footsteps on the porch jostled Carl, who braced against the wall near the door hinges, Luger in hand.

"Dieterman!" Kretschmer called as he entered and closed the door.

"I'm here."

Kretschmer turned to the voice behind him. Carl was lowering his gun staring at Kretschmer's disheveled, dirty and bloodied appearance.

"Good," said Kretschmer acting like nothing happened to him. "You're alert. I'm going to wash." He turned.

"Wait. What happened?" The bruised face and dried blood foretold tragedy. "Where's the farmer?"

"Be more concerned about me, Dieterman. He almost killed me."

He headed for the kitchen. Carl followed.

"Did he escape or what?" Carl asked, somehow hoping he had. They had time to escape, to leave this farm and not worry about the girl. But he didn't like the thought being pursued either.

Kretschmer reached the sink and answered without turning to face Carl. "He didn't escape."

He began unbuttoning his shirt being patient, like a father whose pain-in-the-ass kid asked many questions. When the shirt opened, he turned on the faucet. Puzzled by Dieterman's silence, he faced him. Carl's face was sullen. He was going to ignore Carl and finish washing, but changed his mind—Patience, for the good of all, for the mission.

"I had no choice, Dieterman. It was hand-to-hand combat. Look at me. Do I look like an executioner in this condition?"

"You never have a choice."

Carl Dieterman's stomach sank. He returned to the living room and sat by the window in disgust. The killing was continuing. He would make sure nothing happened to the girl. He didn't have to worry about Lassen and Lehmann. They gave their words. Kretschmer had to be contended with but how long would Kretschmer tolerate him protecting 'the enemy'.

Kretschmer came in shirtless the upper body cleansed, opened a suitcase and changed clothes. Carl watched him.

"They're wrinkled," Carl said looking at the wardrobe.

"They'll do for now."

"What are you going to do about the girl when she gets here?"

Annoyed, Kretschmer placed his hands on his hips and stared.

"Why do you ask?"

"We've left a trail of bodies behind already. Four now."

"I can count, Dieterman. Who'll know it was us?" His voice rose. "Nobody! Because there are no witnesses."

"We don't have to kill."

"What do you suggest we do? Beg them to say they never saw us?"

"We can tie them up. By the time they get free, we'll be on that train."

"Idiot. Idiot! If the authorities know we're in this country, the entire Island will be looking for us and we'll be trapped on that train, or elsewhere. You keep forgetting we're at war!"

"And you keep forgetting you're a soldier."

Rage boiled within Kretschmer. With gritted teeth and thinned mouth, he pointed a threatening finger at Carl's nose.

"Don't you ever question me about that again!"

Carl didn't flinch. "What about the girl?"

Kretschmer backed away. "Why are you concerned about her?"

"She can't hurt us."

"She can recognize us. Therefore, she can kill us—by pointing us out."

"We can tie her in the barn. And hide her. It will be a long time before someone finds her. She may never be found."

"You should have been a priest, Dieterman." He was exasperated. "So you prefer she starves to death?"

"It's better than killing another child."

"How do you know she's a child?"

"I saw her picture in the bedroom."

"How old do you figure?"

"About seventeen."

"I see. How old are you, Dieterman?"

"Eighteen."

"Eighteen. You're both children and dangerous. Very dangerous."

SEVENTEEN

MELISSA AND PATRICIA were nearing the
Shuller woods where birds chattered a late afternoon
cacophony. An amphibious plane from the Coast
Guard station flew high overhead where gray clouds
opened to show blue.

"Are you coming home with me?" asked Melissa.

Patricia pondered, realizing she shouldn't.
Suppertime neared and her mother would need help.

"On second thought, no. I should help Mom get
dinner ready. Say hello to your father for me. I'll call
you tomorrow night or Saturday. I want to spend
tomorrow with Buddy, and see how it goes."

"Have a ball—and don't do anything stupid." She
smiled.

Patricia raised her brows in jest, waved a goodbye
and headed for home.

Before Melissa entered the woods, she turned
and watched Patricia heading away. Somehow, she
had to convince Patricia to attend college with her.
Patricia *had* to go to college. If she didn't this

semester, Melissa believed she would never go—and anyone who wanted to become a teacher as badly as Patricia shouldn't be deprived the opportunity.

One reason she loved Patricia was her unselfishness. To Patricia, the Griffin family needs came before her needs. It didn't seem fair. But since it wasn't the Griffins restraining her, Melissa decided to spend the next few weeks convincing Patricia to be selfish.

She watched and admired Patricia. Then she thought of her father who must be impatient by now, and hurried into the woods.

This summer would be lonelier if Patricia went steady with Buddy. She would see her less often. Maybe she should try to go with Scott more often by double dating with Patricia and Buddy. The summer would pass faster.

She realized a point in her life had been reached where she wanted to share her feelings, her emotions with a boy. Someone to take long walks with, to philosophize with, to share romantic moods and to share dreams about the future. But it couldn't be Scott or any boy she met thus far. Her future lover and husband didn't live in her present world.

Convinced her male counterpart wasn't to be until college, she promised to pay more attention to her father, to get to know him better and to see him more as an individual than a father. If she didn't this summer the opportunity may be postponed indefinitely. And time for him to know she no longer was a child to be raised, but a young woman reaching adulthood.

Yes, she would spend more time with her father. With these thoughts she continued through the woods. No need to start a *different* relationship with Dad by getting him mad by being late for supper.

EIGHTEEN

LASSEN SAW MOVEMENT in the woods and jerked his head back into the barn.

"Someone's coming. It must be her."

"How shall we do it?" asked Lehmann.

"We can confront her on the road or make her come in here. I have it. When she gets closer, go and upset the horse somehow. That might attract her. She might think her father is in here."

"Good idea."

Melissa took her last breath of the leaves and pine-scented woods as she came out into the field. She maintained her quickened pace, scanning the area hoping to see her father.

About fifty yards from the barn, she heard Warrior's neighing and angled toward the barn. Without hesitating she walked in, looked around and went to Warrior's stable. He was standing, passive.

"Dad, are you in here?"

Her eyes adjusted to the diffused daylight in the barn as she looked for her father. Warrior began to pace as she neared, always delighted to see her. She opened the gate and hugged him stroking his mane.

"There, there baby. What's the matter? Were you calling for me? I see Dad already fed you, so he must be in the house. You behave now. Maybe we'll go for a ride later and you'll get your exercise."

Melissa gave him a final pat and closed the gate. She heard a sound and turned. The gasp caught in her throat when she saw Lehmann with a gun. She backed away and pressed against the gate. Her eyes shifted to another man as he rose from behind the tractor and came toward them. Lassen was holding a dagger.

Fear jostled her like a storm pitching a rowboat. The weapons of death made her shake. Sound became difficult. Panic shouted, "Dad!"

The absence of a response made her look around for some object for protection. She pressed harder against the gate and wrapped her arms around her body to withdraw from this dream. She blinked several times to calm her eyes.

"He's not here," said Lassen approaching menacing looking at her in sections from the bottom up. He stopped and stood near her.

"What's your name?"

"Melissa," she said in a meek tone.

"You look frightened. Don't be frightened."

Melissa tried to hide her shaking. She hardly felt the slap across her face that knocked her off balance. Lassen slapped her again. The pain came sharper. Melissa screamed and held her crying face.

"I said, don't be frightened," Lassen commanded.

She forced herself to obey to avoid additional punishment. She straightened, lowered her hands and covered her body again. Her face was wet and blushed.

"Come over here," Lassen demanded backing away. "Over to this side where the light is better so we can have a better look at you."

Hesitant, she shuffled toward the light.

"Hurry up!" Lassen barked.

The feet moved faster, and stopped where the sunlight formed a rectangular spread of light on the floor.

"That's better. Now, raise your head so we can see what you look like. Good. You're pretty. Lower your arms."

She did, hunching her shoulders to lessen the rise of her chest.

"Please, can't you tell me where my father is?"

Lassen's mind was elsewhere. He turned to Lehmann.

"Peter, watch the door. We didn't get it at the other place. We're going to get it here."

Lehmann grinned, approving. Lassen returned his attention to Melissa.

"Take off your shoes."

"Wha-why?"

"I said, take off your shoes."

His arm rose, threatening. With the other hand he brought the dagger closer. She stepped out of her penny loafers confused by the demand.

"Now your socks."

More confusion.

"I won't try to run away. Where's my father?"

"Take them off!" he screeched.

She lifted each leg and removed the white bobby socks.

"Now the blouse."

"No. Why?" She was afraid to answer her own question. The answer was unthinkable. The dagger came closer, menacing and demanding.

"Where's my father?" A tremor was in her voice.

He replied, "Take off your blouse."

With shaking fingers, she undid the buttons, took off the blouse and held it. Her arms covered the top of the pink slip.

"Who are you? Why are you doing this to me?"

"Now, take everything off. Slowly."

Lehmann's eyes were beginning to fill with excitement and lust expecting what was to happen. Something he considered a sensuous, erotic happening, a war prize. Melissa disobeyed to divert the inevitable.

"Why are you here? Where's my father? Why don't you answer me? Please don't hurt me. Leave me alone."

Lassen raised the dagger and the tip touched her neck.

"I'll cut you if you don't do as you're told. Do you want me to scar your pretty face? Do you want to go through life ugly with hideous scars all over your face?"

She dropped the blouse and undid the skirt with trembling fingers hoping against odds something would happen to make him change his mind. The skirt fell. The light flickered off the silk slip. She hoped he was satisfied and the undressing would end.

"Keep going."

She slid out of the slip to her white panties and brassiere, pressed her legs together and wrapped her arms over her chest.

"Take off the bra then the panties."

The dagger once again threatened in an extended arm. When she moved, he stepped back for a better and wider view. Reluctant, she removed the panties keeping her legs tight, turning away from them to hide the blond hairs. Hopelessness enveloped her and her insides cried. She watched them, eyes pleading.

Why wasn't something happening to stop this! She reached behind to undo the brassiere, again keeping her body partially turned. The brassiere fell and her arms immediately covered the breasts. Her body was turned, but she was naked.

Lassen was satisfied and turned to Lehmann.

"Peter, keep the gun on her. Shoot her if she moves away from me like you did the other bitch that disobeyed. Now, Melissa, turn toward me." She turned—her arms and legs tight. "Spread your legs apart and extend your arms."

Melissa didn't move. Irritated at her failure to listen Lassen took a step forward and slapped her hard. Her face flushed as she stood the blow and held tight.

"Do you want to die?" Lassen asked. Her head quivered. "Then do as you're told."

Her instinct to live began to pry her arms off her body. They moved away from her chest and stretched out. Lassen and Lehmann's eyes were on her exposed body. Her legs moved just inches apart.

"Open them wider," Lassen said. "About two feet—more—more. That's better."

He sheathed the dagger.

He moved closer to her, attempted to kiss her and stepped back when she turned her head. His hand touched her thigh and moved upward.

"Please don't. Don't touch me."

She bent her body to get away from him, frightened to move with the gun pointed at her. Did he shoot someone else? What did "like the other" mean? She tried to muster the strength and bravery to stand up to them to fight back somehow, but fear weakened her, and her body and mind shook in terror. His hand moved up then both hands until they caressed and massaged her breasts.

"Please let me go. Don't touch me," she pleaded through tears. He continued to fondle her. She cringed and pulled away and covered her body with her arms again.

"Stand still!"

"Dad! Dad! Help!"

"Shut up! Your father's dead! Dead! He won't help you!"

The added trauma fired her eyes. Her mouth fell. Then the internal mixture of fear and anguish swelled and quaked in her blood, pulling this way and that way. It rushed in dizzying hurdles to her head until, crashing and receding, the light allowed to enter from her eyes became dimmer—and darker until her body lost its strength and she collapsed.

Light began to enter again and she felt the sensations, something touching her body. Fingers, that's what they were—fingers moving up and down, here and there, and the sensation was hazy, misty, not painful—and she didn't care. She was oblivious to everything, but passiveness and the acceptance of death.

Her mind worked in slow motion and her body was detached from her senses, void any sensation as the light in her mind increased and the room and Lassen came into focus. She lost all sense of feeling and his image no longer frightened her. She no longer cared about his threats or what he did.

She was beaten and defeated and the victor owned the universe.

Then she felt some feeling in her face. A hand moved back and forth. She was lying on her back and could see the roof as Lassen moved out of her vision.

Lassen had been slapping her face to revive her. When her eyes opened and stared at him, he was satisfied and moved away.

He spread her legs and knelt between them.

He leaned forward on her and probed with force until he penetrated her virgin body.

Melissa sobbed softly, unresisting. Pain came suddenly to her senses with sensations never felt before. His mouth roamed her face and neck with panic breathing and the clouds in her mind cleared and she screamed aware what was happening to her. She fought desperately to get him out of her. Her body collapsed in the losing battle. Her eyes closed wet in anguish.

The weight lifted. She opened her eyes and through the moisture saw her rapist buttoning his pants. She was conscious of everything again. The pain came stronger. She watched as Lassen moved to the door, took the gun from Lehmann, and then Lehmann came toward her.

He kneeled next to her. She turned her face to avoid looking at him and then felt his hands roam her body and massage her breasts. His eyes were closed with visions of soft nights with his wife.

Melissa was a lamb again when his weight pressed.

Melissa didn't move. The ordeals over, her father's death overwhelmed her and she wept hysterical.

NINETEEN

SATISFIED, LEHMANN WIPED himself and went to Lassen.

"I'll go and get the Sergeant."

He checked the outside then jogged to the house. Lassen watched Melissa in her grief without any compassion. Thoughts of raping her again later were in his head.

Lehmann knocked on the door and Carl Dieterman opened it. Kretschmer was shifting dials on the radio, searching for news.

"We got the girl in the barn."

He looked away from Dieterman's eyes.

"Excellent," said Kretschmer. "Excellent."

He hurried out. Lehmann followed then Carl.

Lassen pointed towards the girl when Kretschmer came through the door. When he saw the position Melissa was in, he froze. Lehmann came in, followed by Carl.

The sight choked Carl's voice.

The nude girl was swaying from side to side on her hands and knees attempting to rise, moaning anguished utterances. Carl had his guard down and was again betrayed, like his uncle kicking him in the groin again as he drank the wine. Rage grew within Carl Dieterman and he screeched at Lassen and Lehmann.

"I thought you were soldiers!"

Lassen smiled. "I said we wouldn't kill her. We didn't."

Kretschmer turned to them. "Dieterman, I don't want your shit, do you understand? Don't say a thing unless you're spoken to."

Lassen moved past Kretschmer toward Melissa. He pulled her by the hair, stretching her neck backward.

"Stand up."

Melissa's body lifted on her knees. Lassen lifted her hair and she stood. Lassen turned her to face Kretschmer. Carl winced at the tortured, wet face. Her eyes were blank, resigned, hands at her sides. Melissa was a broken human being.

Kretschmer approached her and walked around her looking at her body, her dirty knees and hands. He noticed the blood and semen. She wasn't sexually inviting.

"What shall I do with her?" asked Lassen releasing her hair.

"For now tie her to that pole."

He pointed to the supporting pole behind Lassen. Lassen pulled her to the pole.

"Put your back against the pole. Get back on your knees and put your hands behind you, around the pole."

Melissa obeyed, pressing against the pole, on her knees. Lehmann brought some rope, went behind her and tied her legs and hands.

Carl watched in frustration. How could he fight them? At least the girl was alive. He decided to go along with anything as long as they didn't kill her.

Melissa fell forward from exhaustion, her hair over her face. The rope on her hands held her weight, a tragic posture. Carl felt deep compassion for the desperate, humiliated and defeated girl. He had seen the blood and the semen.

"Don't you want her, Sergeant?" taunted Lassen. "She took good care of Peter and me."

Kretschmer smirked and thought about it. A smile stayed on his lips. He approached Melissa and placed his hand on her right breast. He weighed the fullness and turned to Carl.

"I was wrong, Dieterman. She's not a child."

He ran one finger around her shoulders and then stopped stilled by Carl Dieterman's yell.

"Are you still a soldier, Sergeant? Or a damned rapist?"

"Shut up, Dieterman! Shut the hell up!" Kretschmer screamed louder. "Lassen, shoot him if he opens his mouth again. Understand? Shoot him!"

His energy in rage and anger shifted to a physical need to release, to vent and to settle him. He pulled Melissa's hair and lifted her head and yanked backward. She didn't resist. Her eyes were closed tight, like her mouth. She felt cold steel at her neck.

"Open your mouth or I'll cut your throat."

Her lips parted but her teeth were clenched. The dagger pressed harder, increasing the pain. Her teeth released. The dagger released and he sheathed it. His anger level was high, retarding the sexual thoughts. His rage burst. Then she felt terrible pains on her head and screamed from the violent onslaught. Kretschmer was punching her, pounding once again like a gladiator with a crazed demeanor in the Füehrer's service. And he kept punching.

Lassen grabbed and restrained Carl, as he was about to go after Kretschmer.

"Kretschmer! You son of a bitch!" shrieked Carl. "Stop it! Kretschmer!"

Startled by the outburst, Kretschmer stopped swinging, pulled his dagger and pointed it at Carl.

"I told you to shut the hell up!" Then he put the dagger back. "Lehmann, give me your gun!"

Lehmann brought the gun to him. Kretschmer pointed the Luger at Carl Dieterman.

"You've been a pain in the ass on this mission, Dieterman, a genuine pain in the ass. You haven't done anything to prove that you're one of us. It's time you joined us. Go and rape her. Move!"

Kretschmer stared at Carl with contempt for a long time. Lassen released him. Carl stared back. And then Carl walked slowly to Melissa and stood over her.

He looked at his staring comrades waiting for him to perform. He took out his handkerchief, went to his knees, and in a voice meant to reassure said to Melissa, "Don't be afraid anymore. I won't touch you. I won't hurt you. Neither will they. This terrible thing is over. Do you understand what I'm saying? It's over."

"Stop talking to her Dieterman and get on with it!"

He ignored Kretschmer. She raised her throbbing head warily hoping the voice was sincere. Skeptical, she looked into the handsome, understanding face of a boy who must have been her age. His voice did seem calm, reassuring and trustful. Carl winced at the anguished face.

"It's all right. It's all right," he kept repeating. "It's all right."

He smiled a little to convince her and placed his hand on her shoulder. He raised her chin and looked into reddened eyes, wet cheeks—and sorrow.

He tenderly wiped her mouth and cheeks. Melissa didn't know what to think, what to make of the boy. She remained untrusting. Then with some hesitation, he wiped her thighs of the mixture then threw the handkerchief on the ground.

"This ugly nightmare is over. Believe me. I won't let them hurt you anymore."

Kretschmer was getting impatient.

"Enough preparation, Dieterman. Get to it!"

Carl stared at Kretschmer in defiance then ignored him, turning his attention to Melissa.

"Try to relax. You're safe now."

The strange boy bewildered her. She continued to be cautious about believing him.

"Move your ass, Dieterman! Or I'll shoot your damn brains out!"

"Go to hell!"

The retort surprised his comrades, and also surprised Melissa. Was he protecting her? Was this some trick? Some sick trick? She hoped not. Now he was talking to her again.

"What's your name, miss?" She remained silent. "What's your name?"

"Melissa."

She was barely audible.

"Melissa. I'm going to go behind you and untie the ropes on your feet. When I do, stand then sit with your legs in front of you. You'll be more comfortable that way. I cannot release you completely.

Trust me, please. I mean it. I'm doing this to make you comfortable. Do you understand me?"

Melissa nodded several times. Carl rose, went around her and untied the rope. She slid up the pole then sat with her legs extended. He knelt next to her again.

"Is that better?"

She nodded again, thanking him with her eyes.

"Dieterman!"

Kretschmer extended his arm, pointing the Luger at Carl's face. "What are you doing? Let's go!"

Melissa watched the boy's defiance and his lack of fear. Carl stood looking into her face.

"What are you waiting for, Dieterman?" Kretschmer barked.

He turned and faced Kretschmer.

"I won't do it. I'm a soldier first. Not a rapist!"

"You're going to or so help me, I'll kill you!"

Rage overwhelmed Carl and he screamed.

"No, you piece of shit! No!" Kretschmer was stunned. "Get out of here!" Carl screamed. "Get out! All of you!"

He moved toward them sweeping his arm. His rage looked for something to grab. He found a shovel near him and swung it hard against Kretschmer's left shoulder. It glanced off. Kretschmer's right hand shook with desire to pull the trigger. Instead, he dropped it to his side.

"Get out, you scum! Animals! Get out!"

Carl's voice resounded; the shovel poised to strike again.

Kretschmer smiled at Carl.

"Very good, Dieterman, very good. Tonight you proved yourself. Not in the way I wanted but you did prove yourself, Corporal." He turned to Lehmann and Lassen. "You two go in the house. It seems Corporal Dieterman is going to take the first four-hour watch. Lehmann, you're next then you, Lassen. Dieterman will make sure she's tied securely and won't get away. Isn't that so, Dieterman?"

"She won't escape."

Carl lowered the shovel and let it fall. He had won, for now.

"You did good, Dieterman," Kretchmer said. "You showed courage in the face of death. Excellent. Excellent!"

Kretschmer spun and left. The others followed.

TWENTY

THEIR FOOTSTEPS NO longer audible, Carl picked up the shovel and leaned it against the front wall with the other tools. He came to the doorway and inhaled to cleanse the horrific tragedy.

The sun was deeper in the west, and some night insects had started their chatter early. The exterior's peacefulness belied the anguish within the barn.

He felt good about his stand to protect the girl. At least now, he thought, the girl had a better chance surviving. If not for him they would have killed her after the rapes. Kretschmer may have punched her to death.

He glanced at Melissa. That part of the barn was beginning to darken. Near him were three light switches. He switched them on one at a time. He turned off two and left the one lighting Melissa's area.

Carl gathered her clothes and placed them next to her. She had watched him as he stood in the doorway. He had defended her, and bravely. She came to realize he was indeed her savior. She watched him with appreciation as he moved about the barn.

Carl came closer and saw her grimacing from pain.

"Are you all right?"

"I'll be fine. My head and body are competing for who hurts the most." She tried a smirk.

"You can get dressed if you promise not to run from me."

"I promise."

He found assurance in her eyes. He untied her bonds. Melissa stood cautiously and put on the brassiere after wiping her neck and breasts with her slip. Then she put on the blouse.

"I'd like to wash, please."

"Is there water here?"

"Near the first stable. I won't move from here. Put some in the pail."

"I'll get it."

He put water in the pail after rinsing it, and brought it to her. She cupped her hands and scooped water to her mouth, swished it around then expelled. She repeated the procedure. She dipped her panties and wrung them then looked at Carl as if she had to do something embarrassing.

"Do what you have to do, Melissa. I'm sorry I can't give you privacy. I'll turn sideways."

She half-crouched, cleansed herself then wiped dry with the slip.

"I must go to the bathroom now."

"I see. Again, do what you have to do."

Melissa hesitated but nothing mattered after what she'd been through. He had seen her raped and naked and running with blood and semen. Nature's call was normal. She moved behind a hay bale and squatted.

Carl looked away and pretended being deaf. She said, "I'm ready now."

She sat again with hands behind her back, around the pole. He tied her hands, checking the knots. He stood and headed for the doorway to stand his four-hour guard duty. She called to him.

"What's your first name?"

He stopped and turned. "Carl."

"Tell me about my father."

"I—I don't know anything."

"That man said he was dead. Is that true?"

He swallowed to get it out with a deep breath. "Yes."

Melissa flinched from the truth, though expected. "How did he die?"

"I don't know. I wasn't there."

"Who killed him?"

"Kretschmer."

"You were brave. Thank you. Who are you people? What are you?"

Carl paused. He wondered if it would be a mistake to tell her.

"We are soldiers. German soldiers."

"Germans? Nazis?"

"Germans."

"Is that why my father was killed?"

"I understand he tried to escape."

"What's going to happen to me now?"

"I don't know. For now consider yourself a prisoner—a prisoner of war. I can't talk to you anymore. I am deeply sorry about what happened to your father. And I am deeply sorry about what happened to you. It was atrocious and inexcusable. I'll bring some food to you later."

Carl left and leaned against the barn door and waited for the sunset, arms folded, his mind heavily weighted.

Melissa's chin sagged to her chest and she cried for her father.

TWENTY-ONE

HE LISTENED TO her grief with compassion, and sympathy.

Melissa's anguish ebbed at late twilight, and shadows had deepened. The western sky was a stunning watercolor painting of pastel shades of purple and pink. But the world wasn't beautiful anymore.

The house lights turned on adding some brightness to the front of the barn. The lights were a reminder and he left for the house.

Kretschmer, Lehmann and Lassen were sitting around the kitchen table having dinner. When Carl walked in they stopped talking mid-sentence. Carl felt the cold reception, no longer a trusted team member. Ignoring their stares, Carl picked up two plates, scraped what chicken was left from the bones, took some salad, napkins and bread then opened the rear door.

"Dieterman."

Carl turned to Kretschmer resenting the interruption of his mission. Kretschmer looked sarcastic.

"What are you? The Red Cross?"

Carl approached the table and took some chicken meat from Kretschmer's plate.

"This is your contribution."

He walked out and slammed the door.

Melissa was exhausted and in physical pain. Her head ached from Kretschmer's punches and her lungs and stomach were dry from mourning. She didn't know why the young soldier left the barn. She had studied him as he leaned pensively against the barn. He never turned to look at her, allowing her sorrow to expire in uninterrupted loneliness. Was he ashamed over what happened, she wondered? Or was he embarrassed for her? Thank goodness he was here. God only knows what else might have happened.

Then she remembered Warrior. Warrior stood passive in his stable. Her thoughts were now spurred by escape. She had to get away. If she could only free her hands and ride away on Warrior. They would never catch her. She forgot her indignity, self-pity, pain and mourning and concentrated on her plan. *If only I could free my hands . . .*

The knots were securely tied. Her wrists struggled for movement but were efficiently restrained. She tried standing for better leverage, without improvement. Maybe if she was able to loosen the pole, to make it fall or maybe break it. Her body hit against the pole repeatedly, solid in place. Frustrated, she sat again. She looked around for some tool, anything within reach of her legs to help break the bonds. She didn't see one. Her hopes faded.

Hearing footsteps on the gravel, she assumed a destitute posture; head hanging low. When the footsteps approached, she looked up and smiled internal. Carl placed the plate and fork next to her.

"Here. It's not much but if you need more you can have my plate."

She looked at him surprised at his consideration. Why wasn't the world filled with people like him and Patricia? She was beginning to feel safe with him. He wasn't about to rape or hurt her. He was unlike the others.

"Will you untie my hands so I can eat?"

Carl paused.

"No, I'll feed you. I'm sorry. It must be that way. I know you won't try to escape, but—" He shrugged.

Melissa might have been able to use the fork as a weapon. Escape was her priority. If she had to hurt— or kill him, she would. Her survival was foremost.

Carl placed his plate next to hers, sat Indian-style and stabbed a piece of chicken with her fork. For the next ten minutes they didn't talk. They looked at each other studying, evaluating, and sometimes communicating in silence—she the war prisoner, he the enemy. He patterned the feeding—first her, her again, then him. When finished, he wiped her mouth with a napkin. As he began to rise Melissa broke the silence.

"Thank you."

Carl smiled. "You're welcome."

He hosed the dishes and forks and placed them on a nearby hay bale. Then he completed the four-hour watch by standing near and leaning against the barn door staring at the moonlit field imagining how the field would look a month from now when the plants were in bloom. He heard Lehmann say this was a potato farm. He had never been on a farm before and never saw a potato plant up close. He couldn't imagine what they looked like underneath. All he knew from school was that potatoes grew underground. How did they get them out of the ground? And then he, too, thought about his parents.

His father had been a doctor, a general practitioner with an office on the first floor of their two-story house. His mother, a nurse, was an excellent complement. Since early youth, Carl learned not to be an aggressive, noisy child over the downstairs office. The patients didn't like hearing thundering footsteps from upstairs. His father was his idol and his mother smothered him with affection. He was the only child.

Dr. Wilhelm Dieterman was educated in England. He taught his son the language believing English would someday become an important language. They would practice English to the chagrin of Gerda Dieterman. She didn't understand all they were saying. She tried to learn English but wasn't enthused. Carl absorbed the language like a sponge and read English literature by the great authors.

He was fifteen when they were killed. His interest in medicine died with them. He learned much from his father who kept him interested in medicine though Carl preferred tinkering with mechanical things.

His aunt and sadistic uncle soon erased his interest in medicine. But he never forgot the lessons of medicine. He had looked upon Melissa as a patient treating her as a doctor would, within parameters, as he tenderly wiped her and prepared her cleansing.

Warm thoughts of his parents erased the viciousness of war and the memories stirred sensitivity to tears. He remembered long ago, when the world was young and the future daring—under his father's guidance.

Melissa wondered what he was thinking, what upbringing did he have? He must have decent parents to have raised such a good son—though he was now a soldier. But like the boys over here he had no choice. She wondered if they, in Germany, also considered war as glorious and splendid. How stupid!—How absolutely stupid of adults to inflict their stupidity on children. War had to demonstrate the stupidity of mankind! She was sure now. It killed her father and devastated her. War turned men into savages. And it may yet kill her. Will American soldiers act the same way in enemy territory?

But for now, she felt secure with Carl standing by the door. Yet, she remained frightened to sleep.

The clouds vanished and a full moon was the dominant object in the sky. Erich Lassen left the house, admired the moon and headed for the barn. Carl quickly dried his eyes.

"Everything all right, Carl?"

"Quite."

Lassen turned on the other lights illuminating the right side. When he approached Melissa, she turned her face away. He checked the ropes. Satisfied, he went to Warrior's stable and opened the gate.

"What are you doing?" asked Carl.

"Kretschmer wants me to tie the horse in the woods on the other side of the house."

"Why?"

"He doesn't want to chance the girl getting free. She could ride out of here and we'd never catch her."

Melissa's heart sank with her hopes. Lassen harnessed Warrior and talked him out.

"Come on, easy—easy. Come on." Warrior followed the rein's pull. "I'll be right back, Carl."

"I'll be here."

Carl closed the stable gate and turned out the lights Lassen had turned on, darkening the right side again. He watched Lassen disappear in the bend of the road behind the house then watched him walk back. He knew little about Lassen. Did the war make him what he was? Or was he like that before the war? Now, he didn't want to get to know him at all, and the others. They were strictly business until the war was over, or they were caught. Lassen had a taut military gait and his feet fell heavily on the gravel. The gravel seemed to complain the weight.

"I'll take over now," Lassen said.

"Where's everybody? Sleeping?"

"Kretschmer's in the bedroom. Peter discovered that the sofa opens into a bed. You can share that with him."

"No, I was planning to stay in here tonight. I'm sure you and the others won't approve, but that's the way it is. Save your fun for another place like New York. I'm sure for a few dollars you can get all you want without killing."

Lassen shrugged.

"Kretchmer was right. You *should* have been a priest. You sleep wherever you want. I'll be on the porch, should you need me."

"I won't need you."

Carl adjusted some hay bales near Melissa, removed his shoes, and lay down on his back. The hay was soft and comfortable.

"You're doing this for me, aren't you? Protecting me."

Carl turned on his side, away from her.

"I'm doing it for me," he lied. "The hay is more comfortable than the sofa. And I'm tired. Good night."

She felt he was lying and knew she would sleep tonight—her personal bodyguard nearby.

Melissa awakened with a start near three in the morning. The light was on. The better for them to see her, she figured. She didn't see a guard and cocked her head to listen. It was quiet. Carl's soft breathing could be heard. He had turned in his sleep and now faced toward Melissa. She studied him. He seemed younger in repose. She liked the facial lines and his high cheekbones, and sensed the goodness within.

She remembered reading a magazine article last month that said the young age fast in war—in suffering and in tragedy.

How much had he aged? He was mature in his courage. She felt a sudden void of whiteness, virgin ideology, pure spring fantasies, and romantic dreams. She felt older, in mind and body, a veteran of man's cruelty and war's reality with a childhood that seemed far away and out of focus.

Yesterday was long ago and she feared tomorrow.

Then a frightening thought brought panic. She prayed she wasn't impregnated. *Not this way!* She tried to remember her last period. What day was it? She was due next week again, and she counted for reassurance. She felt sure she was safe. But, doubt lingered.

She began to cry, hiding her fright by mourning for her father until sleep returned.

TWENTY-TWO

CARL'S EYES OPENED at seven and saw Melissa
sleeping restful. He tried to remember the last time
he used the bathroom. He avoided sitting on the U-
boat facility until absolutely necessary, remembering
his father telling him it was possible to contract syphilis
from a toilet seat and he never forgot. When he had
to go, he rubbed the seat vigorous after washing it.

The morning was pleasant. The sky was white and
blue. The sun was hidden over Montauk, its rays
piercing through the trees. Warrior was standing in
the distance, tied to a tree. Lehmann was doing his
guard duty on the porch—in the rocking chair,
snoring. Carl thought about leaving him that way for
Kretschmer to find. Instead, he kicked Lehmann's
shoe. Lehmann reacted spasmodic and came alert.

"Wake up, Peter."

"Ah—thanks. Thanks, Carl. I guess I must have
dozed for a minute."

He stood and stretched and scratched his groin.
Carl walked past, entered the house quietly to let

Lassen sleep then enjoyed the moment of the clean bathroom. He shaved and washed under his arms. Shaving was easy with his light growth. When he exited the bathroom a sleepy Kretschmer, with a heavy beard, waited against the wall opposite the bathroom. Carl nodded.

"How's your prisoner, Dieterman?"

"Asleep."

"Get ready. We'll be leaving here in a few hours. Don't look sorrowful, Dieterman. Now move out. I have to go."

Carl moved, detained by the thought that soon he would have a confrontation. The door closed. He adjusted the Luger behind his belt ready to influence the decision regarding Melissa.

Lassen was awake propped up on elbows, bare-chested. Carl sat on the couch.

"What's going on?" asked Lassen.

"Nothing. We had to use the bathroom."

"What time is it?"

"Seven thirty-five."

Lassen shook his head in disgust, annoyed at being awakened early. He rose, in shorts, turned on the radio and found the highest frequency area. The news was ending. " . . . and that ends our morning report. And now a word from you local Pontiac dealer right here in Patchogue . . ."

"Carl, where is Patchogue?"

"I never heard of it. Where's the map?"

"It's still in the carton." Lehmann opened the carton and unfolded the map.

"It's farther west, and local enough. Kretschmer has a feeling the naval team somehow bungled their end. I think he's praying they do. He's pushing for that Iron Cross. You were with the girl all night?"

"I slept on the hay. It was comfortable."

"I don't understand you, Carl. These people are dead anyway. So what's the difference? You know as well as I that we can't take the risk being discovered."

"We're not killing this girl," he said firm.

Lassen shrugged avoiding an argument.

"War is war, Carl."

"Sometimes but not here. We are creating the war."

"Did you just sleep last night?'

"Yes."

"Amazing. When was the last time you slept with a woman?"

"Before we left."

"I could have sworn you were virgin."

"I've been around. Raping that helpless girl was vicious and sadistic. I didn't expect that mentality from you and Lehmann. Just Kretschmer."

"Sorry you were offended. But it happened. She was there for the taking. What's the difference?"

"You raped a virgin."

"How do you know that? She was tight, but I didn't think she was a virgin."

"Didn't you see the blood?"

"Ah, so what. She had to do it sooner or later. It's not the end of the world. Somebody else will have her about two thousand times before her lifetime is over—that is," he smirked, "If she lives that long."

"You're turning into vomit, Erich. You're getting as sick as that sex deviate in Berlin. All you need is a mustache."

"I wouldn't talk like that if I were you, especially in front of Kretschmer."

"He's vomit with a capital Vee."

"Don't be harsh. We're not on a youth movement camping mission. We die if we make mistakes. They hang spies remember? Don't expect us to lead ordinary lives. Stop acting like a holy man. You'll get credit for all we do and the blame equally. I suggest you watch out for your own ass."

"Do you want to kill the girl?"

An instrumental of "All or Nothing at All" played on the radio.

"I don't think we have a choice."

"We do. We can tie her good and leave her."

"What the hell are you, her lawyer? It's too risky."

"Will you think about it?"

"I'll think about it."

"We're intelligent. I see no reason in the future why we can't talk our way out of a threat instead killing our way out. Leaving a trail of corpses is dangerous. That's traceable."

Lassen stretched out on the bed.

"Let's talk later, okay? I need more rest."

Kretschmer came out, shaving soap on his face.

"Did you catch the news?"

"We just missed it," replied Carl.

"Leave it on. Maybe we'll hear it at eight o'clock. Dieterman, make some coffee and something for breakfast. We should all eat well before we leave." He retreated to the bathroom.

Carl followed orders. He made a full pot of coffee, scrambled twelve eggs, and made a dozen buttered toasts. He filled five cups and divided the eggs among the plates. He put toast, a fork and a cup of coffee on three plates. He carried the three plates cautiously as he hollered out that breakfast was ready. He gave Lehmann, still on guard on the porch, a plate.

"Here you are, Peter. Stay awake."

"Thanks, Carl. Again."

"Do you feel you owe me a favor?"

"At least one."

"I don't want the girl killed." He looked deep into Lehmann's eyes for emphasis. There was no reaction from Lehmann.

TWENTY-THREE

MELISSA STIRRED AS Carl approached but she slept. He put the plates down and sat on the floor. The gun and dagger didn't bother him last night. They did this morning. He removed them, placing them at arm's length behind him.

Something was different about her face. He had seen it only in terror and mourning—now replaced by a peaceful quality, as if the storm had passed and the sun was breaking through. He wanted to touch her skin, as he once wanted to touch a beautiful sculpture in a museum. But a sign demanded, "Do not touch." She was beautiful in slumber with an angelic quality. Carl looked at her in a way he never looked at a girl before. He studied her nose, mouth, cheeks, eyebrows and golden hair and felt regret that vandals damaged his beautiful sculpture.

Carl touched her shoulder, nudged her three times and whispered her name. She stirred. He nudged again, gentler, so not to frighten her.

"Wake up, Melissa. It's me, Carl. Wake up. Don't be alarmed."

His calm voice opened her peaceful eyes. She smiled, feeling relaxed. Carl noticed her attractive teeth for the first time.

"Why are you looking at me like that?" Melissa said.

"You have a pretty smile. It becomes you." Yesterday's fright had passed. Was it because the gallant boy was there and being charming? She thought so. He smiled. She rolled her tongue inside her mouth.

"I wish I could brush my teeth."

"That's a luxury for now. Black coffee all right?"

"I usually take milk and sugar."

"I'll get some if you like."

"No. Black's fine. Doesn't matter."

Carl held the cup and she sipped, her eyes absorbing his face. He fed her slow to pass the time. He looked at her, but his mind was elsewhere. In fewer than two hours, Landwolf 337 would have a confrontation over her life. How could he win? The odds were against him.

"Carl?"

"Yes, Melissa."

"Do you come from a large family?"

"No, I'm an orphan. I lived with my aunt and uncle in Leipzig."

"I don't know where that is."

"It's in the southern part of the country."

"What happened to your parents?"

"They were killed."

"I'm sorry. Can I have more coffee? The war?"

"No, an automobile accident. Your mother, I assume, is not living?"

"Now both my parents are dead." She blinked back moisture. "Now we're both orphans. We have that in common, don't we? What will happen to me?"

"Nothing."

"I don't believe that."

"Believe it." The firmness in his voice was reassuring.

"How old are you, Carl?"

"Eighteen."

"Do you have a sweetheart back home?"

"Nobody special."

"How long have you been in the war?"

"About six months."

"Did—you ever kill anyone?"

"No."

"I didn't think you could."

"I could—if someone was shooting at me, or if someone wanted to kill me. I would kill to defend myself."

"I guess everyone would. Why are you here? Is Germany going to invade America?"

"I don't know. I can't tell you why I'm here. I think you're feeling better."

"Why do you say that?"

"Because you ask a lot of questions. Girls always seem to ask questions."

Melissa grinned.

"Just making conversation."

"What else would you like to know?" Conversation would ease the tension.

"What's it like in Leipzig?"

"It's an old city, but beautiful. Bach, Schumann, and Mendelssohn, the great composers, once lived there and Richard Wagner, he wrote opera, was born there. Do you know classical music?"

"A little. I've heard of them. I took music appreciation in school."

"Are you finished with school?"

"I graduated this week."

"You sure have an appetite this morning." Melissa gulped the eggs as soon as the fork reached her mouth. He slowed the process. "Congratulations. Do you have boyfriends?"

"Some."

"Serious?"

"No," Melissa replied.

"You're not getting married soon?"

"No."

"Most girls in my country can't wait to get married after finishing school. They're obsessed with the idea."

"It's the same here. But I'm going to college first."

"Where? To a university?"

"Yes, in New York City."

"Good. Good for you."

"My father—my father used to say to me that there was a big air bubble in the brains of all teenagers and the only way to get it out was to fill it with education."

Carl smiled.

"Maybe when the absurdity of war is over, I'll also go to college."

"What would you like to do?"

"My father wanted me to become a doctor, but I want to study mechanical engineering. I like working with mechanical things, like engines, and I'm fascinated by how they work."

"That's an interesting field."

Carl had a faraway look; his eyes glistened. "I wish I were in the mountains again. There, the world is pure and clean."

"I've never been to the mountains."

"None near here?"

"Just flat land. Some small hills."

"Melissa, what happened to you was horrible."

"It was."

"I wish I could change what happened."

"You can't." Melissa tried to be light toned. "It's not the way I wanted it to be—for the first time. Why are we talking so open like this? My goodness. Two days ago I would have been shy to talk to a new boy. Since you now know the secrets of my private life, how about you?"

"What?"

"When did you lose your virginity?" He paused, stabbed a ball of eggs a few times and brought the fork to her mouth.

"Come on, Carl. When did you? Did I embarrass you?"

"No."

"Then answer. You look as if I did. Did you ever do it?"

"I'm a soldier. All soldiers are experienced at that sort of thing."

"Was it a prostitute?"

"No."

"A girlfriend?—Somebody's wife? You never did it?" she asked with an inquisitive expression.

"If you must know," he grinned embarrassed, "I almost did."

Melissa smiled at him. Her eyes were affectionate.

"That was hard for you to admit, wasn't it?"

"Yes."

Sharing his secret seemed to draw them together adding security to her environment.

TWENTY-FOUR

BREAKFAST ENDED AND Lassen appeared in the doorway at ten minutes before eight.

"Carl, Kretschmer wants to see you soon."

"I'll be right there. We just finished."

He wiped her mouth. "I'll be right back."

The confrontation was about to begin. He began to feel he had offered her the last supper. He picked up his gun and dagger, and with reconfirmation of firmness and a steady gait, he left Melissa.

"What does Kretschmer want?"

"He didn't say. He's calling a meeting. But first, I have to ask the girl something. You go ahead."

"No, I'll wait for you."

"What's the matter, Carl? Don't you trust me?"

"Not at all."

"All right, then wait for me." Lassen moved closer to Melissa. "Miss, I'm going to ask you a question and I want a truthful answer." He didn't have to say he would kill her if it turned out she lied. He conveyed the message by his looks.

"Ask."

"Were you expecting anyone today?"

How should she answer? Should she lie and say yes? Would they leave then, or leave her behind tied to be found? No. They would kill her if they thought someone was coming. Or kill whoever came. Patricia said she would call, but that's all. Melissa hoped she wouldn't decide to ride over to talk about her day with Buddy.

"No, we—no one is expected. The planting is all done. That's the truth."

"Good."

He turned and Carl followed him out.

Kretschmer was pacing impatient in his undershirt. Lehmann was in bed, sitting up.

"What did the girl say, Lassen?"

"No one is expected."

"Do you believe her?"

"I think she told the truth."

"Let's hope she did. I have good news for you, Dieterman. We're staying another day and I'm assigning you to watch the girl and the east road tonight. We'll cover the west. That should make you happy." He turned away and headed for the kitchen. "Lehmann, tell him why if he wants to know."

"Carl, do you want to know why we're staying another day?"

"Don't be an ass. Of course."

"We heard on the eight o'clock news there are rumors someone saw some men landing at Amagansett last week and they may be Germans. Officials believe they took the train to New York. It's unknown if they were caught, but Kretschmer doesn't want to chance traveling today if there's an alert. He figures tomorrow, Saturday, would be a better day to travel. There should be more weekend tourists and we'd blend in better."

"With all the corpses you guys left around they're bound to blame the naval group and if they draw a straight line, they'll find us here."

"You see too many movies, Carl. That's improbable. Besides, there are no witnesses to say they saw four men together near the scene. We're safe here. *No* witnesses!"

"I got your message. I still don't like it. I'll bet Kretschmer would have been happier if the naval unit got caught."

"He'd be thrilled. We would win, but more important, if they did get caught no one will be looking for us. No one saw us land. *No one.* There won't be a need anymore to stay on back roads and woods. I hope they do get caught and take the pressure off us. They could land others elsewhere. We won't be the last, I'm sure."

*　　*　　*

Melissa again thought about escape, but the bonds were unyielding. Even if she could free her hands how could she escape without Warrior? She damned Kretschmer for having the foresight to move Warrior. Where could she run unseen? No place to hide in the fields and the woods were far. They would see her. Daytime escape was out. Would she live until night?

Carl came back and sat on a bale near her.

"How are you doing?" he asked.

"I feel weary sitting in this position, but fine under the circumstances."

"You should know we're staying here another day."

Her confidence fell, shuddering like an avalanche—another day's mental torture. What if Patricia came? Damn, why didn't they leave and leave her alone?

"I think the coffee is running through me. Can I go to the bathroom?"

He untied the ropes. She rose, stretched and went behind the bales. It was clinical. He was the doctor, she, the patient. He listened to the rush of liquid and again pretended deafness. She returned to the pole.

"You can walk around if you like."

"Thanks. I can use the exercise."

Melissa walked to the stable slow then quick three times, did some knee bends and stretched, and sought to find a weapon to overpower Carl. But she was weak, and the effort would prove futile. If she failed, she would lose an ally. Night was the proper time. She sat against the pole. He tied her hands. The knots weren't as tight. When he moved away she discovered the ability to manipulate her wrists better. Hope.

"I'll be waiting outside," Carl said. "Call if you need me."

Alone again, she struggled with the rope. Her hands were mobile, but unable to get free. Defeated again. She had stayed alive thus far. A good sign and was optimistic about seeing tomorrow.

Her hero was holding the others at bay.

Somehow she had to find a way to take advantage of his protection—and to ensure he stayed on her side.

At eleven o'clock, she called him.

"Can I have some water?"

Carl brought her water then left. She thought she was ready, but had to think more about strategy. At one o'clock, Melissa called him again.

"I'm hungry. Can you get a sandwich? Anything."

He nodded and left. He brought the bologna and lettuce sandwich and fed her.

"Carl, you haven't looked at me since this morning and you're quiet. What's bothering you?"

"I have things to think about."

"I enjoy talking to you. Can't you stay and talk?"

"It's best we don't become more familiar."

"It's talk. To pass the time."

"End of conversation. It's wrong. You're a prisoner. One shouldn't fraternize with the—" He was going to finish the statement with enemy. "—prisoners." She wasn't *his* enemy.

"Horseshit!"

Her language jolted him.

"What's the matter?" Melissa asked seeing his reaction.

"I didn't expect that language from you."

"Why not?"

"No, you're right. It is horseshit. How can there be principles when no principles exist in war? Still, I can't sit and talk to you."

"Do you like me, Carl?"

"I think you're nice."

"Would you like to—to touch me?"

"Do you want me to?"

"I would like it."

"Why?"

"Because I like you. You're nice and you did save my life."

"You want to reward me?"

"Not exactly."

"You want to be the first to break my virginity?" Melissa grinned.

"I like you, Carl. It won't be raping me. For you, I'd be willing. I don't know what will happen to me. I might die tomorrow and I'd like to know the nice side of lovemaking now that I know the ugly. Before I die, Carl. Just once. Please kiss me."

Carl remembered thoughts as he stared into pleading eyes—thoughts he had in the U-boat when he was frightened. What if he got caught? How would he react? Spies were hung. Would he be brave knowing he was about to die? Would he beg for mercy? Would he do things he normally wouldn't do to save himself? Would he crawl on his knees and beg, void of pride and humility to live?

Was Melissa doing the same to him? Doing anything to try to save herself? The positions were reversed and he understood, and he patted her shoulder, consoling.

"I'm flattered you want me, but you're going to live. No, Melissa, save the nice side for the man you will love someday. You will not die. And after tomorrow, you will never see me again."

She acted disappointed. "Will you remember me someday?"

"I won't forget you and what happened here."

"Then I won't forget you either and what you did for me."

"Melissa, no more conversation please. I must go back to my post."

"Don't you think I'm pretty?"

"I think you're beautiful."

"You do?"

"Under any other circumstances, I would be pounding on your door every day to take you out."

"You're just saying that."

"I think you're beautiful and feel good being with you. Someday, if the fates will it, we may meet again. And if you're still single and I'm still single, who knows?"

A gleam was in his eyes. Reluctant, he went to his post and leaned against the barn glancing at random at the east road.

At first Melissa thought her invitation to Carl was an attempt to ingratiate him more to her—to tighten the security blanket. But then realized she would have liked him to love her.

There came feelings that lifted her spirits. She refused to accept what they meant. It couldn't be happening here, in this ugly environment with him. It wasn't supposed to happen until college. *It's not the way it was planned!*

Melissa was beginning to fall in love on the brink of death.

TWENTY-FIVE

SIOBHAN GRIFFIN FINISHED her shopping at
Leon's Grocery in East Hampton and watched the
boy with a white grocer's apron load her boxes in
the pickup truck.

Siobhan looked up and down Main Street
searching for Patricia, who was to meet her here
fifteen minutes ago. Patricia was normally punctual
and methodical, so it had to be an exception for her
to be late. The answer was obvious to Siobhan: boys.

The town was busy today getting ready for the
weekend invasion from New York City. Yet, there
wasn't the usual hustle and bustle of this summer
town. The pace was now leisurely, the war a
tempering burden.

It wouldn't be the same during the summer
anymore, she reflected watching the activity in the
town. The war would diminish the summer tourist
trade. Though fuel was becoming difficult to obtain,
the trains from Pennsylvania Station ran on schedule.

If the tourists came at all, it would probably be a mother with children.

The war had already affected food supplies and shortages were something to learn to live with. This week, she shopped for two week's supplies opposed to one. She would shop twice a month now due to the gas-rationing problem. She had filled up the truck's tank and two five-gallon cans in the back for Sean's equipment. She saw Patricia hurrying toward her.

"Hi, Mom. Sorry I'm late."

She was breathing hard. Siobhan thought about chastising her tardiness but suppressed the urge.

"How was your day? Did you see Buddy?"

"Let's discuss it in the truck."

The grocer's aide finished placing the boxes in the rear and slammed the tailgate. Siobhan waved to thank him. As soon as the truck started, Siobhan asked, "Well?"

"I don't know, Mom. We're going to go together for a while, but I don't think it will turn out to be anything serious."

"I thought you liked him. Then it won't be something meaningful?"

"No, I don't think so. Somehow something's missing, you know?"

Siobhan nodded knowingly.

"No gut feeling?"

"Exactly."

"But you're still going to go out with him?"

"It'll pass the summer."

"You two have anything planned this weekend?"

"I was thinking about it. I hate to leave Melissa alone for an entire weekend. I told Buddy I'd let

him know tonight when he calls me. I thought I'd
go and spend the weekend with Melissa and her
father. You know, keep him company as well."

The considerate side of her daughter was
speaking and Siobhan admired the quality.

"I don't think you should do that," Siobhan
replied.

"You don't?"

"This is Melissa's last summer with her father most
likely. She may meet someone next year and spend
the summer in New York or transfer somewhere else.
I think it'd be better if they had more time alone
together—to get to know each other. Since this is
the first weekend, it might be nice if they spent it
together. Of course, it's different if she calls you."

"You think so?"

"I know so."

The firmness of her mother's wisdom made
Patricia withdraw. Mother was right. The Shullers
should have time together.

"I guess you're right. I'll wait for her call. If she
doesn't call me by tonight I'll go out with Buddy."

TWENTY-SIX

EVENING SHADOWS CAME before long and Melissa and Carl shared a supper of pork and beans, and carrots and peas from a jar.

"I wish you wouldn't be stand-offish with me, Carl. You don't have to treat me like a stranger. You don't look at me like a stranger. I get the feeling you're becoming more distant."

"Distant? Actually, I'm beginning to enjoy being with you. Maybe that's why I've been staying here all day."

"But you haven't said much."

"Let's say I like being in your presence."

"Now you're playing with me."

"I'm not. Please eat. It's that there's a conflict within me about you and if I keep talking with you, the conflict intensifies."

"What's the conflict?"

"It doesn't matter. Forget it."

Lehmann appeared at the entrance.

"Carl, Kretschmer thinks you should join us at the house."

He came in and checked her ropes.

"I'll see you later, Melissa," Carl said.

"Bye."

When they left the barn, Melissa began struggling with the ropes. She had to get away! She determined the conflict in Carl's mind was whether to kill her or not.

Melissa struggled harder, nearly crying from the frustration.

Kretschmer and Lassen were lounging on the house steps drinking beer, gazing at the emptiness. The night insects were singing among the random tones of tree toads. The moon was rising.

"Ah, Dieterman. Did you have a pleasant day with your girlfriend?" Kretschmer and Lassen laughed. "On second thought, Carl—" He never called him by his first name. Carl became defensive toward what was coming. "—no need to stand guard out here at night. I realized one could see headlights approaching at a distance. Relax tonight. Forget the prisoner and let's be comrades again. Here, have a beer. It will remind you of home."

Kretschmer extended a bottle of Rupert Beer and Carl took it.

"Damn," Kretschmer sighed. "I got lazy today. I didn't realize how fatigued I was." He patted his sheathed dagger. "Forgot to go look for my weapon. I'll get up early tomorrow."

Carl leaned against the railing. Lehmann sat in the rocking chair. Kretschmer opened another quart of beer.

"There's a case in the backyard under a wood awning if anybody wants more. There's two more bottles in the refrigerator. We should make Riverhead by late tomorrow night if we get an early start.

Lehmann, you double-check everything before we leave and make sure nothing is left behind to connect our being here. Dieterman, your job in the morning is to secure the girl. Tie her up well. I want to make sure she starves to death." He smiled.

So did Carl. He had won. They would let her live.

"You make me feel better, Sergeant."

"I think it's a mistake, but I need you on this mission. I can't afford to have you sulking. We must be loyal to each other to succeed. The Fatherland is counting on us to complete this important mission. We will make historic strikes. Now, let's talk about what we do when we get to New York."

Carl fraternized with them, content his way would prevail, that they now understood he wouldn't tolerate killing outside of their mission. No further need to remain antagonistic toward them. He listened carefully as Kretschmer discussed procedures to follow and at what hotels they would register. The hotel's name where he would stay with Lassen, under assumed names, became lost with the Melissa conflict.

She refused to leave his mind.

At nine o'clock, Carl and Lehmann went inside to listen to the radio. Kretschmer and Lassen stayed on the porch.

"Beautiful night," Kretschmer said looking up at the Little Dipper. "You can almost touch the stars."

"Are we going to leave the girl?"

"Like I told Lehmann, he's to make sure to leave nothing behind to connect us. He knows what to do."

He smiled and Lassen understood, and approved.

They sat there drinking beer and talking about possible targets in the New York area and the future rendezvous with a U-boat for information as to where explosive supplies could be found. Their prime objective in the New York area would be the Hell's Gate Bridge, a major railroad bridge linking Long Island with the mainland. The Consolidated Edison facilities along the East River would be next, crippling the city.

Dieterman was a simple fool, Kretschmer thought. The girl had to die—as pretty as she was. But before he had her killed, he would use her body. No one would interrupt him. She did have a beautiful body and it would be a shame to let that go to waste.

Kretschmer rose and stretched.

"Wait here. I'm going to check the girl—make sure she's tied securely. I still don't trust Dieterman."

"Have a good time." Lassen grinned assuming he knew what Kretschmer planned.

"I'll be right back."

Lassen wasn't wrong. The beer had provoked Kretschmer's sexual urge and Melissa stirred him to the point where he had to have release. His temperature was rising as he approached the barn. Visions of lust were propelling his blood, stimulating the animal instincts.

Melissa didn't hear Kretschmer coming and he watched her as she wrestled with the rope. Her battle had twisted her body. She was sideways to the door. Then she sensed his presence and turned abruptly.

She shuddered.

Kretchmer loomed like a giant against the darkness coming toward her, menacing. With insecure eyes she watched his approach and an alarm began ringing in her ears. He wore a shroud of evil.

Melissa cowered from the crazed look in his eyes. He hovered over her, silent. His hand moved to the sheathed dagger. He watched Melissa's eyes as the gesture frightened her.

He's going to kill me!

Kretchmer grinned at the power he had over her, delighting in her helplessness, his victim.

He knelt next to her and leaned forward nearly face-to-face—close that she saw double images.

"You owe me one," he rasped unbuttoning her blouse. Her senses dulled at his touch. She didn't smell the beer on his breath. She could hardly breathe. His hands were massaging her breasts, over the brassiere. His mouth wet her neck, anger in his fingers. She flinched from the pain and the squeezing. Her body shook and tried to escape. He was relentless. He released one hand and unbuttoned his pants.

Melissa battled captivity and wept from failure and hopelessness.

"Please, leave me alone. You're hurting me."

He stopped gouging her breast and kissing her. He stood and pulled the dagger. She gasped. He walked behind her and cut the rope.

"Now, move over there." He pointed to an area where the hay was about six inches thick. "Come on, stand up." She hesitated and he slapped her hard across the face.

She moaned from the sting and stood then went where directed under his watchful eye. Impatience began to stir him.

"Hurry up and lie down. Pull up your skirt and spread. Hurry."

Melissa tightened her body, protecting her front with her elbows, fingers covering her mouth, refusing to obey. He was intent on threatening her with the dagger, but instead sheathed it and went after her.

"You bitch! Are you deaf? I told you to lie down!"

He slapped then punched her on the side of the head and she went sprawling to the floor. He leaped on her and tried to force her knees apart. Melissa struggled, arms flailing.

His hand reached for her panties trying to rip them off. Her legs were spread wide between his knees and his strength ripped the panties off. He fell on her, struggling to penetrate.

He probed wildly, unsuccessful. She kept punching, screaming for him to stop. And then her hand felt the handle of the dagger. His concentration was on finding the opening and wasn't aware of her hands as they groped to get a firm grip on the dagger. Her mind ignored him now, concentrating on the weapon.

Melissa grasped the handle, pulled the dagger from the sheath and in one circular move plunged it into his neck.

For an instant, time stood still as she waited for the effect of the thrust.

Then it came in a grotesque gurgle, then his horrified eyes looked at her as if to say—What have you done? And then came the blood—first from his neck and it dripped on her forehead, and then spurts from his mouth. Then his rigid body relaxed and collapsed on her. He stopped breathing.

With all the strength she could muster aided by a scream as warm blood streaked her face, she pushed him off onto his back. Breathless, she was muttering, "You pig. You damn pig!" And she entered into a revenge rage. She pulled the dagger from the throat and plunged it into his chest holding the handle with both hands.

"You killed my father, you bastard!" She plunged again, and again. Six times. "You bastard! You filthy bastard!"

Melissa dropped the dagger when sudden sanity made her aware of her surroundings and the danger she was in. Was someone coming? She listened hard—only her breathing, no other sound.

She wiped some blood from her head and face with the torn panties and discarded the cloth behind the tractor. Smeared blood still remained on her face. *What to do now? What shall I do? Escape! Or die!*

No, wait. First hide the body. Straining, she dragged the body behind the hay bales. Yes, the right thing to do. Hide him in case someone came in before she could escape. But she was dead, too, if they caught her.

Melissa squeezed her head to force her mind to think. Leave the light on. If they see it off they may get suspicious. Go to the door and see if anyone is coming. If it's safe then run to the fields keep low and make for the trees. That's the only way.

But first the blood stains on the hay where she killed him. Hurried, she moved the hay around and in her mental confusion covered the dagger beneath the hay inadvertently, forgetting to take it as a weapon to help in her escape. Fear of getting caught and her flight from the barn allowed no room for the dagger.

Then she thought about the back door. The best way out was through the back door. All she had to do was shift the heavy board.

In the meantime, Lassen thought he heard a distant scream. Probably his imagination, but decided to check. If Kretschmer was doing it again with the girl, so would he. It may be a long time before he had a woman again. He began to feel sensations in his groin spurred by the fantasy.

He peeked inside the house to check on Dieterman and Lehmann. Lehmann saw him in the window. Carl had his attention on the radio. Lehmann was about to react at seeing Lassen when Lassen put his finger on his lips. Lehmann understood. He watched Lassen leave the porch and disappear into the darkness.

Before Melissa could leave by the back door, she had to make sure no one was coming. She pressed against the front doorway. It had to be all right. She hoped the bright moon wouldn't betray her when she ran through the fields. She peeked out toward the house.

She saw Lassen approaching and her heart quickened.

Melissa began to pray then thought of Carl. Carl would save her life if she got caught. She could explain her killing Kretschmer. Carl would be outraged that he tried to rape her. It was self-defense. They would understand that. She wanted to run to the back door. Now she couldn't run through the fields. She would be seen. She thought about running to the back of the house and hiding in the basement. They wouldn't think to look for her there. They would search the woods first.

Hide in the barn!

If he saw the barn empty Lassen would run to the house for help, and when he did that she would run to the basement. But what if he didn't run for help? What if he found the body? Her thoughts went into chaos and she retreated to the darkness by the tractor. She had waited long to make a decision and could now hear Lassen's heavy footfalls crunching the gravel near the barn.

Lassen walked heavily on the gravel to alert Kretschmer he was approaching. He didn't want to walk in on him without warning. He had no desire to be a victim of his wrath. He imagined what Kretschmer was doing at the moment and liked the vision.

Lassen stopped at the entrance. To his surprise he didn't see anyone, but no need to be suspicious, he thought. He assumed Kretschmer was making love to her somewhere. He listened for sounds of sex. Disappointed and curious, he entered.

"Sergeant?"

His tone was almost apologetic. The barn remained silent as he walked farther in. Then he heard a noise from behind to his left and turned.

Melissa ran out of the shadows with the pitchfork held high and buried it into his chest before he could react to defend himself.

His death bellow was long and sustained his eyes fixed in disbelief. Then the bellow faded as he stumbled backward until the life in his legs left. He fell and crumpled on his back near the stables. His body jerked, as his hands tried to find strength to remove the pitchfork. They stopped lifeless holding the handle, his shirt covered with blood.

Melissa watched him die without compassion or remorse. She had eliminated the enemy. She was amazed at her achievement, her ability to kill him, to remain victorious thus far.

Then she heard somebody whistling, and the whistling was coming closer.

"Oh, God!" she choked.

Lehmann was approaching the barn. He had told Carl he was going for a walk. If Kretschmer and Lassen were up to something with the girl, he wanted some of the action.

Melissa tried to think quickly. Chaotic, she threw hay over Lassen's body. She moved back into the shadows where she hid before. She had to resort to surprise again.

Surprise is my strength, my only strength!

She had to take on Lehmann. There wasn't time to hide Lassen's body. The body was in the shadows but visible. With the pitchfork sticking up like a marker, she'll never have the opportunity to run. Lehmann had to be dealt with, but how?

Melissa had tried to pull the pitchfork from Lassen's body to use it again but didn't have the strength. She had plunged it deep.

The whistling came nearer. Lehmann entered the barn without hesitating at the doorway and when he didn't see anyone, he stopped. The whistling ceased though the shape of his mouth remained oval.

"Sergeant? Erich?" Then he saw the figure in the shadows by the stable. "Who's there? Erich, is that you?"

He headed for the shape on the floor. Melissa, creeping silently, came out from hiding without being heard and swung the ax into his back.

The scream was piercing, chilling. His arm's effort to remove the object from his back was futile. His knees bent backward then forward then they buckled and he fell face down. She watched his dying movements with coldness. She had won another round.

Melissa was the triumphant gladiator.

Now she felt free and took a deep breath to regain composure. Carl had to be in the house. He wouldn't stop her from escaping. Fear had left her now because she didn't fear Carl. She began to move to the back door and stopped. She had to check the front again to make sure he wasn't coming. Carl was friendly, but the enemy nevertheless.

Melissa turned and became petrified.

Carl stood in the doorway pointing a Luger at her bloodied face.

TWENTY-SEVEN

WAR RETURNED AND they stared motionless at each other on the battlefield—enemies.

The weak and abused captive had retaliated.

Once friendly enemies, they now stood in the way of each other's freedom.

The gun menaced Melissa. He made the first move.

The gun lowered to his side. He turned on all the lights. Carl grimaced at the grotesque methods of death. The ax and pitchfork handles were like grave markers. Blood covered both bodies and the dirt and hay absorbed the overflow. Melissa relaxed when the gun lowered, knowing he wasn't going to shoot her, not right away if at all.

Carl pointed to the blood on her face.

"Are you hurt?"

"No, it's Kretschmer's blood."

"Where's Kretschmer?" he asked. She pointed to the hay bales. He raised the gun again. "Move in front of me, Melissa. Go back to the pole and don't move."

She obeyed, not frightened—yet, doubt lingered. Carl looked at Kretschmer and flinched.

"He tried to rape me, Carl. I had no choice. He tried to rape me and was beating me like before."

Melissa's excuse was ineffective as he looked for new rope. He found rope on the wall behind the tractor.

"Put your hands behind your back and stand. Same way."

Carl tied her hands—shaking his head unbelieving Melissa had killed his comrades by herself. He stood in front of her, hands on hips, incredulous.

"Well, it looks like the end of Landwolf Three-three-seven. You sure did a job of it. Amazing."

"What's Landwolf Three-three-seven?"

"It's the code name given to our mission."

"What now, Carl? It's only you and me. Are you going to kill me?" She hoped for a response, but could see his mind working behind the stare. "Are you going to release me? What are you going to do?"

"I don't know. I don't know. I have to think this out. First I must hide those three bodies. I can't afford to have them found. Nothing must be traceable to Landwolf Three-three-seven."

He dragged Kretschmer by the feet to the middle of the barn.

Melissa turned away to avoid the distorted face. Carl then braced a foot against Lassen's body, pulled hard and the pitchfork freed dripping blood, three lines. He threw it to the ground. The ax had buried up to handle width and resisted his pull. The ax released its hold of Lehmann's spine. Carl threw the ax near the pitchfork. Lehmann's blood rushed out the chasm. He dragged their bodies near Kretschmer's.

Carl looked at his fallen comrades staring hard to feel pity. He found himself without any sensitive feelings for them.

They were victims of the war environment they created.

There was one thing he would do for them, one gesture of human kindness. Someday, if asked by their families as to how they died, he would tell them they died in the line of duty with honor. He wouldn't tarnish their memories.

Their dishonor paid the ultimate price.

"Is there anywhere near the house we can hide the bodies? A well, or a ditch?"

"There isn't anything like that around here."

That's that, he thought, and decided to bury them in the barn. He walked to the last stable, opened the gate and felt the ground. It was soft. Satisfied, he took a shovel and a pickax from the front wall. With the pickax he scratched a rough three-by-six outline on the ground. He removed his shirt and pants and hung them over the gate, placing his weapons nearby. Dressed in beige shorts, he began to dig and shovel, piling dirt around the outline.

Melissa watched his labor, intent on his job. Carl was a gentle person, but his muscles rippled and responded to the weight of the pickax as he raised and thrust it with power into the ground. When the ground loosened, his strong shovel heaves moved the dirt with efficiency.

Carl's body was up to the task. Melissa admired the masculine body as it discharged its strength. She kept watching his labor and soon the body was shining from sweat. His rhythm and the flexing muscles communicated a stirring in Melissa that wiped fear and speculating what would happen to her after he buried the bodies.

He was venting his frustration and indecision with the pickax and shovel.

The trauma of her experience and the continuing nearness to death created a feeling within her she had never felt before from a boy—a man. For the first time in her life she wanted a man to take her and make love to her with passion and desire and understanding that she wanted to do the same to him. She admired his activity, as would a lover.

After an hour, his body aching and exhausted and calluses on his hands sensitive to touch and screaming for relief, he was finished with the grave. He had dug over three feet deep. His legs were covered with dirt. Melissa had listened to his splendid grunts, and now listened to his heavy breathing as he leaned against the stable gate.

Then he searched each body, removing all jewelry and weapons. He searched their wallets, took the money and burned their identification cards with a cigarette lighter. He placed the wallets and the personal effects near his clothing.

Carl dragged Kretschmer first. He lifted and dropped Kretschmer, who hit the edge of the grave and fell in face down. Carl stepped to the opposite side and pulled until Kretschmer's body lay flat in the grave. It wasn't important whether he faced up or down. Dead was dead. He'll never know the difference. He couldn't complain about it. He earned the right. He deserved to face hell.

Then he dragged Lassen, whose body bounced when landing on Kretschmer. Lassen faced up. Carl avoided looking at their faces for he knew that someday those grotesque expressions of violent death would haunt him in nightmares whenever he thought about this night or the mission of Landwolf 337. He breathed relief when Lehmann's body was in place on top of Lassen's. He, too, faced up.

Then reluctant but dutiful, after wrapping his handkerchief around the calluses of his right hand, he began to fill the hole refusing to look at the grave until the dirt had covered Lehmann's face. He rested, massaging his sore hands. He looked at Melissa to make sure she was still tied in place. She was watching him. From her angle, she couldn't see how much of the grave he had covered.

"Almost finished?"

"No. There's more."

Melissa's voice was a signal telling him the rest period was over. He plowed into the dirt and finished the assignment. Fatigue made him careless as he scattered the dirt making the level uneven. He accepted that because when the earth settled again and compacted it would probably settle evenly. Besides, he was tired, damn tired. When all the earth was returned, a small mound formed. He scooped handfuls of hay and covered the dirt.

Carl gathered his clothes, the wallets and jewelry and headed for the house leaving his wallet behind—fallen from his pocket when the pants were thrown over the stable gate.

"I'll be back, Melissa," he said taking the shovel with him.

Her mind lost the romance and doubt returned.

Why did he retie her? Didn't he trust her? What was he going to do now that he was alone? Would he leave her tied up and leave? Vanish? Would he complete the mission on his own? Would he now go out and kill Americans? The questions kept coming, and she had no answers. He wasn't a rapist or a cold-blooded killer, but wasn't he a German soldier with a duty to perform?

And wasn't it her duty as an American to stop him?

She wanted to prevent him from continuing his mission. It must entail killing Americans. But she couldn't kill him. He saved her. Befriended her. She owed him life. And didn't she like him? Kretschmer, Lassen and Lehmann deserved to die. If she had been able to surprise Carl, would she have killed him?

Melissa wasn't sure.

Reasoning gave no further answers. She was the prisoner again and the question, the only question she needed to answer now was what was he going to do with her? She knew about his covert mission. Her future was in his hands.

Carl returned in less than a half-hour with the shovel and sat on a hay bale near Melissa holding a Luger. He had buried their wallets, jewelry, clothes and the two suitcases of dynamite and explosive equipment and placed the weapons in the living room. He never missed his wallet; never realized he had it with him that night.

"Why are you holding that gun on me, Carl?"

"Instinct, I suppose. I'm sorry."

He tucked it behind his belt.

"Well, here we are," she said in jest.

"That we are. That we are."

"Carl, if I promise I won't tell anyone what happened here, would you let me go?"

"No."

"Then what?"

"I don't know what to do yet, Melissa. I think the world of you, but I know I can't release you. If I'm caught I'll be hung. Can you understand that?"

"I'll testify for you. Tell them how you saved me."

"You don't understand. People, your people, besides your father have already been killed and . . ."

"Where is he, Carl? What did they do with him?"

"I don't know. They didn't tell me. I'll try to find him tomorrow if I'm still here. Your authorities will blame me for their deaths. And then they'll hang me as a spy."

"You can trust me, Carl. I will protect you. I owe you that much. I will protect you with my life if necessary. Your courage to save me at the risk of your life will make them believe that you didn't kill anyone."

"Logic doesn't exist in war, Melissa, though what you say is logical. I'm a spy and our countries are at war. That's the only logic. If I'm caught, I will be made an example—with appropriate publicity—to stimulate the masses, to continue to breed hate so that our peoples can go on with killing one another. There's only insanity in war bred by those who promote it." His anger faded. "If the world can only be what we want it to be. But our countries are at war and we can't change that. Victory is the only criterion with the authorities regardless of loss of life. No. If I'm caught, I'm dead—in spite of what you say or your efforts. I'm sorry, Melissa, but my instinct is to survive."

"Regardless?"

"No, without hurting you. I don't want to hurt you. You've had your quota of pain from his war." He smiled. "We have a date after the war, if we ever meet again, remember? I wish I was as strong and as brave as you think I am. I'm a bit insecure right now. Afraid, I guess and confused."

"Carl?" He stood between life and death. She had to overcome that.

"Yes?"

"I think I can speak frankly with you after what we've been through. We spoke about this before and now that we're alone, and after what's happened—I wish you would make love to me—to remember you by. To cleanse the ugly with someone I've grown to admire. Even if you don't trust my being untied then leave me tied."

"I think you mean that."

"I do."

Then he remembered the survival thoughts in the U-boat. Of course she was frightened. She again needed to overtake the threat of death. Once again he assumed understanding her predicament. He would have loved to make love to her having grown fond of her, but the circumstances were vile.

"Let me ask you something, Melissa. You just killed three men—an incredible feat. Incredible. How do you feel about that?"

"I did what I had to do to survive."

"Right. So please understand I must do the same. I have to come to grips with my problem."

"Are you going to make love to me?" she asked.

He stood, cupped her face with his hands and kissed her passionately, releasing his emotions. Their tongues met and rubbed. He felt her body prepare for submission.

He stepped away, leaving her perplexed.

"Don't leave, Carl. Don't stop."

"I'm not leaving, but I'm stopping."

"Why? Don't you like kissing me?"

"Yes, I loved kissing you. It's all crazy. Maybe I love you. I don't know what being in love is. If it's caring about you, thinking about you, wanting to be near you then I guess I love you. That's why I won't make love to you. It's not the proper condition for something beautiful to happen in this place of death. Sounds stupid doesn't it?"

"No, no. It's very beautiful."

"So here we are. Two young people held prisoner by the demented wisdom of adults. I'm going to untie the rope. Then I want you to walk ahead and go to the kitchen. Do I have your word you'd do that without a problem?"

"You have my word."

After untying the knots he kept the long rope. The short strands were left behind. On the way out, he turned the lights off and said, "Good night, Landwolf Three-three-seven. You should have been soldiers."

Carl followed her to the kitchen via the back door. They entered. Carl pointed to the far chair on the other side of the table. "Sit there."

Melissa did, and he tied her hands behind her back around the chair. Then he wet a dishtowel and wiped blood remnants blood from her face and hair, tenderly holding her face.

"What now, Carl?"

"Are you hungry?"

"No."

"I have work to do. I have to pack."

The living room was a mess. He took all the weapons, placed them in the bottom of one suitcase, covered the top with his clothes, and clicked the lock. It locked secure. He placed the radio next to the suitcase. He'll need the radio to contact a U-boat.

He would decide later what to do with the empty suitcase and the carton with the forty thousand dollars. He brought the empty black leather suitcase to the kitchen.

"This is a nondescript suitcase. Where do you think I should put it?"

Melissa shrugged. What a dumb question to ask. He must be confused.

"In the basement."

"Good idea." He did.

On the way back to the kitchen, he tried to answer the questions: What do I do now and where do I go? Do I try to complete part of the mission, or hide until I contact the U-boat and go back to Germany? The explosives are already buried—the hell with them. It's over, no longer a mission. Should I stay in America and wait out the war? I have enough money. Shall I go to New York? I should probably try to contact the U-boat off Fire Island next month. If I go to New York, shall I take the train from East Hampton that is shorter to reach or take the long road to Riverhead as planned? But now plans are changed. Think!

He entered the kitchen and sat next to Melissa.

"You are a dilemma to me. Tomorrow is a dilemma to me. I can't think being with you. I'm going for a walk and by the time I get back, I will have made my decisions. And whatever my decision is, it will be firm. But before I go—" He leaned over and kissed her mouth. "I've come to one decision already. And that is that I love you. But that won't affect my decision."

Melissa wanted to hear how he felt. But what did it mean? She was more confused. He straightened and opened the door.

"Carl, wait!"

He paused.

"Does that mean if you decide to kill me, your decision is final? Even though you say you love me?"

He didn't answer, left, and closed the door.

The sound of the door closing reverberated—as a tympani drum at the end of a frightening symphony.

Melissa began wrestling with the rope.

Carl Dieterman walked westward on the soft earth without changing stride, unconcerned for the planting mounds. He wasn't optimistic about a harvest this year. His head was low, hands in pockets, the posture of a man with a heavy burden. He watched as his shoes kicked up the dirt and followed the puffs of dirt clouds. As he approached the woods, he saw Warrior his white body tainted a light blue by the moon. He approached the horse and patted him.

"You can't talk. But I can't free you either. You may wander off and a neighbor may recognize you and bring you back. Then all you'll be doing is adding to the problem. What do we do with Melissa? What do we do—with Melissa? It's obvious! I'm going to tie her up real good and then release you. Maybe you'll bring help. Maybe a friend or neighbor will call and release her. I'll lie to Melissa about where I'm going and then go the other way. To make sure she gets free, I'll call the authorities in East Hampton in two days and tell them where she is. Maybe someday, when the war is over, I can meet her again. Or maybe even write. Goodnight, horse. I've still got things to think out."

Carl walked back casually same posture following the same path he took to minimize raising dust. He knew it now. He loved Melissa, and was impossible for him to kill her.

If he didn't love her, he still couldn't kill her. It wasn't in him to do that. He never killed before. Was that a weakness as a soldier? He considered it a weakness, but found strength in his decision.

As he neared the house, he checked the area where he buried the other items. The burial place was obvious because of the mound of earth. He felt it wasn't necessary to dig deeper. No reason why anyone would suspect the mound was a burial place. It looked like a normal mound of dirt, a low mound at that. He should have spread the dirt, sprayed it into the field. He shrugged off the idea as being late.

Carl continued, proud of his decision regarding Melissa and convinced it was the proper one, the one to make. He reached the back steps and opened the door.

Melissa was gone.

TWENTY-EIGHT

THE INSTINCTS OF a soldier returned along with panic.

With alarms ringing everywhere in his body, he bolted from the doorway into the fields searching for a running figure in the bright moonlight. He checked between the house and barn, in the barn, the potato storage barn, the east field, the south field, the west field and the north field. Then he ran completely around the house. The panic increased.

Melissa couldn't have reached the woods. They were distant. She had to be nearby. The basement! She had to be hiding in the basement.

He was fifty yards into the north field when he came to that conclusion. Then he froze from terror. The guns! They were in the living room. She must be opening that suitcase!

He ran to the house, time running out on his life. Now he was the one afraid.

He prayed she couldn't open that suitcase. He cursed himself for being stupid, for being weak. He should have remained the soldier instead of a love-struck, stupid teenager.

Maybe there was time enough to stop her. He flung the door open running at top speed, bolted through the kitchen past the partially open hall closet, pushed the living room door open and dashed in.

Carl didn't see her.

He breathed a sigh. The suitcase was on the bed next to the radio as he had left it. Good. She had no weapons. The basement. She had to be hiding in the basement.

How stupid to allow herself to be trapped down there.

"Hold it, Carl,"

Her words traveled up his spine.

He turned quickly. She was standing against the wall by the hinges. The door had hidden her when it opened.

Melissa pointed the shotgun at him finger firmly on the trigger. The two black holes stared menacing and his breath remained in his lungs.

The little girl was now the tower of strength, the keeper of life and death.

The tide of war had changed.

Carl's arms rose away from his body to indicate surrender. The enemy looked terrifying without compassion. And her voice was cold and authoritative.

"It's over, Carl. It doesn't matter anymore what decisions you arrived at. I've arrived at my own. One must do what one has to do—to survive. Isn't that right? You're the one who said it. And like you also said, Carl, it's the end of Landwolf Three-three-seven—completely. Now move. Walk in front of me and go outside."

PART II

TWENTY-NINE

MITCHELL PAPPAS CURSED and gave the world the finger—another Monday morning. With exuberance, he attacked the keyboard and his literary characters. The butler was really doing it.

He had worked long and hard the past week jumping the hurdles of intrigue in Part Two of his novel. Part Three, the final portion, was solvable and easily written without additional research or added intrigue. The butler did it and the world would believe he did. Then he would do rewrites and the final draft.

Toward late morning, however, conflict was in his creative flow, an interruption. Another drum was beating, another story and another intrigue—a mystery: the Luger, the dagger, the abandoned truck and the German soldier, Carl Dieterman. They clung persistent as barnacles to a hull.

"Mitchell, my boy, if you don't find out what this is all about, they'll haunt you for life. So move your ass and start somewhere. Everything must begin somewhere. Check the neighbors. It doesn't mean they were here when any of this happened, but they are the closest. Maybe we'll be lucky and find an old neighbor who'd know what these artifacts mean."

He showered, shaved and dressed. His hair became long for him and decided to cut it at first opportunity when in East Hampton. All he needed was a trim. He didn't have the patience to wait in a barbershop.

He wore a blue short-sleeve pullover, jeans, sandals, and was ready for visiting. But before he could leave the house its past started to haunt. The house began to have a new ambience, a new aura, a connection to his new mystery, and he thought about its past inhabitants.

Who was Henry Shuller? Where did he come from? Was he born here? Did he have a large family? How many people lived here? What happened to them? Were they still alive? What did they look like? Was this furniture the same or did the real estate office bring in new furnishings? They didn't look new, but maybe the agency bought them used.

Mitchell went outside to the porch and gazed at the south field and the lower portions of the east and west fields now weed fields. He envisioned them when the ground was rich-brown and sprinkled with the green plants, when the earth had life and vitality, and when the great oak provided shade for the house.

He changed his mind about taking the jeep. Being a nice day he would walk. He needed the fresh air after being cooped. It wasn't that far to the adjacent farm and the walk would do him good. He headed eastward. Passing the barn, he looked at it with mystery. Now it had meaning in his life, a challenge a puzzle to solve.

"I'm going to find out your secret, you decrepit derelict. There's more to you than old age, a reason why no one had lived here for years. I give you my word. I will expose you." Then he added, "But how? I'll be back to explore you like a crime scene investigator searching for clues."

The hard earth road had lost some encounters with weeds. Though predominant road, the weeds had encroached in good strides. Yet the line of weed along the borders was nearly straight. The field didn't do as well against the invading seedlings. The pines had possessed nearly forty yards of the rich earth and seemed to be growing firm and upright, rising in ascending order from front to back. They nearly smothered the new oak seedlings that took longer to grow, each fighting for the sun's rays. Today was sunny and they seemed relaxed with the abundance of light.

The road through the woods had fared better, the shade helped keep weeds to a minimum. The Shuller woods had thickened. The scent of decomposing leaves and pine needles was cathartic; a refreshing scent that made one glad to be outdoors beneath the rustling leaves in a soothing breeze.

He came to the outer Shuller field, a contrast to the first weed field. This field was a lush green pasture with over one hundred cows milling and grazing on the north end. Now the scent of grass and clover replaced the forest—cowbells added a melodic flavor. The cows were standing. Rain wasn't expected.

The trees had remained contained in this maintained field with no encroaching forest. The neighbor's woods passed and Mitchell stood at the edge of the forest and viewed the adjacent farm.

The land was no longer a potato farm but a dairy farm as well with its collection of silos and buildings beyond the two-story house. The house was painted white, the dairy buildings red.

The road cut through grazing land with more cows and other dairy animals. Now he knew where the roosters, cows and sheep came from. He wondered who lived here now, and what happened to the original tenants of the war days. Maybe they still owned the place. He hoped they did.

The oak trees stood tall at each corner of the house, as if human activity beneath them kept them young and full of foliage. The two near the playground had tire swings, and the playground on the eastern side was well equipped: metal swings, a sliding-pond, monkey bars and obstacle courses of sorts, but no children. Once he reached the house, he saw four persons in the distance talking near the white post-and-railing fence.

A new Dodge pickup truck and a station wagon parked in the driveway. A two-car garage had been added to the original house. He decided to head for the foursome and forget the doorbell. As he moved in that direction two turned and waved to him. He waved back. A man and a woman in jeans opened the corral gate and came towards him to greet part way.

The wind rushed and a foul odor came and passed. Mitchell had smelled that before; chicken waste from beneath the chicken barn and coops.

The couple looked friendly, though curious, approaching the stranger. To make the stranger feel welcome the man hollered "Hi," from a distance of about one hundred yards. Mitchell waved back. The distance diminished and they met and shook hands.

"Good day to you. I'm Jack Griffin and this is my wife, Emily. What can we do for you?"

Jack Griffin's face had been creased by the outdoors; yet sparkled with youth after all these years. With his brown hair now tinged with gray and some remnants of freckles on the round face, the Griffin look was reminiscent of Siobhan and Sean Griffin. Emily's complexion was a contrast; blue eyes, blond hair, and a sculptured face with natural makeup, attractive in jeans—beautiful, thought Mitchell. Her smile was warm and cordial.

"Hello. I'm Mitchell Pappas. I rent the old Shuller place next door and thought I'd come over and say hello. Did I catch you at a bad time?"

"Well, we're pleased you did come. Anytime is a good time to see a neighbor. How are you doing over there?"

"It's quiet. Too quiet sometimes."

"We understand you're a writer, Mr. Pappas," said Emily. "I guess quiet and privacy suit you. I told my four children you needed privacy, to stay on our property. Mr. Borden, the real estate agent, called to alert us. The kids are in school today. That's why it's quiet. Believe me, we appreciate quiet, also." She smiled.

"Listen, let's not stand here," Jack Griffin said. "Let's go in for a cup of coffee. We were about to break anyway. Why don't you stay for lunch?"

"Please do, Mr. Pappas," encouraged Emily.

"Thank you, okay. But Mitchell is what you'll have to call me."

"Great!" Jack exclaimed slapping Mitchell's back as greeting an old friend. "It's nice to have a neighbor to the west again. It's been a long time."

They walked toward the house that looked bright and clean as the sun gleamed off the white paint.

"Mitchell," said Emily, "how long are you renting for?"

"I took it for six months. I don't think I'll stay that long though. I'll probably finish my project before then, about two weeks earlier. But I sure love it there."

"It's a great piece of land," Jack added. "Maybe someday, someone will give it life again."

"You sure have a nice place here," said Mitchell.

"Hey, why don't I give you a tour? Ever been on a dairy farm before?" Jack was enthused with the idea.

"No, I haven't, only to some place that raised chickens."

"Now wait a minute you two," complained Emily. "Don't go running off on me. Do it after lunch."

"All right, honey. After lunch it is."

Mitchell wanted to continue his investigation. "How long have you folks been here?" he asked.

"Mitchell, this place has been in my family for years. It used to be all potato farming until about a dozen years ago. It still is, you might say. The two eastern fields are potatoes and the western portion is where the animals are. Dairy farming is more profitable. But we love potatoes and didn't want to give them up. It's a great crop and still one of Long Island's main crops."

"Jack's parents," said Emily, "had a large family—seven children—but none wanted to become farmers. Now they're scattered around the country. Jack and I decided this was for us, so we converted some land to dairy."

"I'm glad we did, too," continued Jack. "My parents lived with us until my father died six years ago. We kept the potato farming interest because of him. My mother died four years ago. Anyway, I was born on this place in nineteen thirty-three. A long time ago, but I love the place. This has always been home."

Mitchell was pleased with the number of years Jack spent in the area. He might know something about the weapons and Henry Shuller.

"It's a nice place to grown up on," Mitchell said looking around admiring.

Nice, warm people thought Mitchell. People like this should have large families and rule the earth.

They reached the house and entered by the front door. The living room was neat and comfortable—an extension of the owners' personalities. A large portrait of a large family hung on the wall behind the brown plaid couch: a father, mother and seven children. Mitchell stopped to look.

"Guess which one is me?" said Jack. His slightly rounded ears were the tip-off.

Mitchell looked at Jack again then pointed him out.

"Good for you. I was eight then in nineteen forty-one. These are my parents, Siobhan and Sean Griffin. And in order; Patricia, the oldest, Mary Beth, Robbie, Sean, Jr., me, Maureen and Kelly."

"You look like you mother. Who's that?"

Another picture was tucked in the lower right-hand corner of the family picture covered by cellophane and slightly yellowed by age; a black and white snapshot of three females with arms around each other in the snow.

"Well, that's mother in the middle, Patricia on the left and a girl who once lived in your place, Melissa Shuller. The photo was taken in early nineteen forty-two. She was Patricia's best friend. The reason I kept that picture—mother always had it there when she was alive to remember Melissa—and I still do, is because we always considered her a family member. It's appropriate to keep her here with the family. I used to be crazy about her."

A nostalgic glow was on Jack's face as he remembered Melissa and how he used to jump on her whenever he saw her.

Mitchell studied the blond-haired girl with the pretty smile. Emily went ahead to the kitchen.

"These old pictures are priceless. I love old family pictures. They have memories and character."

"I agree, Mitchell. I have an entire album of the family in the early years."

Mitchell grinned.

"I won't ask to see it."

"I was hoping you wouldn't!" Jack laughed.

He led Mitchell to the kitchen.

The kitchen was still decorated in yellow; the color Siobhan had loved. Emily hastened to gather the sandwich ingredients, a salad, and coffee then brought the items to the table.

"Emily, please sit," Mitchell offered. "Don't extend yourself for me. I'm not that hungry."

"It's only sandwiches. I'll make the salad and join you."

"Jack, I'd like to ask you a few more questions, and not about chicken odors. Can you tell me anything about the place I'm staying at? Why is it vacant? Who else lived there besides Henry Shuller and Melissa?"

"Mr. Shuller and Melissa were the only ones to live there. I believe Mrs. Shuller died sometime in the thirties. I'm not sure I know the whole story, but I'll tell you what I know. I was nine years old then and unaware what was going on. Let's see, where to start." He squinted his eyes searching his memory. "Henry Shuller was killed in an automobile accident on the property. His truck went off the road and into the gully. Head injuries. Melissa found his body in the wreck. After the funeral, Melissa moved away. I don't know where she went. College I think. But she never came back, ever. That's why that picture of Melissa in the living room was so dear to my mother, and to us. She became a family mystery."

"She disappeared?"

"Yes."

"When was all that?"

"Sometime in nineteen forty-two, I believe. June."

"And no one's lived on the property since?"

"That's right."

The waters of intrigue were overflowing the dam in Mitchell's mind. "And Melissa just vanished?" he inquired again. "Is there more you can tell me?"

"She wrote a letter to my sister, Patricia, a few days after she left, the last time anyone heard from her. I mean, except for the Christmas card she sent to my mother every year. But there's never a return address. The card is always signed 'Love you always, Melissa.' The cards still come addressed to Siobhan Griffin. I guess Melissa doesn't know that my mother died."

"How old was Melissa in nineteen forty-two?"

"Then?—About seventeen or eighteen. Same age as Patricia."

"Did Mr. Shuller collect artifacts of World War Two?"

"That's a strange question."

"I found an old German dagger in the barn. I thought maybe it was his."

"I don't know. Nineteen forty-two was still early in the war. Maybe some hiker dropped it or something after the place was abandoned. We have hikers out here. Somebody may have taken refuge in the barn in a storm. Who knows?"

"Have you ever heard of someone called Carl Dieterman?"

"Never heard the name."

"He never stayed at the Shuller place?"

"Can't say. He may have visited. All I know is that no one has lived on the property before you."

"I understand the taxes are paid and the house is maintained. I have to say it's in good shape. Do you know who's paying for it?"

"Maybe Melissa is doing that, or maybe she sold it and the new owner is maintaining it for resale value. Property has skyrocketed around here, you know. I suspect Melissa sold it a long time ago, otherwise why wouldn't she have come back to see my mother and Patricia? My mother, rest her soul, could never understand why Melissa never came back. She worried sick about her until the first Christmas card came. Melissa used to spend time with us, almost always it seemed. My mother was her substitute mother. Mom loved her as her own. Melissa broke her heart by staying away. The real estate people should know the new owners."

"He's secretive. I think it has something to do with client relationships and such stuff. Were German soldiers ever on the Shuller property?"

"You mean World War Two Germans?" he looked incredulous.

"Yes."

The positive response surprised Emily and Jack.

"No, not around here. What would Germans have been doing here anyway? Oh, I get it. The dagger. You're still curious about the dagger. No wonder you're a writer. Some imagination."

Mitchell laughed. "Imagination makes life interesting. But you see, now we have a mystery, don't we? No one knows where Melissa Shuller went, and we don't know where the dagger came from."

"Mitchell, you do have a way arousing curiosity," said Emily placing the salad on the table.

"What were the Shullers like?" inquired Mitchell.

"I don't remember," Jack said taking salad. "Like I said, I was only nine then. My sister Patricia would know—if you need to know for whatever your reasons. Patricia would remember all about Melissa. And she knew Henry Shuller. If you want, I can give you her number and address. She continues to live on Long Island."

"Terrific."

"Patricia is now Patricia McGuire. She's a principal at the Chestnut Hill School in Dix Hills— the Half Hollow Hills area."

"Where's Dix Hills?"

"It's in western Suffolk County, in the southern part of Huntington Township. The school is right off Exit Fifty on the Long Island Expressway. Here, give me the pencil. I'll write her phone number at work and her home address and number in Huntington."

Hassling the real estate agent for information regarding the present owner of Shuller's Land was intriguing, but valueless if there wasn't a story here. Also, he could check the tax records at the Town Hall, but that could take time.

First, he needed the solution to the riddle of the German weapons and Carl Dieterman. Was Dieterman on Shuller's Land when Melissa was there? Or was it afterward when abandoned?

What was a German soldier doing in America during World War Two? Was Carl Dieterman here during the war, or did he come afterward as a summer tourist? But then, why would he come to an abandoned farm and lose his weapon in a crashed truck where Henry Shuller died, and drop his dagger and wallet in the barn?

The mystery was more intriguing when he reckoned Dieterman was on Shuller's Land during World War II—and when Melissa was there. And served as fuel.

He wanted a connection to exist between Dieterman and Melissa, and so he had to learn more about Melissa Shuller.

The solution had begun with Jack Griffin.

Step two was Patricia Griffin McGuire.

THIRTY

CHARGED WITH ENTHUSIASM he wanted to get home to call Patricia, but couldn't be rude to these people. He took the farm tour with Emily and Jack.

Educational as the tour was, Mitchell remained impatient to leave. He would never enjoy eggs again without remembering the conditions under which they came into the world.

Mitchell couldn't stand to see animals caged or killed. That's why he hated hunting. He didn't consider it sport but murder. Caging was an outrage.

He liked Emily and Jack Griffin. They were real people, down to earth with rich, basic qualities—the type he likes to have as friends. And Jack did provide a necessary link to his new mystery. Jack offered to drive him home.

His mind began to fill with intrigue: fact and fiction about the possibilities of a new story. If the truth turned out to be uninteresting then fiction would make it exciting. A new novel was beginning to take shape. He had his theme for next year's bestseller, and another million or more dollars— another masterpiece that the world expected and demanded from him.

At the house he reconnected the phone and dialed the school's number. How should he approach Patricia? How would it sound to have someone call suddenly and mention a revered name from the past? How would she respond? Would she see him, talk to him, care or have an interest in Melissa after she abandoned her family? He was certain she would be curious.

The phone rang twice and was answered by a happy, singsong female voice.

"Chestnut Hill School. Mrs. Feldman."

"Mrs. McGuire, please."

"Who is calling?"

"This is Mitchell Pappas."

"May I ask your business? Are you a parent?"

"No, and it's not exactly personal. I'm an author and I need to talk to her about an old acquaintance."

"Please, hold. Thank you."

Mitchell held patiently. Mrs. Feldman returned.

"Mrs. McGuire is still in conference, Mr. Pappas. Can she call you back?"

"No. It is important. I'll hold."

She may reject talking to a stranger, especially an author. He had success with the 'hold' strategy forcing the other party to make another statement.

"It's an important meeting and should run for a while."

"Can you please tell her it's about Melissa Shuller?" He sensed reluctance. "Please, it is important. Can you pass a note to her?"

"I'll interrupt her again."

Mitchell drummed his fingers on the lamp table determined that if Patricia McGuire didn't come to the phone, he would drop in on her tomorrow without an appointment. She had no right to detain him from writing his story. He liked his stubbornness, calling it assertive action. Know what you want and go get it—full speed ahead. His wife, Helene, called it Greek thick-headedness.

"Mr. Pappas?" The voice was different. He broke through and grinned at his success. "This is Mrs. McGuire."

The voice seemed shaken, doubtful and anticipatory unlike the stern authoritative tone of a principal.

"Thank you for coming to the phone, Mrs. McGuire. I appreciate your interrupting your conference. I need to meet with you regarding Melissa."

"Who are you, Mr. Pappas?"

"I'm an author who rented the Shuller place."

"The same Mitchell Pappas who wrote *Murder by Murder?*"

"Yes."

"I know your work. I'm sorry I didn't make the connection. What about Melissa?"

He could feel her voice tense, bracing against possible bad news. *Good, she was curious.*

"I'd prefer it if I can see you. I have some questions to ask."

Patricia was silent, surprised at the meaningless answer.

"Where is Melissa? Why are you writing about her? Is she all right? Has something happened to her?"

"I don't know?"

"You don't know? You don't know Melissa?"

"No, but I must talk to you about her."—A long pause. "Mrs. McGuire, please. Can't we meet?"

"I'm free after school tomorrow."

"That's fine. What time is good?"

"Three-thirty. Tell me why you're interested in Melissa."

"I'll explain tomorrow."

Success!

*   *   *

Patricia cradled the phone and sat staring, unseeing, stunned—a blatant and insensitive unraveling of her history.

When Mrs. Feldman entered the office to inform her that a Mr. Pappas needed to speak to her regarding a Melissa Shuller, Patricia had a tremor hearing the name only her family mentioned. It was like a holy name being blasphemed, and the memories became vivid once again.

Patricia wasn't in conference. Mrs. Feldman's method of protecting her from a handful of harassing and meddling parents who thought their children couldn't get properly educated unless they were on top of things themselves. She had a dozen mothers who should have found something better to do with their time.

How did Pappas become interested in Melissa? How did he find the school? Maybe Jack told him. It had to be Jack. He's the only other family member on Long Island.

And now, all she did was think of Melissa, long after school hours were over.

Mrs. Feldman popped her head in and said goodnight and Patricia knew all the teachers had left. Mrs. Feldman was usually the last staff member to leave the building.

Everything about Melissa returned and Patricia missed her much. She had lost her best friend, a sister. She and Siobhan never understood Melissa's mysterious behavior. Why didn't she come back? When Patricia entered New York University, she checked the roster of registered students. Melissa never went to NYU. Why? She had been accepted. Why didn't she ever leave a return address? Why didn't she ever call?

Did her father's death disturb her that much? Would coming back to the area remind her of her father and mother? Would staying in touch with people who knew her father cause the trauma to continue? Was it more than that?

Patricia and her family had asked these questions with each Christmas card and whenever Melissa's name came into conversation.

Patricia and Siobhan grieved for Melissa with every card, almost as if she had died each year after the card was read. The words Melissa had written always brought tears to Siobhan's eyes.

But life went on. Patricia graduated from New York University, became a teacher in the New York City school system, and two years later married John McGuire, a chemical engineer with Union Carbide. She raised four children: two boys and two girls. The eldest girl she named Siobhan, and the second, Melissa. And thus, Melissa Shuller was forever with her in name and spirit.

The McGuires moved from the city to Lloyd's Neck in Huntington, after the fourth child was born. The children all married and Patricia and John now had six grandchildren. She became a principal when

School District 5 was expanding with the population growth.

Patricia was an outstanding teacher in her day, exacting and demanding with her teachers who she felt were beginning to lack pride in their profession. But she couldn't change the system. All she asked was that her teachers measure up to her standards.

Patricia resented Mitchell Pappas's intrusion into her world. She had accepted Melissa's way of life, and respected—though she never understood—her reasons for privacy.

But Pappas had made her memories vivid. Melissa was alive and vibrant in her mind. What had she been doing all these years? What did she look like? Did she have a family? Children? Grandchildren? Wouldn't it be wonderful if both families got together? Did she have a happy life? Where did she go?

Why didn't Melissa give a return address?

THIRTY⋆ONE

MITCHELL DROVE THE Long Island Expressway to Exit 50 and waited at the red light on Bagatelle Road. Over his left shoulder, he saw the sprawling one-level structure Chestnut Hill. He made a left at the light, crossed the Expressway overpass and made the first left to the eastbound service road.

He found a space in the crowded parking area and parked. He was ten minutes early. School buses lined up, waiting for the daily evacuation. The bus drivers, all females, were holding court by a bus. He entered the silent, hallowed halls of education and signs directed him to the office. He waited at the counter that opened to the secretarial and administrative area.

Mrs. Feldman saw him—a short, stout woman in her late thirties whose hair had already turned white. Her skin was light and fair.

"Can we help you, sir?" she asked from behind her desk.

"My name is Mitchell Pappas and I have an appointment with Mrs. McGuire."

Mrs. Feldman rose. "Yes, she's expecting you."

The silence around Mitchell abruptly ended. From all corners of the school, children poured out and filled the halls.

"Come in, Mr. Pappas," Mrs. Feldman encouraged. "Before you get trampled." Twins, Luke and Sam Birnbaum—Fourth Graders—entered the area. "You two wise guys sit over there until your mother gets here," she ordered.

Mitchell opened the door and followed the smiling Mrs. Feldman to the rear office. She was pleased by her trample remark. Mrs. Feldman opened the door, and standing in the doorway announced Mr. Pappas was here. He heard a voice "Send him in," and Mitchell entered the office.

Patricia McGuire looked serious and stern. Mitchell thought she must have been a beautiful woman in her day because she remained attractive and elegant. This woman had a proud look and posture though seated.

Her red hair had prominent traces of white and gray. Mitchell felt she would look younger if she dyed it. Patricia remained seated as he approached her desk. She remained stern and defensive, preparing to handle this intruder.

Mitchell tried to be exuberant. "Thank you for seeing me, Mrs. McGuire."

"Please sit, Mr. Pappas." He did, in the desk chair facing her. Before he settled in she added, "Mr. Pappas, you are here because you mentioned a person dear to me. If you have, in any way, used her name and evoked memories in vain, I will consider your joke cruel."

Her stare lacked warmth—a terse, somber pronouncement. Mitchell kept a business attitude.

"I assure you, my being here is genuine and related to Melissa Shuller. It wasn't my intention to alarm you. Your brother Jack mentioned that you and Melissa were once best friends. He suggested I should speak to you for additional information regarding Shuller's Land and Melissa."

"Why?"

"Well . . ."

"How do you know Jack?"

"I'm renting the old Shuller place now. We're neighbors." She seemed satisfied with that, confirming her suspicions. "I'll clarify it by starting at the beginning. If you know my other work, my style is to take actual events, add intrigue and some mystery and write a novel. Why do I do that?—Because real events, sometimes, are stranger than pure fiction. In any event, I am currently writing a novel and I rented Shuller's Land last month for six months because of its remoteness and privacy. The other day, as I was walking around the property, I came across a German Luger, a German dagger and the identification card of a German soldier."

He thought that would intrigue Patricia. It didn't.

"What does that have to do with Melissa?" she asked, expressionless, like a prosecuting attorney.

"Probably nothing."

"Nothing?"

"It depends on what you say."

"To what?"

"Did any Germans visit Shuller's Land when Melissa was there?"

She looked puzzled by the question.

"None. I'm sure none did—maybe after June, nineteen forty-two. The land was vacant then. Anyone could have come."

Mitchell took out Carl Dieterman's picture and showed it to her.

"Have you ever seen this man?"

Patricia studied the picture.

"No," She returned the card. "You found this on Shuller's Land?"

"In the barn."

"Interesting."

"Being a person who sees intrigue in everything, the German's card and the objects stimulated my imagination."

Patricia looked disappointed her hopes waned.

"You don't know anything about Melissa, and she's secondary to your need to know about Germans?"

"I want to know if there's a connection."

"No connection, Mr. Pappas, none at all. I know because I knew the Shullers better than anyone else. It is also indignant and presumptuous to barge into people's history for your own profit. You can write anything you want to write, but erase mentioning my family and the Shullers from your mind."

Mitchell didn't answer. He didn't know how. He kept quiet, not to say the wrong thing. She continued irritable, upset.

"I'm familiar with your work and almost all your material is based upon public knowledge, news and newspaper stories. You are now dealing in private matters and I don't approve. And Melissa is a private matter. Why she chose to remain distant all these years is her business, not yours. And when you come right down to it, not mine either. We have no right to expose her life in any way. You, especially have no right. You want to know if there's a connection to Melissa? That's ridiculous. I'm a bit disappointed in your visit, Mr. Pappas. I was hoping you'd shed some light for my benefit to at long last find Melissa. Instead, you're here on business. Your selfish business."

Patricia rose and stared pensively out the window toward the expressway and Bagatelle Road, across an expanse of field where children played soccer on weekends. To the right the school buses were loading. The drone of children's voices reached them.

"I am disappointed, Mr. Pappas."

"There may be a connection. The Luger was found in the truck, in the gully."

She turned, inquisitive. He had reached her.

"In the truck?"

"It was wedged between the passenger seat and door. Did Henry Shuller collect guns or something? Did he have it for protection? What about the dagger? The ID card?"

Patricia stared in thought.

"I see what you mean, Mr. Pappas. From your view, it could be intriguing. Like I said, I knew the Shullers. Mr. Shuller never owned a Luger. I don't know how it got in the truck. Maybe some hiker forgot it there after taking refuge in the cab. Conjecture. The only weapon the Shullers had was a shotgun. Everyone had them in those days. There isn't any information I know about the Shullers that can help you regarding the German weapons."

"Do you mind if I probe your past a little? I know it's a sensitive subject. Your objections to my work are well taken, but since you say that you know about the Shullers, please let me ask. When was the last time you saw Melissa? That is, before the funeral."

"I don't see where this is going to lead us."

"Please. With your help, regardless my needs, I may be able to locate Melissa. I'm a small flickering light at the end of the long tunnel. I may help."

Patricia sat again. He was a gamble to take with nothing to lose.

"I saw her on the final day of school, Thursday then on Saturday. She called us Saturday afternoon to tell us about her father's accident in the gully. We saw her again on Sunday. And the funeral was on Monday."

"You didn't see her on Friday?"

"No."

"Isn't it possible that during the time in between . . ."

"Unrealistic. If Germans were there during those two days, I'm sure some harm would have befallen Melissa. Henry Shuller was killed in the truck accident. He wasn't murdered. And that's a fact. I can't stop you if you want to believe something else happened. If you dare insinuate or blemish the good name of Shuller or Griffin you will be making a bad mistake."

Her eyes implied and confirmed a threat of horrendous proportions.

"It sounds as if fiction is taking precedence here."

"I can't stop you from writing fiction, Mr. Pappas. From the sound of it, you can make an interesting novel. Change the names and the locale and I'm sure with your talent you can make it believable. But that's contrary to your style, isn't it?"

"I need some reality to stimulate the fiction. I would be cheating my readers if I deviate from what they've come to expect."

"It sounds like you have principles."

"I do."

Patricia liked that because, she, too, was principled. She became a bit more compassionate for his mission.

"Forgive me, Mr. Pappas. Please understand my desire to protect an old friend and my past. I have a hunch all this might come to some good. I'll tell you what I know providing you keep me informed on any progress. Not just hunches, but real progress involving Melissa."

"I will keep you informed. You have my word. It will be my great pleasure to tell you that I found her."

Mitchell was pleased. He had broken through her defense.

"Melissa and I were as sisters. We spent the last day of school together, as I said, and then two days later she called. She was hysterical. I had answered the phone and she said that she found her father dead. He had an accident with the truck. I'm surprised to hear you say the truck is still there. My parents and I drove over to her house and found her in tears sitting on the porch steps.

"I hugged her and we cried to each other until she was able to compose herself. She led us to the truck in the gully. Her father was slumped over the wheel. I believe he died of head wounds. My father and mother extracted him from the truck and we took his body to the house. I remember the decaying odor. We had to put him in a room where we opened the windows and closed the door. Then we called the authorities. Melissa said she went looking for him after he failed to return after telling her that he was going to East Hampton. When he didn't come home the next morning, she assumed he had stayed at a friend's house.

"After the funeral, my mother and I tried to persuade her to come and live with us, but she said that she needed to be alone for a few days; to mourn privately. She said she was going to New York City. The next day, we drove her to the train station and she left. And that was the last we saw of Melissa. A week later, I received a letter from her in a thick envelope containing two thousand dollars."

Patricia's face was framed with nostalgia; she was no longer the principal, but a young girl. Mitchell didn't interrupt her nuance because her eyes were misty. She blew her nose softly in a tissue.

"I still remember the letter. I've reread it a thousand times since looking for a clue between the lines. It said: 'In the event we never meet again, I want you to know I love you, and always will. It is my wish that you become the teacher you must be. Now you have no excuse not to go to college. I'll never forget you. I love you, dearest friend, my sister.'" The eyes were mistier.

"From then on, the only way we knew she was alive was by the Christmas card she sent to my mother each year. Mother and I never understood why she left and why she never came back. And that, Mr. Pappas, is the mystery of Shuller's Land. Not the Germans."

"I know you'll never believe it, but maybe there's a connection with the Germans."

"That's pure fiction. But it's remotely possible a German may have accidentally come upon Shuller's Land after Melissa left."

Mitchell sat up. "Are you admitting to the existence of Germans on Long Island during World War Two?"

"Yes."

Mitchell's curiosity ignited. "When?"

"Nineteen-forty-two."

"What?" Mitchell stood and paced, his mind floating in a bucket of possibilities. He abandoned the formalities visiting with a school principal.

"Don't get excited, Mr. Pappas. The FBI caught those Germans within two weeks. Maybe a hunter or hiker found some of their weapons and lost them or left them on Shuller's Land when they trespassed."

"You mean Germans were actually caught landing on Long Island?" He was astounded.

"It's known to many who live on Long Island. There have been various articles about it over the years in local papers. I think someone once wrote a book or an article about the entire mess. The *New York Times Magazine* writes about it on occasion, as does *Newsday*."

"Can you tell me about it?"

"Sometime in nineteen forty-two, in mid-June six German sailors were seen landing near Amagansett. Four moved inland and two returned to a waiting U-boat. They caught the first train that morning to New York City from Amagansett station. So you see, they weren't in the area long. And Shuller's Land is far from Amagansett for them to have traveled there. Someone must have found some of their weapons, probably in the dunes or on their route to the station. I'm sorry I misled you before about Germans going there. That's not what I meant to say. Anyway, the FBI caught those four. I don't remember the entire story, but there were also four more Germans who landed in Florida near Jacksonville at about the same time. Ponte Vedra Beach, I believe. They were also caught—all within two weeks. One in each group turned informer for the FBI. That's how the rest were caught. No damage was done. I believe six were eventually executed as spies by our government. They spared the informers. I always thought it common knowledge since they were the only Germans to land in America during the war. Also, an unconfirmed sighting up in Maine."

"Interesting. I'm surprised our government would kill them."

"We were at war then," she said to justify the government's action. "War justifies many things. President Roosevelt approved the execution."

"But there's variance here. Carl Dieterman was a soldier. Not a sailor."

Patricia wasn't intrigued. "They could have been soldiers dressed as sailors. Who knows?"

Mitchell entered his world of intrigue again. "Mrs. McGuire, what do you think of the possibility of another group of Germans landing that weren't caught or seen at all?"

"Fascinating, but unlikely."

"Why not?"

"It would have been made public after the war or should have been. It would have been incorporated with the latter stories of those captured. And someone would have interviewed them at home in Germany. But no evidence exists others were here. Besides, German spies or soldiers or sailors did no damage to American industry or transportation, or whatever other name they are given—the mission of the groups captured. If any other group came here and didn't get caught, wouldn't they have done some damage? No damage was reported because there was no damage, and no Germans other than those caught and punished."

"Sounds logical."

"Of course. I can't imagine them just vanishing right?"

"I can't find fault with that, Mrs. McGuire."

"The only other recorded incident that I know of Germans being near Long Island happened on the last day of the war in nineteen forty-five. A German U-boat was attacked and sunk by our Navy near Block Island just east of Montauk. As I remember, she went down with forty-four men on board."

"Any survivors?"

"None."

"That eliminates that possibility."

Patricia folded her arms and looked at Mitchell whose mind still probed the past and future.

"Mr. Pappas, now that your German mystery is over, what about Melissa? Can we leave her alone now?"

Mitchell returned to the present and shrugged.

"You've aroused my curiosity about her. Her actions are curious. I know you're sensitive about her. What was she like?"

"She was sweet, soft, not the type to be mysterious and inconsiderate about those who loved her. I wish I knew what came over her. I guess her father's death. No, my family and I never resented her for acting mysterious. We accepted whatever her reasons. She was family. We had family forgiveness. And her Christmas cards held her close to us, as if she wanted to reach out to us but couldn't."

"I think I'd like to find out her reasons, also. Maybe something dramatic happened to change her."

"Now the fiction in you is talking. Still think there's a story here, Mr. Pappas?"

"I don't know. Nothing seems to make sense."

"Will you still try to find Melissa?"

He paused. "I'm unsure. I'm sure she had good reason to do what she did. She did stay in touch. If she had vanished mysteriously or died violently—forgive me—then maybe a story might have emerged. The German connection would have made it fascinating somehow."

"I was hoping you'd tell me good news about her."

"I'm sorry if I evoked sad memories."

The air between them had grown friendlier, drawn together by a common subject. Patricia didn't seem as hostile or offensive.

"The sadness is that I've never seen her again. But I know writers, and your curiosity will haunt you. If for some reason someone or something urges you to find Melissa will you tell her to call me, and give her my home address and telephone number? It would be wonderful to see her again—for many reasons."

"I think Melissa might have to wait. I still have a book to finish. Maybe after that I could create something out of it all—a touch of truth, spiced with fiction. The fiction will be Melissa confronting the Germans. Maybe my readers won't mind."

"Like I said, Melissa was a gentle person. You'd have to create a Joan of Arc." She smiled, almost approving the entire project now. "As I mentioned, Melissa was going to go to NYU. I went there hoping to find her. But she never registered. That could add to Melissa's mystery. Why didn't she go to college? And where did she get the two thousand dollars? We checked later at the bank because my father was Henry Shuller's executor. No money was withdrawn. We deposited the insurance money. As far as I know, the money may still be in the bank. It's all in her name."

"Which bank?"

"I don't remember the name. The bank was on Main Street in East Hampton."

Mitchell's eyebrows rose with curiosity, and with a realization.

"The mystery goes deeper, doesn't it? Are you inspiring me now to find Melissa?"

Patricia laughed lightly. "I'm hoping you'll find a way, of course. I'd love to see her at least one more time before my time on this good planet ends."

"Regarding the Christmas cards, do you know where they were postmarked?"

"The first year's was from New York City. After that, they came from Boston. One came from Maine, I believe, but primarily Boston. I'm not sure anymore. The cards were how we tracked her movements. We tried to trace her, but after a while we stopped. We realized if she wanted to be found, so to speak, she would have informed us or she could have returned to visit. Melissa, for some reason, didn't want us to know where she lived. It had to be a powerful reason. I wish I knew why."

"That is strange, isn't it? Maybe I'll probe a bit, have somebody research and investigate for me and see what develops. I promise to keep you posted when I have something concrete. It will give me enormous pleasure to see you two reunited, to be the fly on the wall when that happens."

"I look forward to the day."

The subject had finished, and Mitchell rose with a sigh.

"I thank you, Mrs. McGuire. I appreciate your time and cooperation."

Patricia rose and extended her hand with a smile. He took it. "I wish you success."

"Mrs. McGuire, if by chance I do see Melissa, is there anything else you would want me to say, besides to get in touch with you?"

Patricia nodded—confident Mitchell Pappas would find her—a man of determination and principle.

"Yes, Yes. Tell her I've missed her and thought of her often. For a lifetime."

Patricia's eyelids were blinking back tears.

THIRTY-TWO

MITCHELL SAT IN his car in the school parking area and watched and listened to the after-school pandemonium of children and grumpy bus engines. School ended some time ago. Why were they making all that noise? There must have been an after-school field activity as three buses waited. The children piled in and soon, silence.

He liked Patricia Griffin McGuire. Because of her, he liked Melissa Shuller. She had to be special for Patricia to love for many years. Then he felt sorry for Melissa for missing a lifetime of friendship with Patricia.

His intrigue was steaming at full throttle. The mystery of Melissa Shuller was as stimulating as the enigma of Carl Dieterman. A story developed and he sat there mesmerized, visualizing its phases.

If Mitchell learned nothing more about Dieterman and his weapons, and Melissa, fiction would place Carl Dieterman on the Shuller farm and somehow explain Melissa's erratic absence—a good foundation for a story. What if Germans did land weren't caught then vanished? Or never returned to Germany? Interesting possibilities. He liked the visual story outline, but it was fantasy. He didn't deal in fantasy, not entirely. He had to pursue reality that thus far was a coffer filled with mystery and intrigue.

Patricia came out the entrance and walked to her left, toward the other parking area. She walked as carrying a heavy burden. It seemed the sun was shining everywhere except on Patricia. His heart reached out to her, and felt sorry he stirred the settled anguish.

Conscious of his sentimentality, he grinned at himself forgetting his sensitive side. He once wrote love poems and love stories to expand the passions and emotions he never gave to a woman—including an ex-wife. He loved Helene Pappas, his new marital combatant. He just couldn't live with her—his fault, and admitted to it. He believed she was too good for him and why he had to get away. He no longer wanted to belong to or be possessed by anyone. The hurt of his other wife cheating on him had scarred his commitment. He would rather hurt than be hurt—if anything at all.

Helene was on her way to becoming a top literary agent because he harnessed her energies into that direction. They agreed to an amicable, part-time separation nearly a year ago—a vacation from each other, they called it. He was her top client, and the commissions from his books provided her with an adequate financial foundation to grow on. She was good, aggressive and hard working. It was like finding a dud that turned into a live bomb, a passive housewife with energy screaming to be turned loose.

Helene had fallen in love with Mitchell the first day she met him at the Four Seasons restaurant in New York City. A mutual friend introduced them at lunch as they sat at a table near the fountain. Mitchell found Helene attractive and felt sorry for her as his friend described how she had been married all those years, was now divorced, and had never worked before. He had wondered if he could use her as a research assistant.

She turned out to be an efficient, relentless worker who stopped at nothing to acquire information Mitchell needed. Mitchell thought about corralling all that energy into bed, but he retained an employee-employer relationship until she maneuvered to get him there.

Helene wasn't sure how it happened fast, but eventually when her life was more secure as Mrs. Pappas, she determined he was the security she needed after a long childless marriage that went on the rocks.

Working for Mitchell was the first job she ever held. She committed herself to the work and to him as she had done when she married. She had allowed her life to be led and controlled by her first husband, living in his shadow and backwash. She had relegated herself to a supportive role to his career and swore that the next marriage would be a partnership.

With Mitchell it almost was, and still could be. Though separated, they remained legally married.

Helene had enjoyed working for Mitchell, almost ten to twelve hours a day—a natural for their time together to expand, until they finally married. After two years of togetherness and one glorious year—the first was a never-ending honeymoon—their stubborn attitudes created a deadlock. Two strong personalities couldn't travel the same road in harmony.

She loved him deeply, and he loved her as much. During long periods together compatibility became their problem. Short periods were sublime. And thus, they created a compatible agent-client relationship ringed by a solid friendship with occasional sexual expressions when the mood was right.

Mitchell pulled out of his parking space after Patricia's car left the area—no sense in sitting there thinking and speculating. He headed back on the service road and stopped by the public telephones on the corner of Bagatelle Road. The expressway rush-hour traffic was beginning. He called Helene.

"You must be getting lonely, Mitch, if you're using the phone."

"Sweetheart, I have to see you right away. I'm on Exit Fifty of the Long Island Expressway in Dix Hills. I should be there at about five or five-thirty, or shall we meet at a restaurant. Let's have dinner."

"Can you make it tomorrow? I have a theater date tonight."

"A man?"

"No, a cocker spaniel. Of course a man! There are others out there besides you, you know."

"Eat with me and tell him you'll meet him at the theater. Is he just a date or a potential provider?"

"Potential, unless you change. He's an old friend. I enjoy the theater and you're not here. Don't feel threatened."

"Well, the hell with him anyway. I'm into a new story and I need your help."

"How's your manuscript coming? Your beloved publisher called me today to ask."

"Good and on target. Tell him he'll have the manuscript a few weeks before my deadline. Now, where shall we meet?"

"Mitch!"

"Oh, honey. Tell him you have a headache. You used to be good at that."

"Never with you."

"You used to be good at that before me."

"That's better."

"Come on. This is your biggest client speaking! And the only man you'll ever love. It's engraved in the stars."

"Someday, Mitchell Pappas, I'm going to say no to you. Why do I always give in to you?"

"Because I fill your purse. Come on, I need you already!"

"All right, for dinner only. Come to the office. We'll decide from here."

"Thanks, baby. You won't regret it."

"I think I will, but hurry. I can't wait to see you."

Mitchell was happy when he saw Helene. He hadn't seen her since he left for East Hampton and realized why he married her: the face and the body. The eyes were wide, dark brown, surrounded by sparkling whiteness, a straight nose with pronounced cheeks and a full mouth that he loved kissing. The makeup was impeccable. The body was curvaceous, masculine enticing at the right places, and she probably had the prettiest legs he had ever seen on a woman who wasn't a dancer. She wore a blue business suit with a light blue blouse.

Helene was the woman he always wrote about— the sexy vixen in her twenties for whom men would die. But his imagination was slightly prejudiced in this case. Helene was now in her forties. Yet to him, she was probably more maturely enticing than a vixen in her twenties, his impression of Helene. To others, she was an attractive woman; nothing exceptional physically, but like the saying goes, "beauty is in the eye of the beholder." He did love her, so he could have seen things that weren't there and not seen things that were. If he wanted to see Helene as a vivacious beauty in her twenties—why not envision her?

She stood at her desk waiting for his hug. The rug was shaggy white, the furniture modern red. The desk was rosewood and the drapes a mixture of interwoven whites and reds. The room had a fresh scent, lightly soothed by her cologne. Plants were in every corner and pictures of the authors she represented were on the right wall over the red couch. His picture was in the middle, in the largest frame—a three-quarter, smiling profile. She kissed his mouth, long and passionately.

"That's because you're my biggest income client."

"That's because you're foolish enough to still love me."

"True, true. I've never stopped and never will. You're preposterous to live with, that's all. I expect you'll come to your senses soon."

"You look terrific."

"Thank you. Did you get lonely out in the sticks? Is that why you came in? For your hugs and a touch of reality?"

"I missed you terribly."

"You're full of your usual bull."

"How well you know me. How's your business?"

She nudged him toward the couch and they sat.

"Excellent. We picked up a few new writers. So far this year, we've published eighteen titles and a bunch of articles."

"Not bad. I knew you'd be a winner. You have the instincts to survive. You'll do well."

"Thanks to you."

"What did you decide about your date?"

"I cancelled."

Mitchell was pleased, and she noticed that. He was about to rise and she pulled him back.

"Let's talk here, give you a chance to relax. I'll fix you a drink and then we'll go to my place for dinner. You do the cooking and no business talk." She winked.

"You always were a wench." He kissed her. "Okay. Fix two drinks, I'll talk. Then I'm your cook and anything else you want me to be."

She stood and headed for the bar and the small refrigerator in the closet. "Start talking, lover."

He told her about the weapons, the identification card, Melissa, Patricia, Henry Shuller and the Griffins, and all else he knew including his theories. He posed questions related to them.

"You were the best research person I ever knew, so I know you'll get results somehow. I don't trust anyone else. This is what I need. If you don't have time, hire the right people for me. But I want you."

"I'm yours. Do you want me to look for Melissa?"

"No. Find out whom the Germans were, who were captured or surrendered. You know the dates. There are articles and a book or books on the subject. Also check the *New York Times Magazine* and *Newsday*. I want to know if any were named Carl Dieterman. Find out what other Germans landed in America and got caught. Let's concentrate on those who landed on Long Island."

She was taking notes. "Next, it's also possible that all the succeeding stories written here about Germans landing in the United States were researched from the American press at the time they occurred or were known. Maybe no one researched Germany. See if you can find some German war records about other U-boat landings on Long Island if Germans landed and were picked up again by the U-boat. Can you get the material from Germany? How long will it take?"

"Two, three days, possibly four."

"Good. Get as much information as you can on Carl Dieterman. What do you think? Do you approve the idea?"

"You can probably get a nice advance."

"Not yet. It's soon. I want to develop it further. Oops, I should say, we."

"I love the idea. German war stories are always popular—something mystical about them with readers. I'm also intrigued as to why Melissa never returned. That's the key question to this story."

"The more I think about her, the more intense I become about the whole matter."

"Speaking as your agent, I hope the Shuller story doesn't interfere with your butler story."

"The butler is nearing completion. I'm delighted that we have a handle on next year's story at this stage. Think about those advance commissions."

"I am. That's why I'm good to you."

"You're the wiliest female I know, so why would a seventeen or eighteen-year-old girl who was a mild person suddenly do something as dramatic as she did? Where did she find the two thousand dollars? Why was she avoiding people she loved to live a secret life?"

Helene rolled her eyes. "I'm as baffled as you."

"Then let's focus on Carl Dieterman. We've got to find out where he came from, why he came here and important, when? When was he released from the army? And where is he today? Is he still alive? Did he die on another mission? If he was landed here in nineteen forty-two the mystery deepens, especially if sometime in June. I have another hunch. Find out if there were any unsolved murders a week or two after each landing. It's speculation but may help us establish a pattern or a movement. If I were a spy on an espionage mission I wouldn't leave anyone around to identify me."

"That's stretching the imagination. Is business over?"

Helene was rubbing his leg, romance in her eyes. He rubbed hers. He kissed her for encouragement.

"Why don't we do it right here on the couch."

"No." she grinned. "I have a headache."

"You lovable bitch," he whispered. "Come on."

"No, because after that you'll lose interest or conk out on me. No, tonight, you are going to wine, cook, dine and romance me. Earn it."

"You know, every time I see you I regret I don't sleep with you everyday."

"You can always come back."

"And in a week we'd fight like cats and dogs."

"Right, Mitchell, my love. But think of the week in between."

"I am. Why don't we do that?"

"What? Spend a week together?"

"I'd love it."

"Make it three days. After that, it's downhill. Then you can leave after you get your information on Dieterman and the Germans."

"Now that's what I call a practical idea, tailored for our love-hate relationship."

"Shall we go?" She rose.

"Lead the way."

"You must be hard up agreeing readily. The boonies must be getting to you."

"No, Helene. This time it's you. I sincerely want to be with you."

Helene was touched and kissed his cheek.

"You do have your moments."

"For three days?"

"That's it. You see how wonderful friendship can be?"

"Helene, I miss your rebuttals and love your body—when you're not using it as a weapon to get your way. The best things about our friendship are your love for commissions, and for my potent physical asset."

"Like I said, isn't friendship wonderful?"

THIRTY-THREE

THE FIRST TWO nights were glorious, physical, compatible and romantic. At eleven A.M. on the third day, Helene called the apartment to say she had the information and asked if he would prefer to come to the office or wait until the evening.

"Let's make it lunch," he said. "I have to get out of this place or I'll go stir crazy. How about going back to where it all started? The Seasons?"

"Let's be different since it's a nice day. Let's go to the park. I'll meet you at the Fifty-ninth and Fifth entrance at twelve-thirty."

"Agreed. That way I won't have to wear a jacket. I'll pick up the sandwiches. Tuna?"

"With mayo."

"Was I right? About the Germans?"

"I'll tell you when I see you. Be patient. I have all sorts of notes, Bye."

He walked from 65th and Lexington where he bought the sandwiches to Fifth Avenue by going west on 65th. Fifth Avenue was crowded, being the lunch hour. He crossed the taxi-flooded avenue and walked south along the edge of the park. It seemed people on every other bench were feeding pigeons. The pigeons moved defiantly among the moving human feet immune by now to the human race.

Helene waited on the corner of 59th. Another trait he loved about her; she was never late. They paired into the park where they found a bench by the lake being vacated by an elderly couple. They quickened their pace before someone else beat them to the bench. It was theirs.

She said, "You get our lunch laid out and I'll start. I have everything you asked for so we'll take them one at a time. The sailors who landed at Amagansett came ashore in uniform on June thirteenth, nineteen forty-two a Saturday, in the early hours. They managed to take the first train from the Amagansett station to New York City. For the record, none were named Dieterman. They were eventually caught within a few weeks."

"That eliminates them."

She shuffled the papers, he unwrapped the sandwiches.

"I have specifics on those four, plus the four who landed in Florida; their names, code names, backgrounds, the purpose of their missions and how each was caught by, or surrendered to, the FBI. Six of the eight were eventually executed."

"The sailors who landed on Long Island are no value to us. Since they caught the first train out after landing, it's unlikely they or their weapons found their way to Shuller's Land."

"Okay, that ends background. This should interest you. It's what you want. The following week, Thursday, June eighteenth, nineteen forty-two, U-boat three-

three-seven, under the command of Lieutenant Commander Guenther Krupp, stopped off the shore of East Hampton and landed four soldiers." *Soldiers!* Mitchell bolted upright nearly spilling the Cokes. "They followed the same procedures as the sailors. They landed in uniform and the two sailors who brought them to shore returned to the U-boat. The soldiers probably changed clothes in the dunes. The names of the soldiers were Sergeant Heinrich Kretschmer, Corporal Erich Lassen, Corporal Peter Lehmann and—Corporal Carl Dieterman!"

"Holy shit. Holy shit! Will you stop being dramatic and go on?"

"Their mission was the same as the sailors. To sabotage and cripple vital industry and transportation."

Mitchell was getting impatient. "What happened to them?"

"No one knows. They landed and were never seen or heard from again."

"All of them?"

"All, they never contacted their U-boat as scheduled and they never returned to Germany. They are officially listed as missing in action."

"This is getting exciting."

"Their official code name was Landwolf Three-three-seven. Now I'll show you how good I am."

She took out a map of the South Fork of Long Island and folded it to show the East Hampton area.

"Now on the same day, an artist was knifed in the neck as he walked in the woods. His name was Gavin Garland. According to the papers at the time, his wife said he was going to paint a scene with a gully on some farm. She couldn't remember the name."

"There's a gully on Shuller's Land. Where the truck crashed."

"Maybe he was headed there." With a pencil she made an X on the shoreline. "The soldiers landed about here. Garland was killed here." She made another X. "And that same day, a woman and her son were murdered as they opened their summer home—Grace Connerly and her son, Douglas. Douglas was found in the trunk of their car, shot in the back of the leg and in the face. She was found nude in the living room, shot in the head. She wasn't sexually molested but there may have been a struggle because of skin and blood in her fingernails.

"The boy was probably running from them and was brought down by the shot in the leg and finished off with the other shot. An aside here—there was vomit all over the boy's shirt, but it wasn't his."

"That's interesting," Mitchell said.

"They were killed about here." She put an X on the spot. "Now where is Shuller's Land?"

Mitchell marked the spot. "Now, Mr. Sherlock Holmes," Helene continued. "If we make a straight line . . ." she did, " . . . it's possible those people were killed by Landwolf Three-three-seven. They all connect."

"Excellent deduction."

"The question now is—Why were they going north-northwest?"

Mitchell shrugged. "Why?"

"The other landing party took the train from Amagansett, right near the shore. Why didn't Landwolf Three-three-seven take the train from East Hampton, also on the southern line of the Long Island Railroad and travel north instead?"

"Good question."

"My guess is that since the sailors took that line, Landwolf wanted to avoid risk by heading for Riverhead to take the mid-island line—a precaution in the event the sailors were caught and the coast was on alert. And looking at the map, if you extend our line . . ." she extended it, " . . . it goes right to Riverhead."

Mitchell nodded agreement, contemplating. If he were smoking a pipe at the moment he would have made a perfect study of a man in deep thought.

"Now what?" Helene asked. "Okay, since you found the weapons and card on Shuller property, we can deduce the following: They rested in the barn unseen, lost or inadvertently left their belongings behind as they left unseen by the Shullers. Henry Shuller wasn't murdered, right? He was killed in an accident. Maybe he found the Luger in the barn and put it in the truck."

"Possible." He passed the sandwich to her and she took a bite.

"Melissa wasn't killed either leading me to believe that the Shullers and the Germans never made contact. It follows that if they killed Gavin Garland and Douglas and Grace Connerly they would have killed the Shullers. Right?"

"Right." He nodded. "We can't dispute logic."

"There were no other unsolved murders between the Shuller farm and Riverhead. It is appropriate and normal to assume, therefore, that they reached Riverhead, boarded the train and made it to New York City. They may have even sat on this bench."

The humor didn't break his concentration.

"Helene, was there any information from the captured groups that they made contact with Landwolf Three-three-seven?"

"It's not in the information I have."

"Now what do you have on Dieterman?"

"I was coming to that. I have information on all four, plus pictures. I spared no expense to get these. They were flown in this morning."

"I said you were the best."

"Still am." She spread the photographs before him. "Heinrich Kretschmer, the group leader. He was a professional soldier, thirty-two years old, unmarried, no family. Corporal Erich Lassen, twenty-one, a munitions expert: in the army two years, only son of Max and Gerda Lassen of West Berlin who confirmed by phone that they never heard from their son. As far as they're concerned, he's dead. Corporal Peter Lehmann, twenty-three: about two years in the army, also a munitions expert. He left a wife in Brandenburg. Couldn't get more on him. Corporal Carl Dieterman, eighteen, the radioman: in the army six months, first assignment, and no parents. He had an uncle and aunt in Leipzig. I haven't been able to contact them. They may be dead."

He picked up Carl Dieterman's photo, and studying the face said, "He does look young, doesn't he?"

"Young, yes but possibly misleading. He could have killed any of those people. Or all of them."

"One more remote possibility," said Mitchell taking the last bite of a half sandwich.

"What's that?"

"What if Henry Shuller surprised them and killed them and didn't tell anyone. Maybe he thought they were burglars or something. You did say they changed into civilian clothes."

"Mitchell Pappas, that's dumb. Even if he did, wouldn't he have reported it?"

"No reason why he wouldn't, I guess, unless he solved his own problems. Don't forget they lived in a desolate area in those days. Maybe he dispensed his own justice."

"Four soldiers against a farmer and a teenage girl? Come on!"

"I'm sorry, but every angle must be thought of."

"Where are we now, besides sitting on this bench?"

"We're more intelligent that's all and left with today's question. What happened to the four Germans? That's the new riddle. It's unlikely all four would defect and stay in the United States after the war."

"That is possible."

"Yes, it is. The mystery does deepen. The riddle is weaving its maze. Do you think you can contact Lehman's wife and maybe find Dieterman's aunt and uncle, if alive, and determine if they ever heard from them? I'd like to eliminate that possibility."

"It will take time."

"Take it."

He looked at Helene admiringly though she had a mouthful of sandwich.

"I keep forgetting you have brains, as well."

"You did say I was the best. But for a few months a year you haven't improved your communication skills. You kept crawling into your fantasies. You're reality was only in bed."

"I was a lousy husband, am a lousy husband and may always be a lousy husband. At my age, it's late to change."

"I understand you better now, but you will. I accept, reluctantly, the client-friend-lover relationship with you. Why don't you stay an extra day?"

"You think you can survive a fourth day?"

"I'll take the day off. Who knows when I'll see you again?"

"You're right. I may not get back to New York City for several weeks. You could come out to East Hampton."

"You mean to Shuller's Land?"

"It's a nice place."

"You're kidding. What do I do while you write and fantasize? Cook and go to the bathroom for excitement?—No, thanks. It'll be worse than going away by myself to a deserted island."

"You're right. I am preposterous."

"Now that you know about the Germans, what about the mystery of Melissa Shuller?"

"Melissa. Melissa. Like you said if the Germans saw her they would have killed her. Finding her will be difficult, and may take months. Even if we find her chances are she won't be able to shed more light on the Germans. Years have passed so a picture wouldn't help us even if Patricia McGuire could remember the towns postmarked on the Christmas card envelopes."

"How are you going to conclude the story?"

"With my imagination, mystery and intrigue that will be appropriately exciting."

"That's the way the world should solve all its problems. Create your own solutions."

"What the hell. We got enough out of the Germans and the Shullers to make a firm foundation for an exciting novel. But still, check the other families. My curiosity demands I know about the Germans, and whether any are still alive."

"Done. Now, how about some peace and quiet while we listen to the birds and the drone of New

York as I finish eating because I'm hungry. Half my sandwich is gone and I don't remember eating it."

They became aware of the city's steady and harmonious breathing. Helene began to unwrap the other half of the sandwich. He reached for her hand and rubbed it.

"How about going to back to the apartment? Your brains turned me on."

THIRTY⚡FOUR

MITCHELL RETURNED TO Shuller's Land on Sunday afternoon.

The time with Helene was utopia; perfect. The Germans and Shullers returned to their conversations only when Helene reported the Germany investigation was in progress. Thereafter, the atmosphere was honeymoon.

But below the surface nagging questions remained. He thought about them in the bathroom to avoid Helene's potential ire. What happened to the German soldiers? How could they leave behind *three* items? Aren't a soldier's weapons the last things he wants to lose?

The nagging and speculation became prevalent on the drive to Shuller's Land. Upon reaching the house he changed into jeans and sandals, and left. He walked in a hurry ignoring his surroundings, impatient to reach the gully searching the road area for other clues. When he reached his destination, he stood on the road and studied the gully and the truck.

Now the area had meaning, substance. He envisioned Henry Shuller struggling to keep the truck on the road and fighting to avoid severe damage after it left the road. He could see the truck bounce off the opposite side and settle in its present position.

And he saw Henry Shuller slumped over the wheel, bleeding from head injuries.

Mitchell descended cautiously, his feet sinking in the fragile earth. He looked inside the cab. The Luger was where left. He examined it again, checking the full cartridge and asked, "Where did you get the gun, Henry?"

He stepped away from the truck and visions played before him: Siobhan and Sean Griffin pulling Henry from the truck as Patricia wept and Melissa remained hysterical at the edge of the gully, the Griffins carrying him up the incline to their pickup truck. The scene faded. He turned detective as he studied the road where the gully began.

Was Henry Shuller drinking? No, he was heading toward town because the truck was facing that way. Did he have a drink too much at home?

He couldn't arrive to conclusions. Holding the Luger he climbed sideways to the deep end of the gully and headed for the house.

Helene came back in pleasant thoughts. She was the perfect woman for him, he concluded. Maybe he could live with Helene for longer periods then see her on a part-time basis during the months he needed to work on his novels. At first Helene thought that suggestion chauvinistic then agreed to evaluate it further—and Mitchell promised an unselfish attitude during the time they would live together. She offered a better alternative. Awaken at 5:00AM

and work until 3:00PM, rest then have dinner ready
when she arrived home at six. He accepted. Time
with Helene was more valuable and important than
his writing.

"What took you this long to arrive at that simple
and practical solution?" Helene asked.

"It takes a while for a narrow-minded fool."

"At long last, the awakening of Mitchell Pappas.
Welcome home after this project. Hurry and
finish."

She understood his world of fantasy, as an agent
and as a research aide—but not as a wife. Yet, he was
the only man she loved, and wanted to love. In their
final analysis, they were perfect for each other as full
partners.

Reaching the house, he went in, left the Luger
in the living room, and came out with the dagger
and the identification card. He wanted to spend time
playing detective in the barn.

He turned on the lights and forced the back door
open to illuminate the barn to maximum. Then he
placed the pitchfork, ax, dagger and identification
card where he first found them.

He knew the dagger and the card hadn't been
moved since 1942. But how about the pitchfork and
ax? The real estate people visited here. Could they
have moved them or used them? He let his
imagination run rampant speculating. A German lost
his dagger as he lay on the hay. Dieterman may have
lost the wallet by the stable as he leaned against the
wall. But the wall was four feet from where he found
the wallet. The pitchfork and ax were close together.
They could be deadly weapons. Were they used that
way? Then he remembered the rope. He probed
the area around the pole and found three strands

each approximately one foot in length. He placed them by the pole.

Let us now assume, Mitchell thought, that the dagger cut the ropes. What does that mean? They were either randomly cut or someone was tied to the pole and the rope was cut to release the hostage. Was it Melissa? Or did Henry Shuller have a German tied here? That answer satisfied him.

Shuller surprised the four—probably with his shotgun—and tied them up. Did Henry kill them? Let's say Henry discovered they were Germans— spies—and decided to execute them. Maybe he became crazed with patriotic fervor and believed the enemy was better off dead. Let's say he stabbed the one tied to the pole then stabbed Dieterman by the last stable. Then the smell of blood could have crazed him and he executed the other two with the ax and pitchfork.

Now he continued, let's say Melissa came and saw what he had done and ran horrified from the scene. Then Henry decided to celebrate by getting drunk and then drove the truck to his death. Or maybe he buried them before leaving. Or maybe Melissa buried them to protect her father after she found him dead in the truck. Patricia McGuire did say that some time passed between the time he left and when Melissa called her. Is that why Melissa ran away? Is that why she never sold the place?—Because the bodies might be found?

The theories were good premise. Writers were workers, not excavators, and why it was rented to a person like himself. Maybe the Germans were buried in the fields somewhere, and farm equipment may accidentally find the graves. All this theory is bullshit if Helene finds one soldier in Germany, he added.

His private conversation made him pace from one end of the barn to the other. He concluded that if they were buried, it would have to be near the barn. He walked around the barn in widening circles, his eyes on the earth, searching for unnatural rises or depressions in the land. He scanned slowly. The planting mounds were deceptive and the fields laden with irregularities. It looked like an impossible mission to find graves there.

Melissa must have a reason for vanishing, and he figured it had to be to protect her father. He kept repeating the thought and kept looking convinced that as the reason Melissa left. He made a full sweep around the barn and started again at the front now looking for subtle variations in the land.

The space between the house and the barn appeared natural and untouched. The area was eliminated. He reached the south field and walked a rectangle among the weeds. Again, the irregularities seemed natural.

Mitchell explored the north and east fields then the lower south field. He wasn't optimistic about covering the west field on the other side of the house. It wouldn't have made sense to drag the bodies far in any direction.

Depressed and hopes dimmed, he went to the other side of the house. The area there was flat, punctuated with scattered weeds before the former planting field began. The uneven rise of earth toward the back of the house was suspicious but small to contain bodies.

"What the hell, let's dig anyway. There's nothing else."

He pulled the weeds and cleared the risen area then went to the barn for a shovel. He wasn't excited about the small mound, figuring it as excess dirt. He shoveled halfhearted and leveled the mound. The limited exercise proved him out of shape and his breathing was labored. He rested, leaning on the handle, searching the western field north and south for better evidence of a mass grave.

The black pine and scrub oak seedlings encroached a wide area on that side as well. Their low-lying branches formed a nearly impenetrable barrier. The meadow in the northern sector fed several cows and sheep, and birds swirled melodic in the taller clumps. A jet screamed overhead to the north, heading west toward Kennedy International Airport kicking off the Sunday afternoon parade of international flights. He was clammy and the perspiration made the day seem warmer.

He became conscious of the desolation intruded by the jet.

All right, he said to himself, you needed a place to vent your creative world. But here you are, digging. You're losing it, boy. You gave up another wonderful day with Helene to do this? Digging? I'm beginning to wonder about your crazy need to be alone when you write. You could as easily have done it in the city in a closed room, and when you want to tell the world to stick it on Monday mornings, go up on the roof and yell. You might get arrested, but what the hell. Dig, you lazy bastard! Dig. Pay penance. Atone for your stupidity.

He thrust the shovel and hoisted dirt. When he thrust again, he met soft resistance and leaned his foot on the shovel for penetration. The shovel barely moved. He pressed harder—resistance.

Mitchell was excited now and removed the dirt faster. He unearthed a dark cloth. He removed more

dirt and lifted the rotted cloth, the remnants of a
black sweater. He held it with fingertips handling it
as if diseased from years in the ground. He put it
aside and began to empty the hiding place. He found
pants, more sweaters, three raincoats, shoes, socks,
shirts, and toilet articles. All rotted, molded, and foul.
But he withdrew each with the fervor of discovery.
All labels were missing.

Beneath the clothes were the three wallets and
jewelry, resting on the two black leather bags—a
wedding ring, three watches, and two other
unidentifiable rings. The watches were Swiss made.
He checked each wallet carefully probing all
compartments. He found nothing. He had to dig
deeper to free the two bags he then lifted and placed
on the ground. The leather had rotted and the clasps
rusted. He lifted the flaps revealing the dynamite,
timing devices, fuses and wire, now ruined beyond
use. He stood with elation among the burial site
contents.

He was right! He was right! Henry Shuller did
kill those Germans and buried their belongings here
and them elsewhere, he concluded. But to make
sure he kept digging.

He dug another two feet on each side and
surrendered then leaned against the house from
fatigue.

You're a genius, Mitchell, he thought. A genius!
The wedding ring must belong to—Who was
married? Lehmann. Peter Lehmann, with the wife
in Brandenburg. The wallets must belong to them.
Dieterman's you found. Now you know why Melissa
left. Guaranteed now. There's no way those soldiers
would have left without their clothing. Why bury
clothing and jewelry? They must have been desperate

or in a panic to hide evidence. There's a basement in this house. Check it out. Maybe he buried them down there. There's nothing in the fields, so what the hell.

He left the articles he had unearthed by the hole and taking the shovel entered the house, opened the basement door and turned the lights on. He stood at the top of the stair with cautious optimism. Could he have buried them down here? Mitchell had been down the basement before and could remember nothing that looked like a mass grave.

Mitchell descended the stair, slowly, adding mystery to his motion, creating his own tension. Even the steps creaked beneath his weight. This time his attention would be on the floor. At the bottom he bent and scrutinized the floor level—solid and straight and concrete. No signs of diggings or patches of replaced cement.

The basement was primarily a storage area, cool and damp. A shipping trunk was near the opposite wall. The other walls were lined with shelves occupied with cartons, suitcases, a sled, bicycle, roller skates, records, a radio, pots and pans, garden tools and supplies and an assortment of useless items that could have been thrown out. All were laden with dust. Spiders had staked their claim with their web fencing.

The dust-covered black leather suitcase was particular interest to him—More black leather? He opened the suitcase. The odor was foul as he lifted the top. His fingers left tracks as the dust clung to them. The suitcase was empty, without identification. He surmised it had belonged to the Germans. That Shuller had emptied it buried the clothes and placed the bag down here since it was a general, unidentifiable suitcase he could have used for some trip. Black leather was expensive; not the luggage a farmer would buy in the thirties or forties. Wasn't black leather a German Army feature?

Disappointed at failing to find the burial place, he went back to the kitchen with the shovel, made a pot of coffee, sat at the table and massaged his deductions: Henry Shuller was a cold-blooded killer. How did one man overcome four trained soldiers, killers? He had to have surprised them as they rested in the barn.

Poor Melissa, the beast in her father was too much and she couldn't bear to live here anymore. Yes, it had to be that way.

Lassen and Lehmann were the munitions experts. They wouldn't leave without their prime weapons. If the jewelry was buried with the dynamite and clothes it meant they were taken from dead bodies. Otherwise, why would anyone want to bury jewelry? The jewelry was removed to prevent identification if anyone found the bodies.

But why wouldn't the clothes and jewelry be buried with the bodies? They had to be buried a distance apart. He would have done it that way. The risk lessened by that procedure. Why were the wallets empty?—To avoid identification, obviously. Think, Mitchell, think!

He slammed the table.

"You ass!" He shouted. "You dumb jackass!"

He jumped to his feet, turned the coffee off, grabbed the shovel and ran out the door.

If they were killed in the barn he would have buried them there! Why drag heavy bodies for any distance?

Mitchell was confident now of finding the bodies as he stood at the entrance to the barn. He crouched for a better look at the floor. It appeared level. Moving toward the tractor, he bent and looked underneath. A good place, he thought, but the ground was smooth. He looked down the entire left side; it was disappointing. Then he checked the first stable, and the other stables in order, thoroughly, a madman looking for that final drop of medicine. The last one had the uneven floor. He swung the gate wide and noticed it passed over the wallet.

He decided the wallet fell out of Dieterman's pocket as he was dragged here. I'm up the creek if you're not buried here, he thought. Don't disappoint me now. Be there and I'll tell the world Henry Shuller killed you.

To be certain this was the place, he ran next door to the potato storage barn. The floor there was level, uninterrupted. He ran back to the barn. It had to be the last stable!

With a quick silent prayer for success, he thrust the shovel hard into the middle of the stable floor and dug with optimism. He kept gouging the earth until the shovel met resistance. He saw bone and shattered clothing, and froze.

"Good God!" he shrieked.

The shock of discovery, the reality of his theory forced him to stagger backward against the stall. When reality sank into his system, he scraped the dirt off carefully, revealing more bones. Then he saw another skeleton and clothing beneath.

He dug furiously now, hands and back complaining of pain. Deeper still until he saw the third skeleton, which was face down.

Mitchell kept excavating. He was up to his knees, ignoring his aching muscles, calluses and burning lungs. The fourth body had to be there. He kept digging. He climbed out of the grave and began digging on the other side, gouging as deep as the other side. Fatigue took its toll and he gave up.

He climbed out and stared into the grave with the three skeletons. Clothing shreds hung from the bones. Who were they? Which one was Dieterman? Where's the fourth one buried?

He jumped back into the hole to determine the cause of death. The top skeleton had broken spinal vertebrae and the rear of the rib cage had been severed. It had to be the ax. He shivered, envisioning the ax entering the back. He moved the axed skeleton off the second one by nudging it to the side. He couldn't determine how the second one died. It could have been the dagger, the pitchfork, or the shotgun. There were bruises on the ribcage, so he settled for the pitchfork. It was difficult to conclude how the one facing downward was killed.

He climbed out, brushing his sore hands on his jeans. His body was damp and dirty. All right, he had found them. But where was the fourth one? Where did Henry bury him? Was he killed later? Was he tied to the pole? Was Henry torturing him, saving him for last while he executed his comrades? The rope was cut. Did he lead him elsewhere to die? Or did Henry have him dig the graves, put his comrades in and cover them? It would save Henry work. Now he had to find that single grave.

He shouldered the shovel like a rifle and stood by the dead tree. Now he looked around Shuller's Land as if it were a cemetery, a burial ground, a slaughter ground, the home of a savage massacre.

Suddenly the place had a foul stench; worse than Emily and Jack Griffin's chicken house.

He thought Melissa did the right thing by Henry. She let the place die. Now, where was the fourth one killed? Where did Shuller take him?—Into the fields?—Into the woods? Why didn't he kill him in the barn? Did he torture him?

He walked the fields for a half-hour with shovel poised to strike looking for any telltale sign of a grave. He was looking for a mass grave before. A single one would be harder to find. Then he tried the woods. He gave up after another half-hour. He leaned the shovel against the house, washed his hands, rubbing the sore points, drank water, turned on the coffee, and sat at the table, exhausted.

He looked around the kitchen wondering again if the furniture was the same when the Shullers lived here. He pictured Henry and Melissa sitting here and talking after the massacre—Henry trying to make her understand and Melissa eventually running to her room, crying. But the added mystery of the fourth soldier gnawed away at him.

Was the fourth soldier in this kitchen before he died?

Why didn't Henry kill him immediately? Was he sadistic? Did he bring the soldier back here, tie him to a chair and torment him with promises of freedom?

Thoughts obscured his vision, mesmerizing images entered his mind's eye, but when he focused on them he found he was looking at the basement entrance. It seemed inviting. An idea jelled.

Maybe the fourth was brought here, killed and stuffed somewhere in the basement. He searched for graves before. Maybe he was hidden down there.

The sudden move from the table forced the chair to fall backward as he hurried down the basement stairs. The first likely place was a deep cardboard box next to the shipping trunk with clothes spilling over and covered with thick dust.

He removed the clothes slowly anticipating a body with each item removed. Halfway down, he reached in and pressed. There wasn't anything hard. Disappointed, he replaced the clothing haphazardly.

Then he saw the shotgun. It leaned against the wall between the carton and the shipping trunk. The shotgun surprised him, puzzled that he hadn't noticed it before. Then he remembered seeing shotgun shells in the hall closet. You would think the real estate people would have removed the shells, he decided.

He picked it up, getting dust all over his hands again, and checked the barrels. One was empty, one loaded. Is this how Henry held them at bay?—With this shotgun? Did he shoot the fourth one?

He put the shotgun back and looked around the basement for possible hiding places for one body. Nothing fit the specifications—except the trunk.

The trunk!

He approached it cautiously, like it was a deadly cobra, and pulled it out to the middle of the floor where the light from the bare bulbs was better.

It *was* heavy, and the weight was encouraging.

He undid the two latches restraining his impatience with the fear of discovery, yet needing to discover. The lock was connected. He pried at it with fingers. It held. What was so valuable it had to have a lock?

He clapped his hands once from excitement.

Who did he save for last: Kretschmer, Lassen, Lehmann or Dieterman? Which one is in the trunk? Is it Dieterman, the youngest? How would he know if all identification was removed?

He ran upstairs for a screwdriver and hammer. He returned, taking the steps two at a time and slammed the hammer against the lock. It fell open. Cautious, he raised the lid expecting to see the skeleton in some contorted position.

He lifted higher and light entered the dark interior. On top was a thick, man's winter coat with fur around the collar. He pulled the coat revealing a woman's coat and more clothing—And more clothing, and more. He couldn't believe it. His arms moved in panic to empty the trunk that should have been a grave.

Angry, he didn't bother to replace the clothes. He went upstairs, turned the basement lights out, slammed the door shut, sat at the table, sprang up remembering his coffee, turned it off, poured a cup, added sugar and milk, sat again and pouted.

Okay, he thought, relax. What do we do now? Call the police? The FBI? No, no. You've come this far, go all the way. You *will* know where the fourth body is buried and what happened here if you find Melissa Shuller.

THIRTY-FIVE

HOW TO FIND Melissa? There was no easy way, only alternatives. He could try to convince the real estate agency to release information on the present owner of Shuller's Land and then trace Melissa backward—if there were additional owners.

But questions remained here. Would Melissa sell the land knowing graves were in it? That they might be found? Or did she assume all traces would vanish with time? Was a new owner holding the land for value waiting for a higher price? And did Melissa sell it knowing he wasn't going to farm the land? Or did she need the money?

Where to begin? He could ask Patricia McGuire for the additional towns, if she could remember them, and then ask Jack Griffin if he remembered other towns or cities besides Boston, or if he saved any envelopes and cards.

If he could assemble a more complete picture of Melissa from friends in one of the towns or cities then he would have a better chance locating her if she moved around. Or, using Melissa's teenage photograph, he could have Helene go through an investigation and a missing person procedure in the areas Patricia and Jack mentioned. But would the picture help after all these years? He wasn't optimistic.

Jack Griffin was a good beginning. He would go visiting in the morning. Tonight he had better cover the bodies before some visitor saw them. He didn't want the world in on his secret yet. He couldn't think of anyone who would visit him today or in the immediate future, but with hikers you never knew—a mandatory precaution.

Mitchell stood over the grave and looked on the skeletons with pity. He took the four photographs Helene obtained for him and studied each one. They were passport size with an inch of white area below the photo. In black ink block-lettering each name was written in the white space.

He wondered which face belonged to which skull, and who was in the field? Who did Henry save for last? Was it the young one, Dieterman or the married one? It didn't matter anymore whom the skeletons belonged to or who was buried in the field. What mattered was finding Melissa. She would tell him.

Mitchell slid the photographs back into his pocket, picked up the shovel and began to fill the hole. A mound formed when the dirt was replaced. He smoothed and spread the dirt and added a layer of old dirt and hay. He was satisfied the barn's secret, and his, was secure.

He picked up the wallet, the dagger, ignored the rope strands, placed the pitchfork, ax and shovel against the front wall and returned to the house. Sitting in the living room relaxing, an unwanted sensation pulsated within—something he never had time with his continuing involvement with intrigue, fantasies, and problem solving that stimulated constant interest. He always remained interested in something, believing an interesting person could never get bored. Only boring people got bored, bored and lonely. And he hated both words.

The sensation was there now. The unwanted sensation of loneliness covered him like a shroud bringing its companions insecurity, fear and depression.

How long could he think about the Germans?— And to hell with the butler for tonight.

Desolation had pursued and overtaken him as he sat in the silence.

What was it he thought about the place as he stood near the dead oak? That the place was foul? He was getting lethargic and passive. He was always optimistic with himself—A personal Pollyanna. His self-analysis computed that it was the active reality of his premise—finding the three bodies.

He wished he were back in New York City. He wished he were anywhere but here tonight. He needed reality, contact with the real world. He connected the phone and called Helene. He nervously listened to three rings. Why didn't she answer? Was she home? Please be home. It was six o'clock. If she were going out for the evening, it was early. She didn't mention anything about going out on Sunday. The fourth ring was interrupted by a hurried voice.

"Hello?" Helene was taking a shower when the phone rang and she stood naked, dripping on her bedroom rug, waiting for a response.

Her voice sent elation through the wires.

"Helene, I need you to know that I love you very much. Talk to me honey. Talk to me about anything except Germans and butlers."

THIRTY⋆SIX

THE WIND WAS blowing wrong again and chicken waste scented the Griffin farm, repulsing Mitchell. He wondered how anyone could get used to the putrid odor. Jack should relocate the chicken coops farther from the house. Today was a school day. The playground area was quiet. As the jeep headed for the house, he perused the fields for signs of Emily or Jack. He didn't see any humans.

He stopped the jeep by the house and knocked on the screen door. Emily came at a rapid pace wiping floured hands on her apron. Her face expanded with joy.

"Hello, Mitchell. What a wonderful surprise," she said opening the door. She wore a green print dress with a dark green apron. "Come in." He entered and waited for her to lead him inside. "Go ahead in," she encouraged. "You know the way to the kitchen." He led she followed. "Today is a baking day, a day to feel like a housewife instead of a field hand. I'll tell you, if I had to do it over again, I wouldn't marry a farmer. The work never ends."

They reached the kitchen.

"Emily, if you had to do it again, you'd marry a farmer. You have the energy to run a house, a farm and four kids."

"Ho, ho. Listen to you. Have a chair." He sat. The counter was cluttered with bowls, eggs, milk, and a cake batter of flour, sugar and butter. Have you had breakfast yet?"

"I'm fine, Emily. I had coffee and a donut before I came over. Forgive me for dropping in on you. I should have called first."

"What for? Around here, folks just drop in on each other. Jack and I thought about dropping in on you the other day, but since you need privacy in your work, we thought it best not to visit. And you missed out on the cake I baked for you."

He was thankful he refilled the grave.

"Don't let that stop you. Next time you get the whim come on over—with another cake. I will stop what I'm doing. I get stir crazy every once in a while."

"Like now? Or are your German weapons still haunting you?" She grinned and sat opposite him with her half-cup of coffee.

"How come everybody thinks they understand writers? But you're right."

"You must be propelled by something or other, since you didn't come for coffee."

"Actually, the mystery of Melissa Shuller has me losing sleep and it's interfering with my work. If I keep wondering about her, I'll never make my deadline on the book I'm working on."

He liked Emily's smile. It was easy to befriend her. He felt comfortable, like he had known her for years.

"I wanted to talk to you and Jack a bit more about her hoping you could provide some information as to where she might have lived."

"Jack's the one to help you with Melissa. He's with the chickens this morning. Packing the eggs. I'll call and tell him you're here. I'm sure he could use a coffee break about now."

The phone was near the door next to a two-foot blackboard covered with notes and yesterday's messages.

"Jack, Mitchell Pappas is here. He'd like to talk to you. Are you almost done? I've coffee on. Good." She hung up and sat. "He's on his way."

"Great."

"Mitchell, what is it you need to know about the Shuller girl?"

"It's a long story, Emily. I'd like to locate her though and thought maybe you and Jack could remember what town or city the past several Christmas cards came from."

"I can't help you there," she replied holding the cup with both hands, elbows resting on the table. She sipped. "I didn't pay attention to the postmark."

"Most people don't," he concurred.

Her cup froze in midair.

"Wait a minute. I think my mother-in-law kept those cards and envelopes like valuable treasures, up to four years ago. I didn't hold on to the cards after that. Maybe Jack did. If he didn't, he might have forwarded them to Patricia."

They were interrupted by a pickup approaching then grinding to a halt in the backyard. A door slammed, followed by footsteps then Jack bounded in through the back door.

"Hello, Mitchell."

They shook hands and he sat.

"You sure got here fast," said Mitchell.

"A lot to do today. Got a tractor-trailer coming for the eggs in a couple hours. But I'll always make time to see you. Besides, I told the guys to work faster."

Emily rose to get Jack a cup of coffee.

"Jack," she said turning away. "Mitchell wants to know if you kept any recent Christmas cards from Melissa."

"Sure did, and the envelopes, too. I'll get them from the basement. I kept meaning to throw the damn things out but somehow I couldn't. It's like the past has a grip on you and won't let go, fighting to be remembered. I guess it's because they meant so much to my mother. I'll be right back. What do you need to know about them?"

"Where they were sent from."

Jack dashed downstairs and came up with a brown paper bag full of envelopes and cards. He emptied the bag on the table. There were more cards than envelopes. Mitchell picked cards at random. All had the same message. Jack sorted the envelopes.

"There are only ten envelopes here. Let's put them in order." He shuffled the envelopes. "Here's an envelope for nineteen forty-two. And here's December seventeenth, New York City, nineteen forty-three, December fifteenth, Boston, December sixteenth, nineteen forty-four, Boston—Nineteen forty-nine, Boston—Nineteen fifty-seven, Boston.— Nineteen sixty-two, Boston, nineteen sixty-three, Portland, Maine, nineteen sixty-nine, Boston, nineteen seventy-two, Boston. Nineteen seventy-six, Boston." He shook the bag and looked inside for strays. An envelope had remained behind. "Nineteen eighty, Boston. Damn, I thought I kept the other years since mother died. But it looks like Boston's it. All Boston after nineteen forty-two, but one."

"Boston is it," said Mitchell. "Maine might have been a visit." He wasn't enthused by the findings.

"Come to think of it, I'm sure the others were Boston," confirmed Jack. "So were the recent ones. Why do you want to know her whereabouts? Same mystery about the German weapons?"

"I promised Patricia I'd try to locate her. I know people who do that."

He thought Jack would get excited about that. He didn't.

"I hope you find her."

"There's a chance if she didn't marry or change her last name. I'll start by checking all the Shullers in Boston and the surrounding areas."

"That won't do any good."

"Why not?" Mitchell puzzled.

"Mother did all that. She called all the Shullers within a fifty-mile radius of Boston. She even called all the Shullers in Portland. She kept checking. You'd think *her* child had run away from home, she was committed to finding her. She even ran ads in the personal columns in the Boston papers. From what I understand, she also checked the local banks and tax records for Melissa's address up to the early fifties, but the only address listed was the local one— Shuller's Land. After a time, the sources were exhausted. Melissa was mother's obsession. But when you come right down to it, Melissa was as her daughter and I treated her like a sister even though I was in love with her in my childish way. Anyway, she didn't find Melissa, and the other Shullers didn't know her or her family."

"She could have married."

"Probably, compounding the problem and the search. Good luck, Mitchell. You're looking for the lost needle. How's Patricia? What was her reaction?"

He stayed for another half-hour. Jack put off his work, and they talked about Patricia, eggs, chickens, farming, and writing.

THIRTY⚡SEVEN

THE REAL ESTATE office on the north side of
Main Street in East Hampton was active. Its long
tenure in town was a guarantee of success, as East
Hampton became a summer Mecca. It was once a
store office that had expanded to the width of three
stores with the town's growth. Their slogan that
Mitchell thought totally self-serving was in gold
lettering in the lower part of the middle window. "If
it's in East Hampton, we know it!"

A variety of awards from real estate associations,
the Chamber of Commerce, women's groups and
restaurant groups, went on ad infinitum; a collage
of many years displayed in the windows. The red sun
of a notary public seal was stuck to the left window.

Three agents were occupied with potential
clients; two secretaries typed. Carter Borden was on
the phone sitting at the large desk toward the back.
He waved to Mitchell when he entered. "I'll be with
you in a moment, Mr. Pappas," he shouted. It wasn't
his enthusiasm to see Mitchell, as a warning to his

associates that the important and famous Mr. Pappas was his exclusive client. A wooden barrier with a swinging gate separated the visitor's area.

Mitchell sat in the waiting area, picked up the first magazine and thumbed through *Life* magazine. Before Mitchell could get involved with an article on the Greek Isles, Carter Borden came anxious into the waiting area. He wore dark-rimmed glasses, a white shirt with a bowtie and blue-striped slacks. His shirt pocket was full of pens in a leather case. He smiled a lecherous smile, to mean; "Come into my web, like the spider . . ."

Mitchell put the magazine down. Borden sat next to him with his back to his fellow workers.

"Ah, Mr. Pappas. How wonderful it is to see you again. How can I be of service? Is anything wrong? Shall we go back to my desk?"

"No, it's noisy back there. Let's sit here."

"If you like."

"Everything is beautiful that I'm considering buying the property. That should net you a nice commission."

"We don't talk about such things, Mr. Pappas."

"Sure. I believe I've found the perfect place."

"You do have it rented for six months, Mr. Pappas, which is just as well because the owner has no desire to sell the land. As you know, we have managed the property's affairs for many years, since nineteen forty-two. We keep our client well advised on the value of the land and each year keeps deferring the decision to sell." He looked around, mysterious to divulge a national security secret. "Confidentially, I believe the property will go on sale in four years."

Mitchell guessed the approximate value per acre and didn't ask.

"Why then?"

"I'm unsure. The owner keeps hinting, planning to rent till then," he said chuckling. "My experience tells me that selling is the next step. I suspect it may be sold sooner."

"You should know. I'm interested today. Tomorrow may change. You're sure the owner won't sell now?"

"Positive, positive. Unquestionable."

"I might be able to convince the owner if we can talk."

"That's impossible."

"Why?" He arched his back as a gesture of firmness.

"I cannot. It's client privilege, constituting a serious breech of confidentiality." Borden looked horrified.

"Nonsense. You want to make sure you don't lose your commission. But you probably have an exclusive listing."

"Mr. Pappas, please. You keep mentioning money and commissions. That shouldn't concern you. We do have an exclusive, obviously."

"I'm sorry, Mr. Borden. I'm a writer, not a businessperson who accepts decorum. I'll tell you what I'm going to do." He leaned forward to talk confidential. "Mr. Borden, I'll give you fifty dollars if you tell me if a woman owns the land. I'm not asking for the name or address."

He flashed a fifty out of view of Borden's associates and those outside walking by the window.

"This is highly irregular, Mr. Pappas." He said it with some smugness. Borden took the fifty quickly and smiled content. "It is owned by a man."

Mitchell nodded with the knowledge that Melissa no longer owned the land.

"Thank you, Mr. Borden. You're a gentleman. Did a woman ever own the land?"

"Yes. Many years ago."

"Okay, now for another fifty bucks. How many owners since the woman?"

Borden took the fifty. "One. The same one who owns it today."

"Mr. Carter Borden, according to reliable sources, you have an excellent reputation for astuteness in business dealings."

Borden nodded agreement.

"I have completed some perfectly marvelous transactions that have made the local papers."

"I'd like to make you a proposition. If you're as astute as your reputation, you'll accept it. I will give you one hundred dollars to tell me who the owner is and where he lives . . ."

"I cannot, sir."

" . . . or I will go to the East Hampton Town Hall, talk to some friends, and check the tax records. Now what does that mean? It may take me some time, a day or two, maybe. But I need the information now. If I get the information from the town, you lose the hundred. I promise that I'll tell the owner I found out about him from the tax records, if he asks. Are you astute, Mr. Borden?"

He took the hundred. "Very."

"Excellent, Mr. Borden. Now that we've come this far, what was the address of the woman who sold?"

"Let me check the file." He went to the file and checked the property's history. He returned, nose in folder. "The last record we have is that the woman was Melissa Shuller, by inheritance. The only address was Shuller's Land. We were then retained by the new owner to manage the property."

"How long ago was that?"

"Let's see. Nineteen . . . sixty-six. Before that, Miss Shuller had the bank across the street handle the tax aspects of the property. They may know her address."

"Good idea. I'll check them after I leave here. But first, the owner's name."

"Ah, yes. Nearly forgot." He checked the folder. "Mr. William Griffin. One twenty-four Hunting Street, Natick, Massachusetts. Telephone, 617-828-2468."

Mitchell wrote the information on a pad Borden provided.

"Thank you, Mr. Borden. It's a pleasure doing business with you." He returned the pad and pen. "Griffin? Any relation to the Griffins next door to me?"

"Heavens, no. I asked him that question. But there are hundreds of Griffins in Massachusetts. Many Irish-Americans up there."

"That's a relief. I thought for a moment there was additional intrigue here."

"I don't understand, sir."

"Forget it, Mr. Borden. Personal stuff. Thanks."

He stood and headed for the door.

"Come back again, Mr. Pappas."

Mitchell stopped by the door and watched Borden grinning like a Cheshire cat—like a spider who beckoned, and having fed. Mitchell knew why he had wanted to punch him in the face the first time they met.

THIRTY=EIGHT

MITCHELL HAD LEARNED more. Now he had two sources left to find Melissa's address: the bank and William Griffin of the many Griffins in Massachusetts. The leads were winding down. William Griffin purchased the property many years ago. Knowing where the seller was today dimmed hopes of Griffin being helpful. Who keeps track of the seller for years after they buy property? No one he knew. The bank was the important source of the two. Melissa may still be banking at a branch office with an affiliate bank in the Boston area.

The bank was a red brick building with a white facade with two Corinthian columns guarding the entrance, letting the world know that what was within was secure. Black lettering over the door proclaimed the bank was founded in 1936. The image was security.

Once inside, he asked a guard if he could see an officer. The guard, who looked like he retired from another profession, directed him to a middle-aged woman elegantly dressed in banker's gray sitting at a desk by the window. The nameplate read *Alice Robinson, Vice-President*. She was on the phone, listening, and watching the street activity. A familiar person walked by and waved. She waved back. Mitchell took liberty sitting before being invited. She looked at him and sat up.

"That'll be fine. Would it be possible to call you back in a few minutes? Good. Thank you. Bye."

She recognized Mitchell Pappas, famous author, and one of the 'in' people in East Hampton though he wasn't the usual socialite. But the community had buzzed with rumors at every cocktail party and gathering, each group content with the knowledge that Pappas was one of them, living among them. Alice Robinson was no fool. Writers made money, especially best selling writers. And serve her purposes financially and socially to say she was Mitchell Pappas's banker in East Hampton.

"How can I help you, Mr. Pappas?"

Her smile was friendly. Mitchell was flattered being recognized—a good beginning.

"Ms. Robinson, I wonder if there's a way to check an old account. As far back as nineteen sixty-six."

Alice Robinson's face remained cordial, though disappointed the elegant prospect wasn't going to open an account—maybe in the future or before he left.

"With computers today, it won't be a problem. It'll take a few moments. What account? Did you have an account here that far back?"

"No, it's not my account."

"We may still be able to help you."

Mitchell was impressed with Alice Robinson. No nonsense or trivia; right to business.

"The account was under the name of Melissa Shuller."

He spelled the last name. She made a phone call, gave the party the information, and held the line. "It shouldn't take long, Mr. Pappas. Please be patient with us."

"That's all right. I appreciate you taking the time to do this. Can you also check if Melissa Shuller has an account in any affiliated branch in the Boston area?"

"Anything we can do to be of service. But we don't have an affiliation in New England."

She listened and watched the street. Mitchell surveyed the important atmosphere of the bank reeking with security. He returned his attention to Alice Robinson when he heard her say, "Thank you." She cradled the receiver and began to write notes. She lifted and read the paper. "You were right. The Melissa Shuller account was closed in nineteen sixty-six."

"Can you tell me the address? She's a distant relative of my wife's and we need to get in touch with her."

"I see. Is that why you're staying at the farm she used to own?" She smiled to impress that she knew he lived in the community.

"Coincidence. It's a small world."

"It's against bank policy to reveal any information regarding our depositors."

"But it's an old account. No longer active."

"Still, it's policy. I'm sure you would want the same courtesy—that is, if you had an account with us."

"I expect to be seeing you again. I need a banker out here. I keep living on American Express, and since I'll be in the area for the season, I'm going to need you. I'm also looking at some property in Amagansett on Bluff Road."

"A beautiful shorefront area."

The Vice-President beamed. Service and security does work, always impressing future depositors.

"I'm sorry I must disappoint you at our first meeting, Mr. Pappas, but I'm sure you appreciate the need for discretion."

"Without question." He began to rise and sat again. "I have no desire to tempt you to violate policy and discretion, but can you tell me if it's a local address? I mean, at the time Melissa Shuller had the account here, did she have a local address or one from out of town?"

She hesitated at the general request. The question didn't violate policy and would probably endear him to her and the bank.

"The address was local."

Shuller's Land, he thought. Nuts.

"Thank you. I'll be seeing you soon, Mrs. Robinson." He stood and turned to leave. "Oh, was that Shuller's Land?" He grinned taking a long shot at violation.

She smiled then nodded, pleased with her first encounter with the famous prospective client. She watched him with admiration as he left the bank. Mitchell was disappointed.

One lead remained—a weak lead.

THIRTY⹀NINE

MITCHELL STOPPED IN the local bookstore opened a road atlas to Massachusetts and located Natick, approximately twenty miles west of Boston adjacent to the Massachusetts Turnpike. He estimated six hours, maybe seven to get there.

He made reservations at the Holiday Inn on Route 9 in Framingham, the adjoining town, for Saturday night. The Holiday Inn operator suggested it as close to Natick. After being convinced the Inn was just yards from Natick, he accepted the reservation, guaranteeing the reservation with his American Express card.

Mitchell wanted to visit Natick on the weekend. Chances were better William Griffin would be home, and Sunday was a better bet than Saturday. He would visit on Sunday morning after a good night's rest following the long and wearing drive.

Maybe he should call first? He rejected that. If the owner refused to give him information over the phone then a visit would prove hostile. He would take his chances on dropping in hoping Griffin was home. After all, it was his final lead. He would do better talking to him in person.

Mitchell packed an overnight bag and a sports jacket and left East Hampton at noon, Saturday. He traveled the Long Island Expressway to the Cross Island Parkway, over the Throgs Neck Bridge to the New England Thruway and stopped at the Stamford service area for coffee, a map, and gasoline. He continued on the Connecticut Turnpike, veered north at New Haven on I-91 to Hartford, where he met route 84, which took him to Route 86 and on to the Massachusetts Turnpike.

By now, his back was tortured. He reached the Natick exit at seven o'clock, paid his toll and veered right toward Route 30 and Route 9. The toll collector gave him directions to the Inn. He reached Route 9 and saw the Inn to the right opposite Shopper's World, a huge shopping center. Route 9 was vibrant. He was surprised at the congestion and the spread of civilization to Natick, a growing area. He made the first legal left, pulled into the parking lot and checked in.

The room was what he expected. He washed, used the bathroom facilities then returned to the front desk.

Signs in the lobby invited him to dine in the restaurant, but he needed to get out and walk a bit after that drive. He asked the young lady behind the desk if she could recommend a good restaurant off the premises. She smiled and suggested Ken's Steak House, across the street or Lou Stamoulis's Seafood and Greek restaurant, across and down the street. He assumed she suggested that because of his last name. He thanked her and winked.

The shopping mall parking fields were packed on Saturday evening. The sun was drifting behind the Inn as he walked to the first traffic light and crossed to the other side. He decided to eat; that would refresh him with energy. He chose the Greek restaurant, savored the taped bouzouki music, had grilled baby octopus as an appetizer then lamb with string beans with a glass of retsina, a cup of Greek coffee, returned to the Inn and tried to sleep. The Greek coffee kept his eyes wide-open like those of a wooden dummy, and it took another two hours before they closed.

Mitchell awoke at seven in the morning to an overcast day. Through the parted drapes he saw the clouds racing eastward. The forecast predicted clear. The blue would come later within two hours. His back returned to normal. Everything was normal except the nightmare.

He couldn't remember when he had a nightmare that thrust him upright with heart racing and pounding. He was about to die, and he awoke just before the dagger was about to be plunged into his neck by Henry Shuller. He chased him through the fields and he fell, and the killer leaped on him in a swirl of dust. He shook his head. It must have been his favorite coffee.

He lay immobile, waiting for his heart to settle. No wonder people die in bed, or in their sleep. *If I had a weak heart, I would be waving good-bye.* Symbolic, he thought, symbolic. His subconscious had lingered on the fantasy for long and was now playing it back in a distorted and alarming way.

The nightmare bothered him. He lay back in bed and tried to analyze it. The conclusion was obvious. Mitchell was getting close and he had to be stopped, somehow.

His body rebelled at rising. He lay there for another hour, half-asleep, half-involved with the Shuller puzzle. The answer to the riddle wasn't far now—he hoped, at the long shot. If Griffin couldn't help him then Melissa Shuller's secret may never be known. The new owner of Shuller's Land may provide a good clue to Melissa's whereabouts. He had seen her years ago but memories fade.

Mitchell thought it phenomenal luck if a picture of Melissa and Griffin closing the deal existed. He discarded that. People don't usually do that. Hell, it wasn't a peace treaty, just a sale of some long forgotten land. But such a picture or a picture of Melissa at that age would help Helene in her missing person investigation. The trip would be a disaster if Griffin didn't have Melissa's last address. His desperation stab of optimism kept hope alive to justify the long drive here.

Melissa returned. How was her life? He reviewed his complicated life and hoped she had a better one. Did she marry?—More than once? How did she make her living? What did she look like?

Then he thought about how he could destroy her life, shatter it by confronting her with the dreaded secret she had lived with all these years. She lived a lifetime of hidden terror never knowing when someone would turn up and confront her with the knowledge that her father was a murdering butcher. Authorities might also consider her an accomplice. The news would make front-page headlines.

No, concluded Mitchell, it was wartime and the people killed were the enemy. No crime was committed. The only thing Melissa had to fear was tarnishing her father's reputation. After all, she did run away to protect him, didn't she?

Mitchell found solace in that. No harm would befall Melissa if he made the story public, and he would have another bestseller from a personal experience. The rewards from that made this story worth pursuing. One couldn't get involved emotionally with the people in his stories. They were the players, they acted the script—he did rewrites.

He forced himself upward, showered and shaved, dressed leisurely and had breakfast downstairs at nine. At ten, he headed east on Route 9 for two miles, made the first left turn and traveled west on Route 9. He traveled the outside lane with the concrete barrier dividing east and west. The young lady at the desk told him to turn right at the bowling alley. He had seen the alley from the opposite direction. He knew where to go.

Mitchell made a right at the bowling alley, closed at that hour, and traveled until he saw Hunting Street. He turned right looking for house numbers; looking for 124. He was early and didn't plan on going in yet. He wanted to get the lay of the land so when eleven o'clock came he could drive straight for it from the bowling alley parking lot. His film director friend would call it location scouting.

Then he saw 124, a white Colonial with green window trim, and immaculate landscaping. He would have a better look on the way back. He drove past the Griffin residence, made a U-turn at the corner and passed the house, slower.

The Colonial sat majestically on a half-acre with rhododendrons, azaleas, yews, juniper, and mountain laurel bordering the front. Four tall sugar maples and two oaks shaded the lawn. A four-foot fence, starting at the rear of the house, enclosed the backyard.

He didn't see anyone. The driveway was empty. The trip didn't look promising, but it was Sunday morning and maybe they were in church. He hoped so. He waited at the bowling alley for eleven o'clock. Several cars turned into the street and he wondered if any contained William Griffin.

Maybe they weren't in church, but away for the weekend. He refused to accept thinking that would waste the trip.

At eleven, he left the parking area and parked in front of 124 Hunting Street. Mitchell was pleased. A blue Oldsmobile was in the driveway. He buttoned the sports jacket and adjusted the shirt collar to lie over the jacket's collar.

The neighborhood was quiet, complacent, as expected on a Sunday morning in this middle-income neighborhood. He looked around at the other houses and concluded this was a nice area to raise children. Nice, typical American community. If anything exemplified America, this did.

Mitchell wished he had grown up in a place like this instead of the streets of New York.

The sky began to clear with the wind soft and soothing rustling through the trees. He walked the concrete ribbon that led to the front door and rang the bell, expecting to hear a barking dog. The dog barked, sounding like a monster.

The green door opened partially behind the screen door, and an attractive elderly woman, well dressed, opened the door wider. The Shepherd was determined to force his way past her to threaten the bell ringer.

The woman's smile was gracious. Her blue eyes were hospitable and the dark blond hair, thought Mitchell, was Clairol. The well-dressed gentleman at her front door returned the smile with a "Good morning."

"And a lovely morning to you," she replied enthusiastic. She found him handsome, yet familiar. As a result, he wasn't a total stranger. She quickly tried to remember where she had seen him before. Had Mitchell known, he would have said from the photo on the back of his books. The dog kept barking.

She closed the door partway to discourage the dog and stood between the door and the screen door. It would seem rude to ask him if they had met before, and embarrassing. She suppressed the urge.

"That dog hates everybody," she said with a smile. "He'll quiet in a minute." She scrutinized him. He didn't look like a salesman and it was early in the year for politics.

"Forgive me for disturbing you, but is Mr. Griffin in?"

"I'm Mrs. Griffin." The dog stopped yelping. "You came just in time. Had you come earlier you would have missed us. We just returned from church. Mr. Griffin is in the backyard. Can I help you?"

She had a curious, pensive expression. The stranger didn't call her husband Bill but Mr. Griffin. He must be a stranger or a customer with a complaint.

"I was on my way back to New York from Boston and being in the area, I wanted to talk to him."

She noticed the New York plates on his jeep.

"Have you met my husband before?"

"No, I haven't, but we've had some business together."

He wasn't lying. He was renting from him.

"If you like why don't you go right to the backyard? This way you won't have to worry about the dog," she said pointing to the walkway. "It'll be easier. I'll tell him you're coming around."

"Thank you." He smiled.

She closed the door wondering whom her husband knew from New York. She hurried to the backyard.

Mitchell walked slowly toward the backyard to give Mrs. Griffin ample time to reach her husband. Griffin approached as Mitchell was about to open the gate.

He wore blue suit pants and a tie, and sleeves were rolled up on his white shirt. He had thin hair, mostly receded and white with touches of gray. His high cheekbones tightened as he smiled, and black-rimmed glasses covered his blue eyes.

"Hi, I'm Bill Griffin. What can I do for you?" he said, brushing his hands together away from his body to loosen the charcoal dust. "I can't shake." He showed his blackened palms. "But we can say we did."

Mitchell laughed. "It's all right, Mr. Griffin. I know you weren't expecting me, but since I was near Natick I thought I'd drop by and introduce myself. I'm Mitchell Pappas, your tenant in East Hampton."

"Well," Bill Griffin exclaimed. "What a terrific surprise. Not only to meet you as a tenant, but as one of America's leading writers." Griffin opened the gate. "Please come in." His speech was obvious New England and educated. "Wait till I tell my wife. She thought you were a disgruntled customer who had work done in the shop."

The backyard was a carpet of sod with trees and bushes. A cement patio extended from the house. He herded Mitchell to the other end of the patio where a charcoal grill lay open with a bag of charcoal nearby. The coals were beginning to smoke. A long rectangular table with benches dominated the patio. A row of eight white chairs aligned neatly along the house.

"When Mr. Borden told me that you wanted to rent the place we were thrilled. How are you doing there?"

"It's probably the perfect place on earth for me. That's why I took it when I saw it. Some writers like to hear the surf. I love the solitude and walking in the woods."

"How's the house? Has the agency kept it up?"

"Everything works," replied Mitchell.

"Good."

Mrs. Griffin watched the two men in friendly conversation as they passed the kitchen window and she seemed relaxed with both men smiling. Yet, there was something about him. Where had she seen him before? And in that instant of doubt, the answer came.

She hurried to the library and searched for his books. She found *Murder by Murder* and pulled it from the shelf. His photo on the back cover confirmed her hunch.

Mitchell and Bill reached the table.

"Please sit. Today is family day and we're planning a cookout. And when I say family, I mean an army." He chuckled.

"How many children do you have?"

Mitchell sat on the bench facing the trees and the adjoining neighbor's backyard, noticeable through the thick foliage.

"Fortunately, they're no longer that. My wife always wanted a large family. We have six—three boys and three girls, and seven grandchildren. That's the army."

"Wow. Congratulations. I'll bet you're not a writer," Mitchell teased.

"No. I own the Texaco station over on Route 9," he said. "Hey, now. Wait a minute. Let me get my wife. If I get carried away talking with you, she'll never forgive me forgetting to tell her immediately. I think she read almost all your books. She bought another one after you rented. You're in our library. She won't let you leave without signing them."

"A fan! Get her out here, quick!"

Bill opened the sliding door to the family room and called out. "Hey, honey. Come on out a minute!"

"I'll be right there," she replied from the kitchen.

She had waited for her husband to call her. Had he not, she would have found an excuse to interrupt the discussion.

Mitchell could hear her footsteps then she appeared at the door.

"Honey, this is Mitchell Pappas. *The* Mitchell Pappas, our tenant," Bill Griffin said.

Mitchell rose as she approached.

"You're kidding. Mr. Pappas, I can't tell you how honored we are to have you here. No wonder you looked familiar. Forgive me for not recognizing you right away."

She extended her hand, smiling. Mitchell took it. Her palms felt slightly damp and Mitchell attributed that to a hasty towel wipe when called.

"The honor is all mine, Mrs. Griffin."

He bent forward, almost a bow, as he released her hand.

Bill Griffin jerked with a thought. "Oops, nearly forgot my manners. Mr. Pappas, this is my wife, Melissa."

FORTY

THE SHOCKED EXPRESSION on Mitchell's face confused Bill Griffin. The unexpected name, the haunting name stunned Mitchell.

Melissa Shuller Griffin wouldn't dare answer her own question. Near panic came when she saw his picture. Why was he here? She knew the answer would be what she feared and ran from almost all her life.

She knew the answer had to come because of the startled reaction on the visitor's face at her name.

Mitchell promptly visualized the young Melissa Shuller in the photograph and superimposed her mentally over Melissa Griffin's features. The resemblance was uncanny. *It was Melissa!* The discovery strapped his tongue. Then he recovered.

Melissa knew from his prolonged expression that this wasn't to be a social visit, but prayed she was wrong.

"Oh, I'm sorry," said Mitchell noticing the confusion on Bill Griffin's face. Melissa's face maintained a smiling mask. "My mind wanders sometimes. You suddenly reminded me of an old friend."

"I hope it's a positive remembrance," Melissa said, cordial, but guarded.

"Whenever I see a beautiful woman, it's positive."

They laughed.

"Thank you, Mr. Pappas."

"Honey, join us."

She sat opposite Mitchell, now looking at her with what she thought to be an inquisitive, yet admiring way. She sensed it. He knew something, but what and how much? For the first time since 1942 she was terrified.

But the terror within was controlled, and the facial mask was confident, positive.

Bill Griffin left the table at a thought and called out into the house.

"Pat, put on some coffee, please. We have a guest."

"Okay, Dad," a girl's voice replied.

Bill Griffin closed the door and sat next to Melissa.

Melissa couldn't contain herself. She had to know why he came. The tension was beginning to crack the plaster of her facade and there was much fright in her to suppress it. She had to know. What did he know? Or was it her imagination?—A self-inflicted beating?

"I'm delighted you dropped in on us, Mr. Pappas. But how did you get our address? I'm pleased you have it. Mr. Borden told Bill it would be kept secret."

"I told him I was on the way to Boston and thought it a good idea to visit my landlord. But he wouldn't give it to me. He's a good man. Protects his clients to the end."

"That's the impression I got," said Bill. "What's the difference, honey, how he got it? He's here and that's the main thing."

"I agree. But I want to know how—if not from Mr. Borden."

"I did want to meet you, so I stopped in at Town Hall for your address. I hope you don't mind."

"Not at all," said Melissa.

She nearly died inside. He went out of his way to find the new owner. Why?

Melissa prayed silently for strength to survive this visit. She was buoyed in that he didn't know who she was. How could he guess? How could he possibly know? He had never seen her. Only the first names were similar. Thousands are named Melissa. She cursed her decision to keep her first name, a weak link to her past.

Mitchell had to act fast. Their family was coming, and soon. He wouldn't have the opportunity to talk if children were screaming and demanding their attention. He would have to leave when the family came.

Before asking William Griffin for the seller's address, he wanted to make sure he was correct about his wife. Was it possible? A coincidence? Was his imagination deceiving him? Was she *the* Melissa? Incredible! He no longer was interested in idle conversation. He had to find out—Melissa or coincidence?

"Mrs. Griffin." Melissa braced. He looked troubled. "Please forgive me, but is your maiden name Shuller? Are you Melissa Shuller?"

The Griffins' cordial masks vanished as their hands met and held under the table as they exchanged glances.

"Are you asking because of similar first names? I know she owned the property before we bought it," Melissa countered.

Mitchell took out his wallet from his inside jacket pocket and withdrew the photo of Siobhan and Patricia Griffin and Melissa Shuller in the winter scene. He extended it to Melissa studying her for a reaction, knowing that if she weren't Melissa Shuller the people in the photograph would mean nothing to her.

Nothing the stranger could say or show her would penetrate the defensive wall she had been building over the years. What was he reaching for inside his pocket? What could he possibly show her? What evidence? Whatever it was, she felt confident of countering.

But then Melissa saw the faces as she took the photo and the earthquake within remained barely stifled by gritted teeth. Distant tremors began as Siobhan and Patricia's faces made the past vivid, and her heart quickened and the teeth tightened. She wasn't as strong as her preparations led her to believe. Emotions became visible by her eye movements. She prayed silently, "Don't weaken, don't weaken, don't . . ."

But the tide Melissa had suppressed all these years could no longer be restrained and it reached the shore. The waves welled in her eyes and they uncontrollably widened as she held the picture tenderly. Nostalgia consumed her senses and the defense mask began to crumble. The facade weakened as her eyes released a wet streak down her face.

Convinced, Mitchell let her have the moment.

Mitchell looked at Bill Griffin's serious expression. Bill leaned towards Melissa and recognized his wife with the two strangers.

"I saw this photo at the Griffin farm," Mitchell interrupted. "Jack Griffin and his wife, Emily, run the place now. The original is in his living room. He told me how he used to love you, and how he jumped on you every time he saw you."

Melissa's sobs became audible.

"Why do you have the picture, Mr. Pappas?" asked Bill.

"I mentioned to Jack that I might be seeing you and he gave it to me to copy. I had planned to ask if you knew where Melissa Shuller was."

"Why?"

"They thought that as the new owner, you might know her address. His family has been looking for Melissa for years."

Melissa broke down and cried. She turned her back to Mitchell to hide her grief then turned back halfway.

"How—how are they?"

She erased the need for Mitchell to ask again if she was Melissa Shuller.

"Sean Griffin died about six years ago. Siobhan Griffin died about four years ago."

"Oh, my God. Forgive me." She hid her face. "What have I done?"

Bill Griffin moved closer to Melissa, put his arm around her shoulder and gave comfort and a handkerchief. Melissa wiped her face and turned back to Mitchell.

"How are the others? Patricia?"

"I saw Patricia. I was told the other Griffins were scattered around the country. You'll be happy to know that Patricia went to college, to New York University looking for you. She did become a teacher and is now a principal of an elementary school in Huntington, Long Island. She's married and has four children. Her name is McGuire now." He took a piece of paper from the wallet. "This is her address and phone, at home and at school. She told me to tell you to please call or write and that she misses you. And she meant it. By the way, she told me about the money."

"She told you?"

"Yes. We had a nice long talk about you. She missed you, still does."

Melissa's fingers rubbed the photograph, massaging Patricia and then Siobhan's face. She took the paper, studied it then passed it to Bill, who placed it in his shirt pocket.

"It's time. It's time." Melissa whispered. "Thank you, Mr. Pappas. I will call her tonight. Maybe tomorrow."

The sliding door grating on metal forced Melissa's face downward to hide the red eyes. A young lady appeared at the door.

"Coffee's ready, Dad."

"Come here, honey. I want you to meet Mr. Pappas," said Bill.

"Hi." She waved, holding her position. "Nice to meet you. Dad, do you want it there or inside."

She resembled Melissa: blond, blue-eyed and attractive.

"Just keep it warm. I'll get it later."

"Okay. Bye, it was nice to meet you, Mr. Pappas."

She closed the door and vanished.

"That's our youngest—Patricia," Bill said. "We named her after Patricia Griffin. The next one in line is named Siobhan. We named our other daughter Martha, after Melissa's mother. In order, the boys are Henry, after Melissa's father; William, Jr.; and Sean, after Sean Griffin."

"That's wonderful! The Griffins of East Hampton should be pleased to know that Melissa married a Griffin," said Mitchell.

"That's one of life's strange coincidences," Bill added, and then laughed. "I think she married me for my name."

"You're a lucky man, Mr. Griffin, to have such a large family."

Bill's arm hugged Melissa's shoulder.

"I am, Mr. Pappas. I am a very, very lucky man, indeed. More than most."

"Mr. Pappas," said Melissa. "I want you to know that I'm grateful you came here today."

Melissa felt better about Mitchell. He had found her, but as long as he was looking for a missing person, no immediate harm could come from it.

"As I said, I didn't expect to see you here. But now that I did meet you and do know your history from the Griffins, I must ask you the questions that have haunted the people who loved you, and still love you. Why did you leave and never return? Why not a return address with your Christmas cards?"

"I suppose it did seem strange and mysterious." She sighed.

"Extremely. You've hurt those people. They looked everywhere for you. Siobhan saved all your Christmas cards."

"You're serious?"

"Yes. I saw them. They called every Shuller in the Boston area because of the postmarks. And Portland, Maine, too."

"Portland? Oh, yes, we spent two weeks there one December."

Melissa was comfortable with Mitchell now. She would think of some reason to say why she left.

That's what he wanted to know. She made up many reasons over the years in the event someone asked.

"How long have you lived here?"

"For about fifteen years," said Bill.

"We've lived in the surrounding area since nineteen forty-four," Melissa added. "I met Bill then. He swept me off my feet and brought me up here."

"But you never forgot the Griffins."

"Never."

"Why Boston?"

"You mean the cards? I shopped there at Christmas. I mailed from there."

"If I were a detective, Melissa, I would say you mailed from Boston because of its size. It might have been easier to find you in a small town."

Melissa acted offended. "That's out of order, Mr. Pappas."

"Forgive me, but you still didn't mention why you left. Did you have something to hide?"

"Now you do sound like a detective," said Bill.

"It's a bad habit. From my books."

"There's nothing mysterious as to why I left. When my father died—did you know that?"

"Yes. The accident in the gully."

"I became disoriented. Confused. I wanted to get away from the farm, from everything and everyone who would remind me of him. My mother died there also. I was alone so I left. Other than the Griffins, it was desolate. And I didn't want to be a burden on them, another mouth to feed."

"Is that what you want me to believe?"

"That's my reason. It's not exciting or dramatic, a personal thing. I loved my father very much. The farm would have been a constant reminder. I needed to get on with my life."

"And you never got over his death? That's hard to believe. I can't believe that. I know why you ran away."

The Griffins looked alarmed, their pulses increasing with anxiety. What did he know? Their hands met again.

"I told you, Mr. Pappas, no other reason."

Melissa was stern, a barrier to hold back this visitor's curious tide.

"And I told you I know why."

"All right. Why?"

"I know that the reason you ran away was to protect your father."

Melissa stared back at Mitchell, thinking, analyzing to figure out how to react to the strange statement. She didn't reach a conclusion. She didn't know how to respond. The Griffins remained silent, their hands tightening.

This visitor wasn't a visitor anymore. The past made him a prosecutor, and she a defendant.

Mitchell found nothing in their expressions. He expected a broader reaction to his startling revelation of the truth. Melissa broke the silence.

"My *father?*"

"Melissa, I don't know if Bill knows any of this, but what I concluded makes a fantastic story. I must admit that I also wanted to find you for selfish reasons."

"You mean you want to write a book around my family?"

"About what happened on Shuller's Land."

"I see. Well, Mr. Pappas, Bill knows all about my past. You may speak freely. What happened on Shuller's Land? What do you imply about my father? What are you thinking about my father?"

"That he butchered the four German soldiers."
Silence.

The Griffin faces were stoic and tense.

"What are you talking about? What German soldiers?" asked Melissa with a cold stare.

"These German soldiers."

Mitchell reached inside his right jacket pocket and displayed the four photographs. He laid them end-to-end facing the Griffins, who were numb.

"They are: Heinrich Kretschmer, Carl Dieterman, Peter Lehmann, and Erich Lassen."

Melissa cringed as the faces stirred the savage memory of rape and self-defense. The prosecution introduced damaging evidence.

"I still don't understand, Mr. Pappas," Melissa countered.

"You never saw these men?"

"Never."

"Mr. Pappas," said Bill griffin. "I'm beginning to resent your accusations and questioning. My wife's past is none of your business."

"It is. Unless you people prefer I discuss it with the authorities."

Melissa calmed Bill. "Let's hear him out, Bill. I don't appreciate any accusations or innuendoes about my father."

Mitchell retrenched. "All right, it's possible you never saw these men's faces. But I know you saw their bodies."

"Not those, either," retorted Melissa.

"Let me tell you what I think happened. Instead of questioning everything I say, let me tell you my theory—we'll call it that for now—and then we'll argue the points. Agreed?"

"Agreed," said Melissa. "Go ahead."

"Sometime in June, nineteen forty-two these four German soldiers dressed in civilian clothes and carrying equipment, found their way to Shuller's Land probably to rest for the night. I first realized Germans had been there when I found a dagger in the barn and this identification card." He reached into the other pocket and put Carl Dieterman's card on the table. He watched for a reaction from Melissa. She stared, suppressing emotion.

"Then I found the truck in the gully, and found a Luger within. Now with this evidence, I began to piece a puzzle. Why did you leave? What were the Germans doing there?

"I checked further with Germany, and discovered that they were landed in East Hampton and traveled north-northwest. They killed an artist and a mother and her son. I drew a line and it was obvious they came to your farm. I could have concluded they left their belongings behind, or lost them when they continued on and that you and your father never saw them.

"I wasn't satisfied. I searched for graves and found a small mound by the house. I dug and found jewelry, clothes, and three empty wallets. The fourth one belonging to Dieterman, I found in the barn. At the bottom were two cases of explosive materials. Now, why would soldiers lose their weapons and bury their explosives and personal effects?—Because they never left the property. I probed further—and found three bodies buried in the last stable."

Melissa gasped, her hand moving late to her mouth to cover the sound.

That spurred the prosecutor. The reaction confirmed he was on the right track.

"Three bodies. Buried in the stable. Then I looked for the fourth body, but couldn't find it. But it's buried out there somewhere and I think you know where it is."

Melissa didn't answer. Mitchell continued.

"I believe your father surprised the Germans as they rested in the barn and tied them up. Then he went berserk or patriotic and killed them one by one. Executed them. I believe he knifed one, axed one in the back and killed the third with a pitchfork."

Melissa's eyes were mesmerized, her mind on the real past and the imagined past. Visions of her killing her attackers were lucid. Bill could feel her blood racing through her fingers. They waited patiently for the presentation of the evidence.

"Then he had the fourth German, who I believe was Dieterman because of where I found his wallet, dig the grave, throw them in and cover the hole. Then he killed Dieterman with a shotgun. I found the shotgun in the basement. I thought he had buried him in the basement, but I was wrong. I looked outside again but the years covered all traces.

"Now to get to you, Melissa. You discovered what your father had done and were shocked—horrified your father could be such a beast. Then he had a few drinks and drove to town. That's when he had his accident in the gully. You stayed long enough to give him a decent funeral and then you disappeared, afraid to stay because you might slip or say the wrong thing. You left Shuller's Land abandoned all this time so that the years would forget its ugly secret."

The Griffins looked at each other without expression. Their eyes communicated. Mitchell couldn't gauge their reactions to his brilliant summary and conclusion from their expressions. It bothered him.

"And that's why I wanted to find you. Germans landed in America during the war. They were caught. These Germans," he tapped the table, "were never captured, and never made it back home. That's a story."

"I can see why you're a writer, Mr. Pappas," said Melissa. "You have a vivid imagination. But what you think happened is fiction. Pure fiction. And you want to do that story with your fictional twists?"

"I believe the world has a right to know what happened to these Germans."

"And you will say that my father butchered them?"

"Yes."

"You will so carelessly and wantonly destroy a good and decent man and a wonderful father's memory?"

"He killed these people."

"No, Mr. Pappas. If you accuse my father then your story will be all fiction. My father didn't kill these people."

She looked at the photographs with disdain.

"I can appreciate your defending him."

"I cannot allow you to hurt that man's memory. I know how you write."

"As I said, the world should know."

"The world need know nothing." Melissa's stare repeated it—*The world need know nothing.* "But if you insist, let them know the truth."

"That's not what I'll be doing? Impossible."

"My father did not kill these Germans. They killed him."

"What are you saying?" said Mitchell incredulous.

"They killed him. So he couldn't have killed them. You look like you don't believe me, Mr. Pappas. You don't?"

"No, I don't. He was killed in the truck accident."

"Believe it, Mr. Pappas, because I killed these Germans. The four of them."

It was the surprise twist, the twist that he always invented to shock his readers. Now he was jolted by reality.

"Melissa, don't do it. Don't go on," her husband begged.

"No, it's all right now. It's all right. Mr. Pappas, you have your fictitious version. Now you'll have the truth. Bill knows the story, as I mentioned, so if I'm unable to continue, he will.

"On my last day of school, I returned home after spending some time with the Griffin family and was confronted in the barn by the Germans. What I didn't know at the time was that my father was already dead. Killed by Kretschmer. Then I was raped, Mr. Pappas. Raped. First by Lassen then by Lehmann and then beaten by Kretschmer. Dieterman was the only one who showed me any decency. He helped me and became my defender.

"The next day Kretschmer came to the barn, untied me—it was I who was tied to the pole, by the way—and tried to rape me. I was able to find his dagger and I stabbed him in the throat. As I was about to escape, Lassen came into the barn and I got him with the pitchfork."

"Incredible," muttered Mitchell.

"Then Lehmann came in and I drove the ax into his back. I was young but had the advantage of surprise. Then Dieterman caught me and retied me to the pole. I was sure he was going to kill me. I even tried being nice to him, to get sympathy from him, but I couldn't. You were right about a German digging the grave, and you were right in saying Dieterman dug it. He placed his comrades in the hole so they wouldn't be found. He didn't want to leave any trace they were on Shuller's Land. After he buried them, he took their personal belongings and buried them where you found them.

"Then he took me to the kitchen and tied me to a chair. He said something about duty and being a soldier. I knew he was going to kill me. He went out for a walk to decide if he should kill me. I managed to get free, found the shotgun in the closet and captured him when he returned. I did what I had to do to survive."

She paused. Her fingers intertwined and pressed until the knuckles drained of color.

Mitchell waited.

Melissa's mind was on the young soldier and his expression when he saw the shotgun pointing at him.

"Then what?" Mitchell coaxed to break the trance. No reply. "Melissa, where did you kill him?"

Her eyes grew mistier and she wiped them.

"Forgive me—but this is a sensitive situation. I loved Carl Dieterman. He was the first man I ever loved. In any event, I—I told him to walk in front of me and to go outside. He seemed brave, and never begged or even made an appeal for his life. I guess he felt sure I wouldn't harm him because he did nothing to harm me.

"He wanted to know why we were going outside and I told him I wanted to check my horse, who was tied up in the woods. I had him walk in front of me as we went out. I remember it was a beautiful moonlit evening as we walked through the field.

"We walked slowly without talking. When he was relaxed, or seemed to be, and sure that everything was going to be all right—" Her hands went to her face and rubbed to erase the memory. She took a deep breath and lowered her hands. "He wouldn't say anything. Maybe if he had said something. I raised the shotgun and aimed, but my hands and body wouldn't stop trembling. I didn't want to kill him. I didn't. But it had to be. And then . . ." Her eyes glared and her mouth formed an oval. She was reluctant to continue. Her hands wrestled again to keep from shaking. Mitchell was spellbound by Melissa's trauma, as her unpleasant memories delayed the past from unfolding. "And then—shot him—in the back of the head." She shivered and looked distant again. "I owed him that much—not to know when. He never felt anything. Then I buried him in the soft earth—near the woods where he fell. After killing the others with a knife, a pitchfork, and an ax the shotgun was easy. And that was the end of Landwolf Three-three-seven. Completely." She exhaled deeply, loudly, and calmed herself.

"I had been through two horrendous days and I wasn't able to think. All my instincts said survive. And I did. They were beasts, savages."

Mitchell believed her. When he found the dusty shotgun in the basement one barrel was empty, one loaded. "Except for Dieterman," Mitchell added.

"Except for Carl Dieterman. Carl Dieterman." Melissa repeated the name with reverence. "Yes, I regretted depriving him of his life. Regretted it very much. Always have and always will. I had killed someone I had loved and admired deeply. He was a wonderful young man. On occasion, I still cry for him when I think about him and our time together." Her eyelids moved quickly to retain the tears. Her lips quivered. The tears loosened. "I put the shotgun down in the basement that night, cleansed my body and mind with a hot bath and then slept. I felt no remorse, compassion or pain. Just tired. The next day, I came to my senses, realized what I had done and mourned for Carl Dieterman. But like someone said, war is war and it has a way of dehumanizing those caught up in it, making death and killing justifiable and easier to accept."

Bill was shaking his head with disbelief as if hearing his wife's past for the first time.

"And *that's* the true story, Mr. Pappas," Melissa concluded.

Mitchell was speechless, stunned by the truth, by her experience.

The silence grew heavier.

Bill Griffin stirred the atmosphere. He stood and walked behind a mourning Melissa and tenderly placed his hands on Melissa's shoulders.

"Melissa?"

"Yes?"

Her voice was soft, resigned. Melissa felt the same as that night in the barn—weak and helpless. Let what must happen, happen.

"I'm glad Mr. Pappas came here today, honey," Bill said stroking the shoulders. "It's time you were able to vent the past that has tormented you all these years. I'm sure Mr. Pappas will use discretion and compassion if he still feels that he must write the story. I believe the time is perfect now, Melissa—to tell Mr. Pappas the whole truth."

The body beneath his hands rebelled. Melissa's head turned upward to plead with him.

"I *have* told the whole truth."

Bill again rubbed her shoulders to calm her.

"You left out a minor detail."

Mitchell became puzzled.

"Bill, are you saying that what Melissa said was not the truth?" He was astounded. "What the hell is going on here?"

"Only that there's more to tell. She'll tell you."

"There's no more to tell!" Melissa insisted, exchanging her plea from Bill to Mitchell and back to Bill, hoping one believed her.

Bill sat next to Melissa again, placed his arm around her shoulder and squeezed lovingly.

"Melissa, you've come this far with Mr. Pappas. It would be wrong to tell an incomplete story. This is the right time."

"No more, Bill. There's no more. The small detail is insignificant and has no bearing and has to do with my father. You're magnifying its importance."

Melissa began to cry and her eyes became frightened.

"But I do want it known now, honey. Please. You've cleansed your soul. Finish the job." When Melissa hesitated, he turned to Mitchell now sitting on the edge of his seat. "Mr. Pappas . . ."

Melissa interrupted, sobbing. "No! Bill, please don't."

" . . . all that Melissa said is the truth except for one aspect of it."

"What is that? What about her father?"

Mitchell leaned forward, cocking an anxious ear. Melissa buried her face in her hands.

"The part about Carl Dieterman," Bill continued.

"What about him?"

"Melissa didn't kill him."

Mitchell's mouth fell. Melissa's head stayed down, sobbing, imploring.

"Bill, you mustn't go on, please," Melissa pleaded.

"I must."

Mitchell was captive to the drama unfolding before him then impatiently asked, "What did she do to him?"

"She let him go."

There was a numbing silence.

Mitchell found his voice.

"But—but he never returned to Germany after the war. I know his family is in Germany and the records show that he never returned."

"That's right." Bill nodded. "He never returned to Germany. He never wanted to go back there again."

"Then where did he go? And how do you know he never returned to Germany?"

Bill hugged Melissa tighter.

"I know, Mr. Pappas, because I'm Carl Dieterman."

FORTY-ONE

CARL DIETERMAN REMOVED his glasses, picked up his picture and held it up to Mitchell.

"Don't look so shocked, Mr. Pappas. If you look closely, you'll see the similarities. The cheekbones and nose are similar."

Mitchell studied the faces. "Yes, yes they are."

Melissa looked hopeless and dejected, and Carl held both her hands.

"I'll continue the rest of the story for you," he said.

"No, no," she insisted. "I'll do it. I'm all right." She breathed deeply. The nightmare was over.

"The next morning, we went looking for my father. Kretschmer had taken him for a ride to survey the property. We figure he crashed the truck purposely in an attempt to escape. We searched everywhere then found his body in the woods after following the footprints in the field where he and Kretschmer fought. He must have gotten away, but Kretschmer caught him and beat him over the head.

The Luger you found was Kretschmer's. We put my father's body on my horse and took it to the gully and placed him behind the wheel to make it look like an accident.

"Carl—Bill—took the train from East Hampton that afternoon for New York City. We had agreed to meet in two days in front of the Public Library at Forty-second Street and Fifth Avenue. Then I sent Patricia the letter and the money.

"I forgot to mention that the Germans had forty thousand dollars with them when they landed. We used that money for Patricia and to live on until we knew it was safe for Bill to find a job where questions wouldn't be asked. Thank goodness for the money, because it was difficult for him to get work. I found a job as a clerk for a nominal salary.

"A few weeks later, we heard that eight other German spies were caught and that six were executed. We panicked. But we decided to stay in New York City because of its size and the millions of people.

"I thought we would be safe there. But during Christmas time, I saw some friends from school, from East Hampton, shopping in a department store and I ran out before they saw me. I realized it wasn't safe for us to be in New York anymore. He came in as a spy, you know, and if he got caught, he would have been executed. We left New York in January of forty-three and came to Massachusetts because of Bill's slight British English accent and its similarity to New England dialect.

"We bought a house with the money. He found a job in a gas station—he liked being around engines— and I got a sales clerk job in Woolworth's. I stayed in touch with the Griffins because I loved them. They were my family, my only family. But I couldn't risk contacting them, or anyone finding me—us. That's why I sent the cards from Boston. You're right. Boston was a subterfuge. I guess you know it all now."

"I could add to that," said Bill. "I'm sure you know by now why we took the name Griffin. If you're curious as to how I got the name William, it's after my father, Wilhelm."

"May I ask a question?" asked Mitchell. "Why did you transfer the property to Bill after all these years?"

"I convinced Melissa that it was time to put the property up for sale. She agreed at that time because there was less risk if a William Griffin sold the property. After the title change, I contacted the real estate people and put it up for sale.

"The next day, Melissa changed her mind. She didn't want to take the chance. Finally, after all these years and with the crushing burden putting six children through college, I convinced her to at least rent it to cover some costs and add towards our retirement. She agreed to the rental. You were perfect. A writer. Someone who wouldn't go probing or digging the earth."

Melissa added, "I couldn't risk selling the land. The land's value would have made life financially comfortable for us. But we were rich in being together, being a family and that was more important."

"I'm sorry I uncovered your secrets. I must admit the truth in this case is more intriguing than what I could have imagined. I would have done a great injustice to your father, Melissa, though I would have given him a fictitious name if I hadn't met you."

"So now," stared Melissa, "you want to do a great injustice to Carl Dieterman."

FORTY-TWO

IN FRONT OF the house, Henry and Theresa Griffin had parked their brown four-door Pontiac. Henry, a lawyer and a Harvard graduate, had a practice in Boston.

Their two daughters, Melissa, ten, and Nancy, eight, jumped out of the back seat and ran into the backyard. Young Melissa and Nancy saw the three adults sitting at the table and called for their grandparents' attention. Mitchell picked up the pictures and the card and placed them in his pocket.

Melissa and Bill rose and greeted them.

"Hi, sweethearts!" Bill picked up little Melissa and kissed her. "Hello, hello, sweetheart." Then he put her down and did the same to Nancy. "How are my beautiful girls today?"

Melissa hugged the children with as much enthusiasm as Bill. The joy was satisfying. The children were heaven sent to release them from the dreadful conversation. She gushed with enthusiasm to forget the past again, to pretend Mitchell Pappas never existed.

Henry and Theresa came into the yard dressed casually for the relaxed family gathering. Henry waved.

"Hi, Mom. Dad."

Henry kissed his mother and hugged his father.

"How are things, son?"

"Good. How about yourself?"

"Couldn't be better. Hi, honey." He kissed Theresa.

"Hello, Dad." They both kissed Melissa.

The depression of history vanished from Melissa and Bill's faces, hidden from their family.

"This is Mitchell Pappas, an old friend who stopped by to visit. Mitchell, this is my son Henry, my daughter-in-law, Theresa, and my two granddaughters, Melissa and Nancy."

Mitchell rose and they exchanged greetings.

"Mitchell, Mom, and I have some minor business to discuss," Bill said. "Why don't you go inside and give us a few more minutes."

"Sure. Mr. Pappas, let me know if you need a good lawyer. Dad's a tough negotiator." They laughed. "Let's go kids, let's go see your aunts."

The Henry Griffins left and they sat again.

"What's the next move, Mr. Pappas?" asked Melissa. "Will you go to the authorities? What will happen to Bill?"

"The authorities? No. I respect your decision to tell me the truth. The best thing, I suppose, is for me to think about what you said. You people went through hell. I'm not a detective, just a curious writer with a wild imagination. But I won't do anything without discussing it further with you."

"So you may write the story?"

"I may. I may not. I might change it a bit so it doesn't reflect upon your present identity."

"You know perfectly well that with your reputation, the world will believe it happened. And will want to know on what truth it's based."

"That's possible."

"Is there anything we can say to stop you?"

"As I said, let me think about it."

Mitchell studied their faces and tried to imagine their lives, their moments of anguish living with their secret, keeping it from their family—the Sword of Damocles dangling by a single horsehair over their heads to fall at any time.

"You seemed disturbed, Mr. Pappas," said Melissa. "Do you have more questions?"

He shook his head, contemplative.

"No more questions. I'd best be going now."

They rose and walked somber to the gate.

Nice backyard, Mitchell thought taking a final look around. Nice backyard.

Melissa and Bill had nothing more to say.

The trial was over and the jury was out.

History had caught up to them. They were the defendants—and they had defendants' eyes—and the prosecutor couldn't say anything as he saw the plea for leniency in their sorrowful eyes.

Suddenly, there was joy and happiness running toward them. The dog barked from inside and three children, all boys, and two adults approached—Sean Griffin and his wife, Stacy. Sean was a carbon copy of Bill Griffin. The rest of the Griffins had also arrived, exiting from their cars. They *were* an army.

Mitchell turned away from Melissa and Bill and walked through the Griffin family, waving hellos. He didn't want to be introduced to them. He wouldn't feel right doing so in his newly found role of judge and jury on the future of their parents. The area turned into a happy greeting hall.

Mitchell walked to his car quickly and silently and sat behind the wheel, watching their faces, and watching Melissa and Bill hug their grandchildren and their children as if the end was near and they wanted to express to them how much they loved them all.

He watched the beauty of the family scene until the Griffin clan disappeared to the backyard.

Melissa stopped at the gate, turned, and looked at Mitchell. It wasn't a long stare. But enough to say to Mitchell—Please, don't hurt my family. Then she turned and vanished behind the house.

Mitchell lowered his window all the way and listened to the sounds of the Griffins on Sunday morning.

How could he harm this magnificent woman who sacrificed her life to be with and to protect the man she loved? He asked that question again and again.

How beautiful, how magnificent their love for each other must be.

Then he thought about Helene, and the family he never had, and he suddenly valued the real world of love, home and family. Togetherness—the real joy, happiness, anguish and secrets. Real emotions. And in the short moment, he envied the Griffins.

It was late for him to create a family like the Griffins, but it wasn't late to salvage his life with Helene.

Mitchell sat there for another five minutes thinking about his life, his values, reality and fiction, Helene, the Griffins—and at what price a bestseller?

Melissa's words repeated. "So now you want to do a great injustice to Carl Dieterman."

All his works were based on some event, but no one went to jail from his revelations. He simply added intrigue to reality. He didn't destroy lives that hadn't already destroyed themselves. His heroes or villains were already dead or in jail.

No, he wasn't a judge and he wasn't a jury, and he didn't want to be either one. By god, he wasn't god and didn't want to play one.

Mitchell opened the car door and walked to the backyard buttoning his jacket. He stood by the gate watching the Griffins. Bill was putting more hamburgers on the grill. Melissa was talking to three women when she saw Mitchell. He waved to her to come to him.

"Melissa, may I see you?"

Curious, she nudged Bill then headed toward Mitchell. Bill Griffin turned from the grill, gave the job to Henry and followed Melissa. Melissa waited for Bill and they approached Mitchell together.

They stood before him, awaiting sentencing.

"Yes, Mr. Pappas?" asked Melissa.

"Like you said before, Melissa. The world need know nothing."

Melissa nodded with an inner peace that glowed in her eyes. She kissed Mitchell on the cheek.

"Thank you. For my family."

"You're a brave lady for what you did. And you, Mister—William Griffin, you're brave and lucky."

"That's what I said before."

"That you did. Melissa, remember to call Patricia."

"I will. Tonight after the kids leave."

"Will you tell Patricia the truth?"

"Only when I see her. I must. She must know why I left. I know she'll understand—and I'll visit Siobhan's grave and ask forgiveness."

"That's good. Good." He tried to envision the tender scene between Melissa and Patricia. "And come down and visit me. At Shuller's Land."

Mitchell shook hands with Bill. The grip was friendly and sincere. He gave them a warm smile, turned slowly and returned to the car. The Griffins returned to their family.

The verdict was in.

Mitchell sat behind the wheel nodding in confirmation of his decision. The world needn't know—the hell with it. It would be his and the Griffins' secret. There was always another story, another mystery another intrigue somewhere.

For now, he knew what the world would never know. And that pleased him.

And he relished the thought that tomorrow morning, early Monday morning, he would tell the world to go to hell with enthusiasm—and give it an extra jab with the middle fingers.

EPILOGUE

A MONTH LATER, Melissa Shuller and Carl Dieterman returned to Shuller's Land.

There was life in the dead oak. Sparrows had discovered the secluded farm—several dozen—a few commuting between the tree and the holes in the barn.

That's the life the William Griffins saw when they stopped their car at the edge of the west woods to survey and to pause before completing the trip to the house.

The tearful and joyous private reunion with Patricia McGuire, yesterday, was emotionally over. Now they had a mission to fulfill at Shuller's Land then visit Jack Griffin and Siobhan's grave, and then return to Natick with the promise to Patricia that their families would get together during the Thanksgiving weekend.

They returned to Shuller's Land, not for nostalgia, or to see Mitchell Pappas exclusively, but to decide on where to rebury the bodies of Landwolf 337.

The risk of someone else finding the bodies could reopen the grief and danger Mitchell had exposed and suppressed. Someone else may not be as compassionate and sensitive.

Mitchell Pappas could be trusted now. They were sure he would help them rebury the bodies somewhere out of the way, where they couldn't be found or turned over by farm equipment, most likely deep in the woods.

Once removed from the barn and reburied far from the house, it would be virtually impossible to ever make the connection again if anyone accidentally found the bodies. Who could possibly connect them to the past? There was no evidence the bodies were German soldiers. There weren't any weapons lying around anymore or luggage or the other identification Mitchell needed to trace them. Yes, once the bodies were moved the William Griffins would be completely safe.

And Patricia promised secrecy. Patricia had to be told the truth why Melissa never returned to Shuller's Land or visited her again. Re-uniting with Patricia was a must for Melissa.

Melissa sensed a special communication in Mitchell's eyes when he said goodbye to them in Natick, a satisfaction in knowing and then suppressing and keeping their secret. She also sensed some strange sense of joy in his subtle grin as if he reveled in knowing what the world didn't.

But though they were on a mission of finality to forever conclude the closing chapter of the story that connected their past, a wave of childhood and family remembrances swept before her. She was saddened by the neglected condition of her former home and the land that her father and ancestors worked hard to maintain and live from. Melissa wept.

When the nostalgia ended, they both knew that once the final secret of Shuller's Land was reburied, Melissa Shuller and Carl Dieterman would always be hidden behind the names Melissa and William (Bill) Griffin.

Bill eased his foot off the brake and the car coasted to the oak where he parked it.

"I don't see his car. A jeep wasn't it?" said Melissa.

"Maybe it's around the back. It sure is quiet. Let's go in."

He started to get out.

"No. I'll wait here. I'll go in later. I'm not ready to face it. Maybe it's best that we forget the past altogether."

"After today, honey. For now, don't force it. He may not be in anyway and the house may be locked. I'll be right back."

Melissa sat passively, refusing and fighting to recall the days of innocence and family that came painfully. She had to go into the house before they left even if Mitchell wasn't in. She would find a way to get in. She had to, but not right away.

Then her gaze focused on the barn.

Bill walked quickly to the front door and knocked. No answer. He looked at the rocking chair, different than the one he remembered, and envisioned Peter Lehmann in it on guard duty, asleep. He knocked again. Absent response or footsteps from within, he tried the doorknob and the door opened. He pushed it open and called, "Mr. Pappas—Mitchell!" No response. He walked in.

Everything was neat and no signs of anything belonging to Mitchell Pappas. He checked the bedroom. The bed was perfectly made and the closet door open, its interior empty. The kitchen was spotless. He went halfway down the basement stairs and called his name. No answer.

Mitchell Pappas had gone.

Bill went outside to tell Melissa and when he looked toward the car, Melissa wasn't there. He turned eastward and saw her. Melissa was leaning against the barn's doorway, hands covering her mouth, her body limp and still—visualizing the rape and her killings.

He jogged to her and held her tight. "Are you all right?"

She nodded. "It's so vivid again."

"It's time to forget that, also. Mitchell Pappas has moved out."

"Gone?"

"Gone."

"That's strange. He knew we were coming today. He said on the phone that he looked forward to seeing us again."

"I guess he went elsewhere to write or he finished his project. Wait here. I want to check the grave."

Melissa took a deep breath and straightened her posture. "I'm fine. Let's do it together."

They walked in slowly, their minds filled with the brutal killings and the mauling of a young girl.

Bill stopped. "Wait let's turn on the lights. It's dark by the stable."

Sparrows fluttered in the loft and flew out the holes, upset by the human intrusion.

He flipped on all the lights. Holding hands, they approached the last stable.

The breath stopped in their lungs.

The grave was empty.

A dark rectangular hole gaped back at them. The dirt was piled in mounds around the former grave.

But before panic could set in, Melissa and Bill saw the note nailed to a stake to the right of the hole. The note read:

> **'Your friends moved to places unknown. The world need never know. And neither will you. May the happiness you deserve be yours forever!! Mitchell'**

Melissa walked carefully to the stake to avoid getting dirt in her shoes, pulled the note, folded then put it in her handbag. Then she smiled at her husband—a smile of peace and finality.

The past was secure, their future safe.

Mitchell Pappas had written the last chapter.

In his way, Mitchell Pappas received his reward. He owned the final secret of Shuller's Land. And Melissa seemed to know that's the way it had to be.

*   *   *

CPSIA information can be obtained at www.ICGtesting.com
Printed in the USA
LVOW08s0337180615

442837LV00001B/128/P